Claws of Fear

Michael Elia

First published 2020
by Rowanvale Books Ltd
The Gate
Keppoch Street
Roath
Cardiff
CF24 3JW
www.rowanvalebooks.com

A CIP catalogue record for this book is available from the British Library.
ISBN: 978-1-911569-93-0

Marion Weisberg, aged forty-one, was on holiday in California and was visiting SeaWorld outside San Diego Zoo. A couple of days back, on the eighth of July, 2017, she had finished work at Munich Zoo in Germany and taken a flight the next day, stopping off at New York before continuing on to Los Angeles. Having recovered from her jet lag, she spent the morning being driven in a taxicab from Los Angeles to San Diego and, by three in the afternoon, she was watching the killer whales and dolphins performing stunts in the swimming pool at SeaWorld.

Sitting next to her was a sixty-two-year-old Chinese man, who began a conversation with her.

"Greetings, Marion Weisberg," he said.

"How do you know my name?" Marion said, her voice shocked.

"Your husband, Klaus Weisberg, in Munich, told me many things about you," the old man said. "How for many years, you had a paranoid fear of dangerous animals, but after a car accident, you were in a coma, dreamt of ancient spiritualism and worship of dangerous animals, and learned animal whispering. When you recovered, you had overcome your terror and you then saved Klaus from a wolf in Germany's Bavarian Forest by killing the wolf with an axe. This was thirteen years ago in 2004."

"What's your name?" Marion asked. "And where did you meet my husband?"

"My name is Lin Wu, and I'm from

Shanghai in China," he replied. "I met Klaus in Regensburg in Bavaria, and we talked about a war between ruthless industrialists, poachers and organised criminals on one side, and dangerous or formidable creatures on the other. The criminals have magical powers granted to them by magical gold. The gold is so strong and hard, nothing but the weight and strength of an elephant's hooves can break this gold and destroy the criminals' powers of witchcraft. The deadly beasts also possess invincible powers of sorcery, but they cannot defeat the poachers and criminals until the gold is destroyed. The beasts' magical powers give them immunity from bullets, but they're up against rogue sharks, ocean killers, killer reptiles and wild dogs that work for the criminals.

"Klaus told me you have perfect detective skills due to finding buried animal bones in certain regions of Germany and France. But you will need clues to find this gold—clues that will lead you to travel by sorcery from one state or country to another and prevent dangerous encounters between animals and criminals. Your sorcery can adjoin far-apart countries in a dreamworld to unite the Beasts of Lin Wu, the fearsome beasts who are up against the criminals, and the Beasts of Li Hei, Li Hei being a ruthless and brutal dealer in animal products. You could join the Congo and Nepal with Colombia and Venezuela, the Congo with Australia, or Wyoming with France or other countries in Europe."

"I see," Marion answered. "How will I gain these powers of sorcery?"

"By eating these three magic bananas from a plantation in northern India," Lin Wu said. "The Beasts of Lin Wu have gained their powers by eating the same kind of bananas. And now, I must disappear."

Lin Wu warped into the mist, and Marion was shocked and amazed. The woman unpeeled the three bananas and consumed them in two or three minutes. She could taste their magical qualities and felt a new surge of strength and power flowing through her slender body. She got up from the row of seats and called a taxicab, asking the driver to pick her up from San Diego Zoo and drive her back to the hotel in Los Angeles.

***

Marion ate an enormous dinner of buffalo steak with jacket potato and French bread, followed by banoffee pie and white wine, before retreating to her hotel room, stripping naked and climbing into a cosy single bed. She slept until seven in the morning, and the last hour of her fast was taken over by two long dreams.

The first dream was set in the Pacific Ocean off California, and the second happened in the dreamworld adjoining the Congo and south-western China with Colombia and Venezuela.

In the first dream, occurring in the waters off California, a huge crocodile and a massive alligator who had escaped from San Diego Zoo journeyed through the water towards Los Angeles. There, they united with an awesome great white shark and an enormous tiger shark. The huge sharks operated alongside three large and savage killer fishes—a barracuda, a conger eel and a moray eel—as they viciously attacked twelve male divers. The sharks brutally savaged and pulverised five men. All the divers' ribs and spines were crushed by the brutes' enormous red jaws and fearsome white teeth. Two of the men's arms were chewed off and the other three had a leg severed. The barracuda, the conger eel and the moray eel bit, chopped and shredded chunks of flesh and bone from three other divers. Then the barracuda and the conger eel each chewed off a foot from two men, and the moray eel cut off a man's right hand.

A stingray and a manta ray joined in the fight, stabbing and poisoning two men with their barbed tails containing lethal toxins, and then the crocodile and the alligator seized the legs of the last two men. The killer reptiles spun round with their deadly death-rolls, twisting off the men's legs before the crocodile snapped a man's arm off with his bone-crushing jaws. All twelve men died in agony from excessive loss of blood or being stabbed by the stingray and the manta ray. The stingray's victim had also been poisoned by the toxins from the ocean killer's tail.

Nearby, five men from another yacht had been constricted, ripped and shredded to pieces by an octopus, a giant squid and a cuttlefish. The octopus suffocated and tore apart one, the giant squid constricted and shredded two others to bits, and the cuttlefish mutilated the last two to bloody ribbons of flesh and bones. With their long, powerful tentacles containing suckers with sharp horny rims, these three ruthless and brutal invertebrates were equally as ferocious as the two sharks and five killer fishes. The two killer reptiles matched the sharks and ocean killers in vicious savagery and cruelty. All these sharks and ocean killers were working for Li Hei, and Li Hei's gang had also opened the killer reptiles' enclosures at San Diego Zoo to release the crocodile and the alligator.

A day later, the sharks and killer reptiles informed the vicious invertebrates that two giant clams, ten crabs and ten lobsters were working for Lin Wu.

The octopus, the giant squid and the cuttlefish set off for the waters off Malibu in Los Angeles, where the giant clams, crabs and lobsters seized two men by the feet and another two by their toes. All four men were dragged down into the ocean depths, and each lost a foot or all ten toes. On seeing the octopus, the giant squid and the cuttlefish swimming over to murder them, the giant clams, crabs and lobsters tried to escape. But it was too late. They had attacked the four men because they were working for Li Hei, but as these men were fatally wounded, the three savage invertebrates finished them off each with two or three blows from their tentacles. The octopus and the cuttlefish ripped open two men just as the giant squid slashed and tore open the last two. Then they turned with brutal savagery upon the giant clams, crabs and lobsters. With flailing tentacles, the octopus slaughtered all ten crabs whilst the giant squid massacred seven lobsters and a giant clam. The cuttlefish tore open three lobsters and the other giant clam. Then the ruthless and brutal invertebrates devoured the four men they had mutilated.

The sharks, the crocodile and the alligator watched two other massacres, each a hundred metres from a cove of water guarded by the octopus, the stingray and the manta ray. Two gangs of divers were constricted, shredded and torn to pieces by the giant squid and the cuttlefish or had chunks of flesh and bone bitten and chopped out of them by the barracuda, the conger eel and the moray eel. The savage invertebrates slaughtered four men, and the ferocious fishes brutally massacred another five. Another eight divers swam to the cove for safety, not knowing that the octopus, the stingray and the manta ray were just inside the cove. The sharks and killer reptiles sped through the water towards the cove to assist the vicious killer fishes. As the octopus ripped and tore apart one man, the stingray and manta ray violently stabbed another two. All three were killed outright. The sharks seized the legs of three other divers, their bone-crushing jaws and terrifying, razor-sharp teeth crunching off the divers' legs before the sharks crushed their ribs and spines and devoured them with no mercy. The crocodile and the alligator crunched their powerful jaws and teeth into the legs of the last two men, before their dreaded death-rolls twisted the men's legs from their bodies. Then the killer reptiles used their fearsome teeth to crush in the men's ribs, and both men were killed instantly.

The great white and the tiger shark saw treasure nearby in the ocean—the reason why the divers had ventured into these dangerous waters before being viciously savaged by the ocean killers and killer reptiles.

The sharks negotiated with the stingray and the manta ray as to whether the two rays wanted to work with the savage invertebrates or the fierce killer fishes.

They chose the giant squid's gang.

Then the sharks, the crocodile and the alligator decided to join with the barracuda's gang.

The great white and the tiger shark negotiated with the crocodile and the alligator, deciding they needed help from the fearsome sawfish and three smaller sharks that were equally ferocious and brutal—the blue shark, the bull shark and the hammerhead shark. Together with the ocean killers, the sawfish and all five massive sharks needed to attack and devour tourists swimming in the waters off Malibu Beach in Los Angeles. But the stingray and the manta ray knew how best to find the three huge sharks and the sawfish, so the great white, the tiger shark and the killer reptiles needed to swim towards the giant squid's gang and persuade the rays to join with them.

Lin Wu's men were in a big boat off Venice Beach in Los Angeles, and they were savagely attacked by the giant squid's group of five ocean killers. The octopus, the giant squid and the cuttlefish shredded and dismembered three men, just as the stingray and the manta ray poisoned or impaled two other men. Meanwhile, the sharks and killer reptiles savagely mauled and mutilated the last four men.

The sharks informed the giant squid that the stingray and the manta ray must search for the sawfish, the blue shark, the bull shark and the hammerhead. The giant squid agreed to this. The sharks ordered the stingray and the manta ray to search out the sawfish's gang and tell them to join the other ocean killers and killer reptiles in attacking the tourists off Malibu Beach. Both fishes swam out into the Pacific Ocean in order to find the sawfish's gang.

The invertebrates and fishes reunited with each other, and then rejoined the sharks and killer reptiles. But the sharks, ocean killers and killer reptiles saw enormous black and white killer whales on the horizon. This was a bad sign.

The killer whales joined the dolphins and walruses, the killer whales and dolphins arriving off California from Mexico and the waters off the northern United States, whilst the walruses had swum over from British Colombia in western Canada and Alaska. They surrounded the three enormous sharks, the massive sawfish, the stingray and the manta ray. The dolphins viciously mauled the stingray and the manta ray until they were dead, whilst the walruses outnumbered the sawfish and used their long, sabre-like tusks to rip them open, and the killer whales ruthlessly savaged and devoured the blue shark, the bull shark and the hammerhead. The crocodile and the alligator attempted to attack the dolphins, having seen the killer whales on the horizon, but the killer whales viciously assaulted and chewed the killer reptiles until they died. Only the sharks and ocean killers were left alive.

The two enormous sharks, three huge fishes and three awesome invertebrates knew the sawfish's gang and the killer reptiles would never return. The larger sharks and ocean killers needed to attack the tourists at Malibu the next morning. First, they would rest for the night.

***

Marion's second dream was set in the dreamworld joining the jungles and bamboo forests of the Congo and China with the tropical rainforests of Colombia and Venezuela. In the Congo, an African elephant and buffalo bade farewell to a white rhino and a black rhino as they decided to search for three massive male gorillas. These giant herbivores and great apes were the Beasts of Lin Wu, and they needed to unite as many large herbivores and apes as possible against Li Hei's poachers. Their magical powers made them immune to bullets fired from the poachers' guns.

The elephant and the buffalo journeyed along the Congo's dreamworld border with Colombia and Venezuela, where they encountered five giant anteaters from Colombia and Venezuela and ten South American wild pigs, called peccaries, from both countries. The giant anteaters and peccaries led the elephant and the buffalo to the bamboo forests of western China, where they met five giant pandas. The giant pandas told the elephant and buffalo that the elephant's group had to head off with the ten chimpanzees from the Congo and ten orang-utans that Lin Wu had introduced into China from Sumatra and Borneo in Indonesia. The giant herbivores and apes would make their way from China back into the Congo to locate the three enormous male gorillas.

When the African elephant, the African buffalo, the chimpanzees and orang-utans were three miles down a wide and muddy pathway, they were confronted by a vast gang of poachers, who fired at them with their rifles. But the beasts' powers of sorcery repelled the bullets, and then the elephant and buffalo charged, flanked to the left and right by the chimpanzees and orang-utans. With long ivory tusks, sledgehammer horns and ground-churning hooves, the elephant and buffalo gored and trampled twelve men together. The elephant bashed a thirteenth with his club-like trunk. Using their fearsome, fang-like teeth and vice-like hands, the chimpanzees ripped eight poachers' faces and necks and tore off their arms, just as the orang-utans tore the faces and pulled off the arms of seven huntsmen. From neighbouring Uganda came fourteen ferocious wild pigs—namely five warthogs, five bush pigs and four giant forest hogs—whilst three savage baboons, having journeyed over from Cameroon, came with four aggressive drills and five vicious mandrills, both species of fearsome primates that were cousins of baboons. The baboons, drills and mandrills brutally mauled twelve men as the warthogs, bush pigs and forest hogs gored, tore open and disembowelled fourteen more.

Also joining in were the five giant pandas—whose tremendous claws were like those of bears—five giant anteaters and ten peccaries with scimitar-like tusks as razor-sharp as those of the warthogs, bush pigs and giant forest hogs. The giant pandas and giant ant-eaters ruthlessly mauled ten poachers with the brutal ferocity of grizzlies or black bears. In the same three minutes of carnage, the peccaries bit and chopped the last three brutes to death. The whole gang of armed men lay in bloody heaps of mutilated corpses.

The chimpanzees and orang-utans thanked the three troops of primates, four sounders of wild pigs, the giant pandas and giant anteaters. The elephant and the buffalo surveyed the whole area, with assistance from the giant pandas, giant anteaters and peccaries, before these smaller beasts split up, going with the other wild pigs and baboons in three directions. The giant pandas, giant anteaters and peccaries headed for China's border with South America whilst the warthogs, bush pigs and giant forest hogs ventured through the Congo's rainforests with the baboons, drills and mandrills. The chimpanzees and orang-utans trailed behind the elephant and buffalo as these giant herbivores searched for the three male gorillas.

The elephant and buffalo watched a large gang of poachers coming their way. The chimpanzees and orang-utans also saw the gunmen and disappeared into the forest flanking the muddy road. The elephant and buffalo withdrew back down the highway with the armed men in pursuit. Then the giant herbivores saw a wide side road leading away from the main road. Coming down the main road was another gang of poachers. Both gangs of men were closing in on the herbivores. The giant herbivores headed down the side road and sensed that the second gang was venturing into the forest flanking the side road.

The elephant and the buffalo ambled down the side road for an hour. The second gang were fifteen yards ahead and aiming their powerful, high-velocity rifles towards the beasts. The men bombarded, pounded and pummelled the giant beasts with a ferocious hail of gunshots, but the creatures' magical powers repelled the bullets. Then the beasts charged with awesome power, speed and brutal ferocity. The elephant stabbed, gored and trampled four thugs whilst the buffalo gored and crushed a fifth brute. All five criminals lay in bloodied heaps in the mud with all their bones broken, their lives ended in the most harsh, cruel and brutal manner.

The elephant and the buffalo doubled back along the side road towards the main road and knew they must confront the first gang of poachers. And they knew the first gang was much larger than the second gang of five men.

The elephant and the buffalo wandered back up the highway. They needed to find the gorillas. But first they had to locate the chimpanzees and orang-utans.

The giant herbivores continued strolling at a casual pace. Suddenly, eight poachers stood in their way, aiming their high-powered rifles towards the enormous beasts. Using their magical spells, the elephant and the buffalo repelled the bullets vomited from the rifles, before they charged the men with vicious brutality. The elephant stabbed and gored one man, bashed, pounded and pummelled a second man repeatedly with his sledgehammer trunk and crushed four men with his rock-hard hooves. The buffalo's formidable horns, like a battering-ram, gored another man and tore his ribcage out. He bashed and pounded the last poacher, then used his flesh-chopping hooves to kick and trample both crooks so they died instantly.

But twenty-one more evil and fearsome brutes charged down the highway to rescue their eight fellow criminals and focused their rifles towards the giant herbivores. The guns opened fire with vicious savagery, but the herbivores' spells destroyed the bullets. The poachers were then a target for the ten chimpanzees and ten orang-utans, now being led by the three male gorillas. With their clubbed fists like giant hams, the gorillas swiped three men—two suffered fractured spines and the third a broken arm and fractured ribs. The gorillas then savagely mauled and pulverised the men with their giant fangs like lions' teeth. The first two men also suffered broken ribs and several bite wounds all over their bodies and legs. The third violent killer sustained multiple bite wounds and a broken leg. All three men were dead in minutes.

The chimpanzees outnumbered and viciously savaged five men whilst the orang-utans repeated this savage assault on another five, severely mauling the poachers' faces, necks and arms with their dagger-like teeth as their strong arms with vice-like hands wrenched the men's arms from their shoulders. The ten men died in agony from excessive loss of blood from ruptured arteries and blood vessels and their skulls being fractured by the apes' fearsome and brutal fangs.

With thirteen armed men slaughtered, the elephant and the buffalo charged the last eight poachers with crushing power and speed. The elephant impaled one man and tossed him through the air whilst crushing and trampling four other men with his hooves. All five men died in a matter of seconds.

The buffalo ploughed into another killer and tossed him repeatedly into the air. The murderer crashed to the ground with all his bones broken, then the buffalo used his sledgehammer hooves to kick a second brute and crush a third. Both men sustained broken legs or ribs and a fractured pelvis. The buffalo finished off all three men by plunging his horns into their stomachs, and the brutes died in minutes from being disembowelled and torn open.

Then two even larger gangs of poachers charged down the muddy road from the east and west, twenty-six thugs sprinting from the direction of South America and China to the east and north-east, and twenty-eight criminals speeding and darting from the rainforests to the west. The harsh, cruel brutes aimed their rifles towards the giant herbivores and apes, but more magical spells burned the rifles red-hot. The evil and brutal men threw their firearms to the ground, screaming, yelling and crying with agony. With the guns useless, the poachers from China, Colombia and Venezuela, as well as Tanzania and Uganda, were viciously attacked by the three sounders of warthogs, bush pigs and giant forest hogs and the three troops of baboons, drills and mandrills. In the same two or three minutes that the wild pigs brutally gored and disembowelled fourteen men, the baboons and their cousins savagely mauled and murdered twelve more. All twenty-six poachers were massacred without mercy by the wild pigs' scimitar-like tusks and the primates' dagger-like fangs.

This left the fifth gang of twenty-eight armed men local to the Congo and neighbouring Cameroon and Nigeria, hundreds of miles away in West Africa. The three gorillas used their enormous hands and lion-like fangs to bash and maul three massive men to death while the chimpanzees ruthlessly savaged and killed ten more. The orang-utans brutally mauled and murdered another ten.

Five men remained, and the elephant and the buffalo charged with awesome, fearsome strength and extreme violence. It only took thirteen seconds for the elephant to bash and crush four riflemen, the same space of time it took for the buffalo to gore, trample and crush the last gunman. All twenty-eight armed men lay in scattered, bloodied heaps of mutilated flesh and fractured bones.

The elephant and the buffalo offered their gratitude to the warthogs, bush pigs and giant forest hogs, together with the baboons, drills and mandrills, who then bade farewell to the giant herbivores and apes. The three huge gorillas ordered the ten chimpanzees and ten orang-utans to disappear into the forest before the gorillas led the elephant and the buffalo down the wide, muddy highway towards a large pond. Once they had reached this pond, they headed south through the forest, towards where the silverback and his two fellow males had a family of ten female gorillas and fifteen youngsters.

But the three male gorillas were in for a shock. The trees were being sawn or chopped down, and the gorillas found their females and youngsters lying dead around their lair, clubbed to death. The men responsible were not poachers; they were criminal developers out to destroy the forest.

Then the elephant and the buffalo spotted the white rhino and the black rhino stalking the men from the south. The elephant, the buffalo and the male gorillas were positioned behind the trees and thickets to the north. The rhinos suddenly charged with brutal strength, power and speed. They stabbed, gored and trampled ten men with their formidable horns and terrifying hooves. The men were petrified with stark terror and blind horror. The elephant, the buffalo and the gorillas charged with fearsome strength and power. The elephant gored and crushed three men, the buffalo impaled another and tossed him into the air, and the last three men suffered brutal deaths, being savagely mauled by the male gorillas. The orgy of deadly violence ended when the gorillas smashed the men's heads open with their enormous fists. The men died within the next second.

The elephant and the buffalo welcomed the rhinos and introduced them to the gorillas. The rhinos offered sympathy to the male gorillas for the deaths of their females and youngsters. The gorillas, the elephant and the buffalo knew this was the reason that the rhinos had attacked the criminal developers.

The elephant, the rhinos and the buffalo had to hunt down the leading criminal developers and murder them, including the ruthless animal dealer Li Hei.

The four giant herbivores doubled back east towards the dreamworld border with China where Li Hei ran his evil gangs of poachers and criminal developers. When the elephant's group reached the hideout on the Congo side of the border, they discovered Li Hei was not at the hideout. The elephant's band overheard the poachers discussing how Li Hei had warped himself with witchcraft to San Diego, and how his men had broken open the doors of the killer reptiles' enclosures and released the crocodile and the alligator. The crocodile and the alligator had swum through the waters off California towards Los Angeles to join up with the sharks and ocean killers. Li Hei and his gang had also driven to Los Angeles so that they could use psychic mind signals to communicate with the ocean killers.

The elephant's gang also had to use witchcraft to warp themselves to California in order to unite with Marion Weisberg and Lin Wu.

But first, they had to massacre the poachers and criminal developers at the rainforest hideout. A patrol of armed men paraded around the front gate of the hideout, aimed their rifles towards the giant herbivores and blazed. The giant herbivores' powers of witchcraft vaporised the bullets and heated up the fearsome guns. The men screamed and cried with excruciating pain and dropped their weaponry. As the elephant destroyed three thugs, the white rhino and the black rhino pulverised five brutes and the last two crooks were stabbed, gored and trampled by the buffalo's lethal horns and deadly hooves.

As the two rhinos kept watch for reinforcements of men outside the hideout, the elephant and the buffalo crashed through the wooden wall and solid gate so they were inside the enclosure.

Five more poachers were taken by surprise before they could reach for their rifles, the men frozen with blind terror and horror. With flailing kicks from his club-like front hooves, the elephant smashed the bones of three men before he trampled another two. Hurrying out of the hideout were the last five men, all criminal developers from China. The buffalo ploughed into two of the men with his terrible horns, ripped one man's spine from his back and tore out the second brute's ribcage. Both men died in four or five seconds. The elephant attacked the last three criminals with deadly ferocity so that his terrifying tusks horribly gored one man just as his ground-churning hooves crushed the other two. All three men perished from broken bones.

The criminal developers were finished, and the elephant and the buffalo made their way outside the enclosure to rejoin the rhinos. The elephant's gang journeyed back through the forest towards the gorillas' lair.

The elephant, the buffalo and the rhinos reunited with the three male gorillas, and discovered that the gorillas had been joined by the ten chimpanzees and ten orang-utans, backed up by the five giant pandas and five giant anteaters. The giant anteaters from Colombia and Venezuela were flanked by the ten peccaries from both countries, the warthogs, bush pigs and giant forest hogs from Uganda, and the baboons, drills and mandrills from Cameroon.

The six troops of male apes hurried up large trees whilst the giant pandas, giant ant-eaters and wild pigs hid themselves behind bushes and thickets, and the elephant's gang made their way behind acacia, baobab and hardwood trees. One last gang of criminal developers and their workers from Colombia, Venezuela and Mexico, as well as China and the Congo, came over to cut down hundreds more trees to make way for large farms. Some of the men had rifles to defend themselves, not wishing to be taken by surprise and attacked like the previous gang who had fallen victim to the elephant's gang and the three gorillas. The armed men were as vigilant as eagles and could sense the giant herbivores hiding behind the mass of trees. The giant pandas, giant anteaters and wild pigs needed to divert the men's attention away from the trees by attacking from the thickets. With extreme violence and aggression, they charged like tigers ambushing their prey. In a matter of seconds, the giant pandas mauled five men, the giant anteaters ripped open another five, and the peccaries chopped and tore to death two more. The last fourteen gunmen fired their rifles at the twenty beasts, killing all the peccaries, felling the giant anteaters and dropping the giant pandas with shots to the heads or chests. But with strength and speed, the other three sounders of wild pigs used the beasts' sacrifice as a distraction, closing in upon the men in a few seconds. The warthogs ripped open five men as the bush pigs tore open another five and the giant forest hogs disembowelled the last four men. Petrified terror and blind horror overcame the mass of unarmed men left alive.

Dropping down from the trees, the six troops of savage primates threw more workers to the ground in seconds, the impact breaking the men's backs. The three baboons, four drills and five mandrills fastened their fangs into the necks and heads of twelve men and killed them in five seconds. The three gorillas, ten chimpanzees and ten orang-utans dug their dagger-like teeth into the chests or heads of twenty-three workers, crushing their ribs or penetrating their brains. The evil men were dead in thirteen seconds. Charging from behind the trees, the elephant destroyed eight workers. In the same period, the rhinos pulverised ten workers and the buffalo gored the leading criminal developer, fracturing his spine, ribs and both his legs. All these men died from broken bones and loss of blood.

Then the ferocious beasts grieved over the deaths of the giant pandas, giant anteaters and peccaries. After ten minutes of mourning, the elephant informed the apes of how the giant herbivores had overheard the poachers at their hideout discussing how Li Hei had warped to California. The elephant told them how Li Hei's men had released the crocodile and alligator from San Diego Zoo, how those reptiles had allied with the ocean killers, and how the sharks, ocean killers and killer reptiles, along with a gang of Li Hei's men, planned to attack tourists in and around Malibu Beach. The elephant told the apes how the four giant herbivores needed to warp themselves to California to prevent the Beasts of Li Hei from committing this horrific atrocity.

At that moment, the giant herbivores were joined by three enormous male lions, ten lionesses and five cheetahs native to the Congo. The male lions commanded the cheetahs to stay in the Congo in order to adjoin the Congo with Nepal and ally themselves with five huge male Bengal tigers. The massive, savage tigers and the ferocious cheetahs would cooperate with the male gorillas in supporting and helping Marion Weisberg to carry out surveillance of Li Hei's rogue beasts in the Everglades of Florida. The thirteen male lions and lionesses had to warp themselves alone to Malibu Beach with the giant herbivores.

The lions ordered the elephant, the rhinos and the buffalo to form a warping spell, and the Congo's most powerful and dangerous creatures disappeared into thin air. They reappeared five seconds later in California, on the section of Malibu Beach not used by tourists so as not to scare off the men and women.

At that point, Marion's dream ended. She awoke in her hotel room in Los Angeles. She was naked, but she slipped on her clothes and then saw a message left on the dressing table: the first clue telling her where she must head.

"To Malibu Beach," Marion whispered. "I must warp myself there now."

She evaporated from the well-lit room. Three seconds later, she met the lions, the elephant, the rhinos and the buffalo at Malibu Beach.

***

Marion's husband, Klaus Weisberg, aged forty-seven, was warped to the tundra of northern Alberta. It was a snowy, icy region of western Canada to the north of Alberta's Wood Buffalo National Park, famous for its American bison or buffalo. Five bison had been warped to the tundra by Lin Wu after his magical spell took Klaus from his farm outside Munich. The gang of male bison were joined by a puma, a lynx, a bobcat, a wolverine and a feral cat, backed up by a wolf, a coyote, a very large mountain fox as big as a Labrador, and a bull mastiff, all of them savage killers from Wood Buffalo. Uniting with them were an American badger and a mink local to Alberta; a common badger, a weasel, a stoat, a polecat and a pine marten warped over from Norway; and a badger and four weasels or mustelids of the same species from Sweden. But just as formidable, ferocious and deadly as the five American bison were two polar bears from Norway and Sweden and three polar bears native to Alberta's tundra. All these beasts were off hunting for food.

"We meet again, Lin Wu," Klaus said evenly. "Why have you warped me over from Bavaria to this region of Canada?"

"It's a long story," Lin Wu said, his voice calm. "I met Marion at San Diego Zoo and informed her of a war between the Men and Beasts of Li Hei and the Beasts of Lin Wu. Because she is a brilliant detective, I involved her in this war, and now you are involved. I gave Marion magical powers by feeding her three magic bananas, and I want you to eat another three magic bananas, which will give you powers of witchcraft."

"We're two wizards and a witch," Klaus commented. "Okay, I'll eat the bananas."

It took five minutes for the long-haired, bearded German to consume the three bananas. He experienced new physical and mental strength and the power of witchcraft travelling through his muscular body.

"Do you feel the power of sorcery?" Lin Wu wanted to know.

"Yes, I do," Klaus replied.

"These magical powers will enable you and Marion to dream of what the Lin Wu Beasts have been doing in other parts of the world," Lin Wu explained. "You will have the power to talk to your wife, thousands of miles away in another country, with mind signals, like using a mobile phone. You can also use this power to communicate with deadly creatures. You and the Lin Wu Beasts can stop bullets hitting you. But the Men and Beasts of Li Hei also have powers of sorcery due to magic gold. It will be a brutal and dangerous war fought with evil savagery. But we must persist."

"I see," Klaus said.

"Talking of you and Marion dreaming of what the Lin Wu Beasts have done in other parts of the world," Lin Wu remarked, "Marion has just woken up in her hotel room in Los Angeles after having two dreams, one of sharks, ocean killers and killer reptiles attacking innocent divers and my sorcerers in the waters off California, the other of giant herbivores, giant pandas, apes and wild pigs combating poachers and criminal developers in the dreamworld joining the Congo and China with Colombia and Venezuela. Both of you will have more dreams telling you what my beasts have been doing. Even more to the point, when Marion executes a mission in one part of the world, she'll find a clue telling her which state or country to warp herself to next. I have left these clues."

"She may need my help," Klaus suggested.

"No, Klaus," Lin Wu insisted. "Marion can look after herself. You're needed here in Alberta to assist me, the five bison, five polar bears and the large predators and mustelids from Alberta, Norway and Sweden. In my psychic mind, Li Hei has travelled from California to Canada, and he and his poachers plan to massacre the bison, polar bears and predators, and kill both of us."

"In that case, we must stay put," Klaus decided.

"The bison, large predators and mustelids are returning from their hunting trip," Lin Wu said.

"They're carrying dead prey," Klaus observed.

"They'll have a feast," Lin Wu said. "Just watch them."

The five enormous bison, being herbivores, carried carrots, cabbages and turnips given to them by workers in a greengrocer's in a nearby village. The massive polar bears were dragging the carcass of an enormous bull moose they had outnumbered and killed. The puma, the wolverine, the lynx and the bobcat had each slaughtered a rabbit and a hare, whilst the feral cat had killed a rabbit, a hare and two mice, and the dog had murdered a rabbit, a hare and three mice. The wolf, the coyote and the fox had each massacred two or three rabbits and two hares, together with ten farm chickens, four of these chickens falling prey to the fox. The American badger and the mink had killed rabbits and hares as ruthlessly as the puma, the wolf, the coyote and the fox; both mustelids had murdered three rabbits and two hares, one rabbit and both hares being the mink's victims. Of the five mustelids from Norway and five mustelids from Sweden, the two badgers had killed two rabbits, three mice and three chickens; the two weasels, two stoats, two polecats and two pine martens had massacred four rabbits, four hares, five mice and five chickens. All these mustelids killed rabbits, hares, mice and rats more savagely than the mountain fox, the bull mastiff and the cat. The puma and the wolverine were the largest and most ferocious of the larger predators, the wolverine being the biggest of all the mustelids, but the bison and polar bears were the dominant beasts due to their huge size and crushing strength.

After the moose, the rabbits, hares, mice and chickens were eaten ravenously and the bison had consumed the vegetables, they stared at a gang of poachers led by Li Hei, who aimed their rifles towards the bison and predators. Too small to attack armed men, the American badger and the mink were warped by Lin Wu back to Wood Buffalo, whilst the ten smaller mustelids disappeared into the haze and found themselves back in the coniferous forests of Norway and Sweden.

The bison, polar bears and large predators charged Li Hei's gang, but had no magical powers to stop bullets. The puma and the cat charged one man as the wolverine, the lynx and the bobcat sped and darted towards three others, the puma screaming viciously and the wolverine roaring with savage rage and fury.

The poachers' rifles blazed, and the puma's gang were shot to death in a hail of bullets. The wolf, the coyote, the fox and the dog charged two men, two large wild dogs to each man, but the men fired again and again, and the wolf's gang died from several shots. The wolf was the last of the four canine beasts to die.

But the five seconds it took for the armed men to massacre all nine predators worked to the advantage of the five bison and five polar bears. Goring and tossing five men into the air and trampling three others, the bison fractured the men's bones, whilst the polar bears brutally savaged five poachers on the ground. The men were covered in claw and puncture wounds, their bones broken. All these men died in fifteen seconds, but the remaining poachers fired dozens of gunshots into the bison and polar bears, and all ten giant beasts eventually died.

As this all happened in front of them, Klaus and Lin Wu ejected lightning bolts towards the poachers, but Li Hei repelled every lightning bolt.

"Li Hei is extremely dangerous and not a man to be underestimated," Lin Wu told Klaus.

"What must we do?" Klaus said.

"Get out of here," Lin Wu informed Klaus.

"Li Hei is about to fire lightning at us," Klaus told the old man.

"I'm about to warp us out of here," Lin Wu said.

With a warping spell, both men disappeared

into the icy mist. Three seconds later, they were in a mountain forest in Wyoming in the northern United States.

"Where are we?" Klaus inquired.

"At Yellowstone National Park, overlapping Idaho, Montana and Wyoming," Lin Wu replied. "Where we are is in Wyoming. With my magical powers, I have united here five rabbits and five hares with two feral cats and three dogs alongside a puma, a lynx and a bobcat, together with a wolf, a coyote and a fox."

"But wolves, coyotes and foxes prey on rabbits and hares," Klaus objected. "Not to mention a puma, a lynx and a bobcat will take their toll of rabbits and hares, and the dog and the cat will eat rabbits, hares, mice and rats."

"My sorcery has united the herbivores and predators as allies," Lin Wu explained. "I have cast friendly hearts into the six large predators and the dogs and cats, and I have persuaded them to respect the rabbits and hares. The dogs, cats, rabbits and hares will be effective in massacring evil rats sent by Li Hei to murder the rabbits, hares and fierce rodents local to Yellowstone. Assisting them will be an American badger, a mink and a fisher marten—the fisher being a cousin of the pine marten and the beech marten of Europe. Supporting the six predators forming the puma's gang will be two massive, ferocious herbivores: a male American bison and a bull moose. Not to mention four huge male bears local to Wyoming, two grizzlies and two black bears, who are the largest, most powerful and savage of all the predators. This army of predators and herbivores are North America's Lin Wu Beasts, and unlike the beasts in Alberta who had no magical powers to stop bullets, Wyoming's Lin Wu Beasts do possess powers of sorcery as well as their strength and ferocity."

"And these beasts are coming towards us now," Klaus said.

"Don't be intimidated," Lin Wu said. "They're very friendly towards noble humans."

The bison, the moose and the four male bears were flanked by the puma, the lynx and the bobcat to their left and the wolf, the coyote and the mountain fox to their right. The fox was a very big beast with long legs, who was as large the coyote. Mountain foxes in the mountains and hills of Europe and North America were larger than the lowland foxes of flat countryside, as well as stronger and fiercer. Behind the giant herbivores, bears and large predators walked the three dogs, two feral cats, five rabbits and four hares, flanked by the American badger, the mink and the fisher. All these beasts looked at Klaus and Lin Wu with friendly, intelligent eyes.

***

On a remote part of California's Malibu Beach, the thirteen lions, the elephant, the two rhinos and the buffalo were hidden behind undergrowth, away from the men and women sunbathing on the sand further up or swimming in the Pacific Ocean's sky-blue waters. Marion was with the beasts. She suddenly saw, closing in on the men and women from the suburbs of Los Angeles, a large gang of Li Hei's poachers, brandishing powerful hunting rifles with which to blast to death these people—and the police officers and coastguards watching over the beach. The poachers started firing indiscriminately at innocent people and policemen, killing and wounding dozens of men and women. These people fled into the sea, where they were vulnerable to attack from the sharks and ocean killers, this being the deliberate intention of the poachers.

The three male lions and ten lionesses bounded behind the beach-huts so the poachers would not spot them. They emerged one by one from behind these hiding places and cantered with tremendous power and lightning speed towards the men, hurling themselves at the men from behind. The lions crashed into thirteen men, throwing their full weight upon the men's backs and hurtling them to the ground. The lions' lethal, razor-sharp claws sliced and shredded the poachers' legs and upper bodies before their deadly, dagger-like fangs crunched through the men's necks or heads, killing them in ten seconds.

The other poachers rained a hail of gunshots into the lions and lionesses, slaughtering all the lionesses so only the three male lions were still standing. The lions hurtled upon three men, their hind and front claws raking through the brutes' thighs, chests and shoulders as their powerful fangs lunged for the men's throats and strangled them. More shots from other poachers bloodied the lions' heads and killed them instantly. But the elephant, the rhinos and the buffalo sprayed lightning spells, which burned up the criminals' rifles and scalded their hands. Screaming and crying with burning agony, the poachers dropped the rifles as the four giant herbivores thundered along the sand with powerful hooves. The elephant shattered four men to death with his heavy hooves, then plunged his tremendous tusks into a fifth man and hurled the brute into the air. The man perished from being impaled again upon the elephant's ivory tusks before the deadly giant slammed the killer onto his back, smashing the crook's head on a rock. The white rhino and the black rhino each stabbed with their horns and crushed three men against their hooves as the buffalo ruthlessly gored one man and tossed him about repeatedly whilst trampling and kicking another man under his hooves. Their bones smashed to pieces; all eight men were killed in a matter of seconds.

Petrified with terror of the now-dead lions and the attacking giant herbivores, the men and women stayed in the sea. This was the moment the sharks and ocean killers attacked with appalling savagery and bloodlust. Three men each lost a leg to the snapping red jaws and enormous teeth of the great white and the tiger shark. Both sharks seized two other men and crushed their spines and ribs, the terrifying ferocity of the attack dismembering both. The other men and women screamed with horror as they helplessly watched these five men being viciously mauled and maimed in this furious attack. The barracuda, the conger eel and the moray eel crunched and chopped big chunks of flesh and bone from three men while the octopus, the giant squid and the cuttlefish tore, shredded and mutilated three other men with their sharp tentacles.

The elephant, the rhinos and the buffalo cantered into the sea to drive off the large, violent brutes, which lunged and slashed at the giant herbivores with deadly teeth and fearsome tentacles. Marion fired spells at the eyes and noses of the sharks and ocean killers, and then the killer whales, walruses and dolphins rescued the people trapped in the water. Attacking with savage fury and awesome power, the killer whales brutally mauled and devoured both giant sharks. The dolphins outnumbered the barracuda and bit large chunks out of him until he perished. The walruses ripped the conger eel and moray eel open from stem to stern. The octopus, the giant squid and the cuttlefish bit and slashed at the walruses and dolphins until the killer whales closed in, crunching their massive jaws and razor-sharp teeth through the giant squid's gang, massacring the three giant invertebrates in a matter of minutes.

"It's all right!" Marion cried to the surviving

men and women on the beach. "These beasts are friendly. The poachers were Li Hei's men, the same men who released a crocodile and an alligator from their enclosures at San Diego Zoo."

"A crocodile and an alligator!" one man exclaimed.

"They're now dead," Marion explained. "The killer whales killed them."

The survivors and Marion thanked the killer whales, walruses and dolphins for rescuing these people from the ocean killers. They were also grateful to the deceased lions, and to the elephant, the rhinos and the buffalo for massacring the savage, brutal poachers.

Then Marion spotted, amongst the rocks, another clue. She read it with inquisitive eyes. "To Florida's Everglades. We must warp ourselves to Florida now," she addressed the giant herbivores.

Marion and the giant herbivores evaporated into the haze.

***

With magical spells, the three gorillas and five cheetahs linked the Congo to Nepal and met up with the five huge Bengal tigers. The tigers knew the gorillas and cheetahs were allies, not prey. With hissing growls and grunts, the cheetahs communicated a tragedy they had picked up psychically. The lions and lionesses had been shot to death on Malibu Beach in California by a vast gang of poachers. The tigers lowered their heads with grief. The tigers, cheetahs and gorillas, all males, knew they must avenge the lions' brutal deaths.

Before the thirteen lions had warped to California, the male lions had ordered the cheetahs and gorillas to form the dreamworld joining the Congo with Nepal and to meet up with the tigers. All three gangs would warp themselves into Florida's Everglades with three other big cats from Nepal and Brazil, namely a spotted leopard, a black panther and a jaguar. The three large male wild cats approached the tigers and cheetahs, all these feline beasts possessing powers of sorcery, and they disappeared into the forest mist.

Five seconds later, they were in Florida's Everglades. The tigers ordered the two leopards and the jaguar to wait for them in the forest near the Everglades Zoo, whilst the tigers, cheetahs and gorillas would search for Marion and the giant herbivores. The gorillas knew there were violent attacks on humans in Florida being committed not only by sharks, ocean killers and killer reptiles, but also by rogue giant herbivores who had warped over from Kenya—another African elephant, a white rhino, a black rhino and an evil, brutal African buffalo. The tigers and gorillas needed to observe what these wicked rogue beasts were doing and where they were hanging about so that the tigers could inform Marion and the noble giant herbivores from the Congo.

The spotted leopard, the black leopard—or

black panther—and the jaguar made their way through the mangrove swamps and forests towards the Everglades Zoo. The tigers, cheetahs and gorillas followed their senses towards Florida's south-western coastline overlooking the Gulf of Mexico, not far from the two islands of Key West and Key Largo. Overlooking the Gulf to the west, the tigers, cheetahs and gorillas glared towards a village and then stared at the tropical blue waters. They spotted a crocodile, an alligator and a Komodo dragon forming an alliance with a great white shark and a tiger shark. The alligator was native to Florida's Everglades, whilst the crocodile and the Komodo dragon had warped over from Uganda and Indonesia in order to ally with the alligator and then the sharks. The tigers knew these were Li Hei's Beasts, for otherwise killer reptiles would not unite with sharks and ocean killers.

Then, eight men approached the beach, totally unaware of the danger they were in, having not seen the sharks and killer reptiles. The tigers also saw another six men away from the beach being stalked by the four rogue giant herbivores from Kenya. The sharks and killer reptiles disappeared underwater, the sharks about to attack five swimmers; the crocodile, the alligator and the Komodo dragon went for three others. But as the men were about to enter the water and the men away from the beach were oblivious to the elephant, the two rhinos and the buffalo about to attack them, the tigers and gorillas thought fast to divert the men away from the water and the beach in order to save them from the evil beasts. Bellowing, roaring and screaming at the tops of their voices, the tigers and gorillas charged towards the beach. The gorillas showed themselves to the eight men in the water and the six men on the opposite side of the beach. The fourteen humans grabbed their clothes, the larger group joining the smaller group in the undergrowth before climbing into a truck. The vehicle moved away along the road flanking the beach.

The elephant, the rhinos and the buffalo panicked upon hearing the ear-bursting roaring and screaming of the tigers and gorillas. The giant herbivores wailed, trumpeted and screamed with blind panic. Their attention was drawn away from the truck full of tourists, for elephants, rhinos and buffaloes in Africa and Asia feared lions and tigers, the top predators in these continents. But due to being corrupted by Li Hei's magic, they fought their fear and charged towards the tigers and gorillas, the giant herbivores bent on revenge. No match for these awesome beasts, even big cats and enormous, strongly-muscled apes as formidable as the tigers, the cheetahs and gorillas regarded discretion as the better part of valour. Sprinting across the road, they sped into the undergrowth, first going southeast and then northeast to confuse the rogue elephant's gang.

In the ocean, the sharks and killer reptiles were highly disappointed and frustrated the tourists had failed to fall into their trap by entering the sea. The quick thinking of the tigers and gorillas bellowing and roaring had saved both groups of tourists.

Knowing the sharks, killer reptiles and giant herbivores would target more humans, the tigers, cheetahs and gorillas made their way back to the coast. They glanced at the village and, with violent chills in their stomachs, were overcome by guilt and remorse that they had failed to warn the village's inhabitants that the giant herbivores were nearby. The beasts rampaged through the village with murderous violence and fury, killing dozens of men, women and children in the street. They smashed their heads, tusks and horns into the buildings, which collapsed upon the people inside. Trampling, crushing and goring as many people as possible with hooves, tusks and horns, the elephant and the buffalo were psychotic and savage in their evil brutality, whilst the white rhino and the black rhino were as murderous and merciless as the much bigger elephant.

The cheetahs heard the terrified, agonising screams of six men who were stranded in the sea after an octopus and a giant squid had violently capsized their fishing boat. Three men were being ripped apart and dismembered by the octopus, the giant squid and the cuttlefish. Three other men were torn apart, chopped and mutilated by the barracuda, the conger eel and the moray eel. All six ocean killers were different individuals from the ocean killers massacred by the killer whales and dolphins off Malibu Beach.

Five male swimmers were being chased towards the beach by the great white and the tiger shark, together with the crocodile, the alligator and the Komodo dragon. The evil, ferocious man-killers thrashed the ocean water with their tails, but the men made it to shore. As these swimmers ran up the beach, the sharks and killer reptiles gave up their pursuit. Sharks could not pursue humans on land, and crocodiles and alligators could only outrun humans over a short distance due to their legs being much shorter. Komodo dragons could outrun the fastest men, but the alligator ordered the Komodo dragon to give up the pursuit.

The men who had escaped were confronted by eight poachers and two large Dobermann dogs, which barked, snarled and growled savagely at the men. Aiming their rifles, the poachers opened fire and riddled the swimmers with bullets, killing them instantly. The tigers watching were enraged by this sickening atrocity against unarmed, half-naked men, and by the village and ocean massacres committed by the giant herbivores and ocean killers. With violent bursts of lightning speed, the tigers, cheetahs and gorillas raced towards the men and dogs, five hissing, snarling cheetahs against two barking, growling Dobermanns. The Lin Wu Beasts, firing spells as they ran, burned up the rifles so the men screamed with excruciating agony and dropped their weaponry. With two or three last sprinting bounds and then a combined assault of leaping and lunging at the poachers, the tigers and gorillas were upon them in seconds. All four sets of claws shredded and mutilated the legs and upper bodies of five men as the tigers fastened their powerful, dagger-like fangs into the men's necks and heads. The men perished in a barbaric orgy of horrific violence.

The gorillas felled three poachers to the sand with bone-breaking blows from their hands, smashing the men's spines before raining crushing bites all over their arms, legs and bodies. Bashing their heads repeatedly, the gorillas spattered their faces with dark red blood, breaking noses, jaws and teeth and splitting open heads. The men's slaughter was as savage and brutal as that of the five men murdered by the tigers.

The five cheetahs wrestled the Dobermanns to the ground. The dogs stood no chance against the thin, slightly-built felines as dangerous as lions or tigers. Their hind and front claws tearing the dogs to pieces, the cheetahs sank their needle-like fangs into the hounds' necks and finished them in three seconds.

But the tigers, cheetahs and gorillas were spotted by the sharks and ocean killers in the sea, and the crocodile, the alligator and the Komodo dragon on the sand. The tigers doubled back and ran with the cheetahs and gorillas cantering after them, and they made it into the undergrowth again. Darting across the highway, they leapt into the mangrove swamps and disappeared underwater. The elephant, the rhinos and the buffalo reached the swamps a few seconds later and knew they had lost the Lin Wu Beasts again. The water was so dark, murky and muddy, even the crocodile and the alligator could not locate the tigers' gang.

***

The Lin Wu Beasts finally located Marion, who was with the noble giant herbivores from the Congo—the elephant, the two rhinos and the buffalo who had massacred the poachers at Malibu Beach after witnessing the heroic lions being shot to death. The gorillas informed the noble giant herbivores that four rogue giant herbivores had massacred a village of innocent people overlooking the Gulf of Mexico. The tigers told the giant herbivores and Marion how six fishermen in a boat had been shredded and chopped to pieces by an octopus, a giant squid and a cuttlefish along with a barracuda, a conger eel and a moray eel, and how two sharks together with three killer reptiles had chased five male swimmers onto the beach. The cheetahs recounted how these men had been shot dead by poachers backed up by Dobermanns, and how the tigers, cheetahs and gorillas had ripped to pieces the men and dogs.

"But the rogue giant herbivores, ocean

killers and killer reptiles are still at large," Marion pointed out. "And my psychic mind is picking up where they will attack next. They're heading through the swamps and rivers, even the sharks and ocean killers who don't inhabit swamps. Fifty miles from Miami are ten boats full of fishermen catching fishes, prawns, crabs, lobsters and giant clams in the river. They'll be the Li Hei Beasts' next targets. We'll warp ourselves there now. You four giant herbivores, head for the Everglades Zoo to join the leopards and the jaguar. The tigers, cheetahs and gorillas are smaller and can hide more easily amongst the undergrowth whilst these creatures and I foil the Li Hei Beasts' attack."

***

Marion and the tigers' gang spotted the ten boats, and then the Li Hei Beasts surrounding and closing in upon the vessels. The sharks would destroy a total of ten men in the first two boats. The barracuda, the conger eel and the moray eel would bite and maul to death five men in the third boat. The octopus, the giant squid and the cuttlefish would bite, chop and mutilate eight fishermen in the next three boats. The crocodile, the alligator and the Komodo dragon would rend, tear apart and dismember five men swimming in the river. And the elephant, the rhinos and the buffalo would smash open four boats and stab, gore and impale all twenty men in these river vessels.

"Do as I do and throw warping spells," Marion

explained. The brunette was addressing the tigers, cheetahs and gorillas.

With a hail of warping spells, Marion and the Lin Wu Beasts evaporated the giant herbivores into the murky mist, and they ended up obstructing the sharks and killer reptiles. Taken by surprise, the sharks, the crocodile, the alligator and the Komodo dragon bit giant chunks of flesh and bone out of the elephant and the rhinos. Meanwhile, the barracuda, the conger eel and the moray eel savaged and mutilated the buffalo. The giant herbivores still fought with vicious savagery, breaking the bones of the crocodile, the alligator and the Komodo dragon and fracturing the ribs of the sharks and murderous fishes.

The octopus, the giant squid and the cuttlefish saw Marion hiding behind the thickets with the tigers, cheetahs and gorillas. The evil brutes advanced through the swamp to slash with their sharp tentacles and massacre Marion and the Lin Wu Beasts. Marion fired lightning through their eyes and into their brains, as well as burning their tentacles. The lightning and electricity roasted their legs, boiled their enormous bodies and fried their brains for three minutes. Going up in smoke and steam, the giant squid's gang died as horribly as the sharks, the barracuda, the conger eel and the moray eel. The killer reptiles and rogue giant herbivores were also floating lifeless in the water. But this was not the end of Marion's troubles.

As the ten boats of terrified fishermen headed back towards Miami, an army of dark sorcerers appeared on the opposite bank of the river. But Li Hei was not amongst these evil men. Before they spotted Marion and the Lin Wu Beasts, Marion cast a warping spell. She, and all thirteen beasts, disappeared into the warm haze.

They reappeared five seconds later outside the Everglades Zoo and met up again with the noble giant herbivores from the Congo. The tigers noticed that the spotted leopard, the black panther and the jaguar were not with the elephant, the white rhino, the black rhino and the buffalo; they were on the hunt for deer and birds.

The army of Li Hei's sorcerers and their pack of hunting dogs discovered in their psychic minds that Marion and the Lin Wu Beasts were near the wire fence closing off the Everglades Zoo. The evil men vaporised themselves from the riverbank. They travelled as invisible spirits across Florida's Everglades and then emerged out of the forest mist. They were outside the Everglades Zoo. But Marion was hiding behind the check-in office at the entrance inside the zoo, where she would not be an easy target for the sorcerers. Carrying out her attack first, she sprayed lightning towards the large gang. It ricocheted and bounced about between the men. The men returned fire.

The crossfire of lightning persisted for four minutes, which became five minutes, and then six. The sorcerers had been rigorously trained for many years by Li Hei, and Marion was weakening from the lightning-fire.

The dogs charged. Marion bashed open the office door, ran inside, barricaded the door with a small chest of drawers and then returned fire again. The dogs were barking, snarling and growling with psychotic fury and violence. They leapt at the door, trying to force their way past the chest of drawers on the other side. How long could Marion keep the dogs outside the office whilst blazing lightning at the Men of Li Hei? They blasted the open windows until the glass shattered and continued their lightning attack for another four or five seconds. When they briefly ceased fire, Marion fired lethal bolts towards their groins, suddenly gaining the element of surprise. As the men crumpled up in agony, she blazed at their feet, shins, knee-caps, then their unprotected eyes and noses.

The Li Hei sorcerers were thrown backwards, but the barking, snarling dogs had pushed the chest of drawers away from the door. The furious beasts bashed the door open. Marion's lightning-fire ricocheted between the savage dogs, and then the tigers, cheetahs and gorillas pounced from behind the thickets, leaping and lunging with the brute power and speed of lions.

The tigers brutally savaged five dogs and smashed the skulls of three other hounds with deadly blows from their bear-like paws and razor-sharp claws. The cheetahs outnumbered and mauled two dogs until they died, then slashed the face and neck of a third dog with their claws, felling him with blows to his jugular vein. The gorillas bashed, pounded and pummelled nine devilish canine beasts until they lay in lifeless heaps.

The gorillas and tigers threw lightning at the sorcerers, and charged. Charging like runaway locomotives or enormous battering-rams, thundering hooves churning the ground, the massive elephant, the awesome rhinos and the huge buffalo also fired bolts, which disabled the men. The elephant's tusks and trunk bashed and pounded two men just as his heavy hooves crushed four men like pancakes. The criminals lay in heaps with all their bones broken.

The rhinos stabbed two other men and tossed them into the air before trampling another eight crooks with their hooves. All these men died from broken bones and excessive loss of blood. The buffalo gored one man with his fearsome horns. He crushed another under his sledgehammer hooves and tossed his first victim through the air. The brute hit the ground, and both men perished from broken bones and fractured skulls.

More men blazed lightning at the giant herbivores, but the tigers and gorillas were upon them in a matter of seconds. The tigers ruthlessly savaged five men, their claws ripping apart the brutes before their powerful fangs crunched through the men's necks and finished them. With their enormous fists, the gorillas smashed the skulls of three crooks before turning on the last three criminals. Their massive jaws and teeth dealt multiple puncture wounds to the men's arms, shoulders, bodies and legs. With broken arms and shoulders, broken legs and pelvises, and fractured ribs, the brutes died slow, lingering deaths before blows from the gorillas' fists bludgeoned the men's heads and finished the deadly massacre.

Marion emerged from the check-in office and sprinted towards the tigers and gorillas. The cheetahs wandered after her. The elephant, the rhinos and the buffalo watched the tigers, cheetahs and gorillas, admiring their courage and bravery. Then Marion realised she was exhausted from this ruthless and brutal battle to the death, and she needed some sleep.

Lying down behind the thickets, she succumbed to sleep in eight or nine minutes, and was unconscious for three hours. During the first quarter of the first hour, the tigers, cheetahs and gorillas picked up psychic mind signals from the leopard, the black panther and the jaguar at the Mississippi River outside New Orleans in Louisiana. As well as California and Florida, this area of the south-eastern United States, overlooking the Gulf of Mexico, was also experiencing attacks on humans by sharks, ocean killers and killer reptiles backed up by more of Li Hei's sorcerers. The Beasts of Lin Wu needed to travel by witchcraft to Louisiana to reunite with the three big cats from Nepal and Brazil.

***

During the third hour of Marion's rest, she dreamt of the three hours of danger the Beasts of Lin Wu experienced in Louisiana. The large gangs of Lin Wu and Li Hei were exchanging lethal spells in a deadly crossfire of lightning. Li Hei's sorcerers were too strong and highly trained to fight off, and they forced Lin Wu's men into the dark, mud-green waters of the Mississippi River. A great white shark and a tiger shark chewed off the arms of two men and severed the legs of another three. These men bled to death in minutes. A barracuda and a conger eel chewed off the feet of two other men before a moray eel joined the savage fishes. All three killers brutally savaged three other sorcerers until they perished. The octopus pulled apart another man as the giant squid ripped apart two more, cutting them to ribbons, and the cuttlefish constricted and tore to pieces the last two followers of Lin Wu.

On land, the elephant gored and crushed five of Li Hei's men whilst the rhinos repeated this attack against six crooks and the buffalo gored and impaled two other criminals. Joining the giant herbivores was a hippo from the Congo who had been warped to Louisiana by Lin Wu.

The hippo crushed three Li Hei sorcerers with his awesome weight and impaled two others upon his long, sabre-like tusks. Then the five giant herbivores, including the towering elephant and the savage hippo, plunged into the river and furiously crunched and gored the sharks and ocean killers, who swam into the Gulf of Mexico.

Seven Li Hei brutes were left alive, trying to flee, but the tigers, the leopard and the black panther charged out from the undergrowth, leaping at the men and brutally savaging them with hind and front claws and dagger-like fangs. The tigers strangled five men just as the leopard and the black panther throttled the other two.

The battle was over. Before this savage skirmish, the two leopards had used mind signals to tell the five tigers that the jaguar from Brazil had gone missing and so too had the chimpanzees and orang-utans from the Congo and Indonesia. The three gorillas set off in search of the jaguar, the chimpanzees and orang-utans, and the buffalo decided to carry out some searching of his own. The elephant, the rhinos and the tigers bade farewell to the buffalo, who made his way through the thick wheat and corn fields of Louisiana.

The giant herbivores and big cats strolled along the banks of the Mississippi until they reached the hippo's new lair, which was guarded by the five cheetahs. The hippo stood guard in the water as the cheetahs patrolled the riverbank flanking the entrance. The elephant, the tigers, the leopard and the black panther indulged in a conversation with the rhinos. The big cats planned to carry out their own hunt for the jaguar and three troops of apes, but the rhinos suggested to the tigers and leopards that they wait for the buffalo to return. Then the elephant heard the hippo bellowing and roaring and the cheetahs hissing with ferocity and fury, and the elephant charged outside the hippo's lair. The hippo was chasing four farmers away whilst the cheetahs were sprinting after three fishermen. The men made their escape in a speedboat.

This intrusion was meant to provide a diversion so that poachers could break into the lair, but the rhinos and big cats detected the men's presence before these gunmen were halfway into the cave. With the element of surprise being their most fearsome weapon, the tigers and leopards came around the corners and lunged towards the seven men. The men bashed and knocked out the tigers, the leopard and the black panther with the heavy butts of their rifles, but the white rhino and the black rhino plunged their horns into two men and trampled the other three until they were dead. The last two men dropped their rifles and sprinted out of the cave, joining five other armed poachers. But emerging from the muddy green water came the elephant and the hippo, backed up by the five cheetahs charging along the grass bank. The elephant gored and kicked two poachers as the hippo chewed and crushed three other men. The cheetahs outnumbered the last two men and tore them to ribbons before their fearsome fangs strangled the men.

The hippo knew that his secret lair overlooking the river had been compromised.

The elephant advised the rhinos and the hippo to return by sorcery to the Congo, due to being easy targets for men with rifles.

The rhinos and the hippo warped themselves into the mist, and then the elephant sent mind signals to the buffalo to return to the hippo's lair as soon as possible. The elephant then insisted to the cheetahs that they hide in the cornfield and keep watch over the river for the sharks and ocean killers swimming in from the Gulf. These ocean killers could attack humans swimming in the Mississippi, so as soon as the cheetahs spotted them, they needed to use their psychic brains to send mind signals to the elephant, the buffalo and the big cats, telling them to guide people out of the river. The cheetahs agreed to this. The two giant herbivores and seven big cats would search for the jaguar and the apes.

The elephant, the tigers, the leopard and the black panther advanced northwards along the riverbank to find the buffalo. The cheetahs sent psychic mind signals to the elephant, informing him that the sharks and ocean killers had entered the river from the ocean. The elephant thanked the cheetahs, and then saw Li Hei's poachers beating up police informants who had told the New Orleans Police Department of the poachers' destruction of endangered wild animals in Nepal, Uganda, the Congo and now here in Louisiana. The poachers chased the informants into the river and fired at them, wounding rather than killing them. At that moment, the sharks and ocean killers from the Gulf of Mexico savagely attacked the informants in the water. The great white and the tiger shark took off one man's arm and the right legs of two other men. The barracuda used his fangs to chop off a fourth man's foot and the conger eel and the moray eel severed two more hands. With repeated slashing blows from their dreaded tentacles, the octopus, the giant squid and the cuttlefish ripped open the last three men. All nine informants died from shock, agony and excessive loss of blood.

Enraged by this sickening atrocity, the elephant and the big cats fired spells at the poachers that burned their arms and hands and fractured the bones in their feet so they could not run away. Dropping their rifles from their scalded hands, the armed men limped away from the elephant and the big cats, who darted after them. The buffalo came from the opposite direction, bursting out of the thickets and attacking two men. The buffalo's horns tossed one man into the air. He landed on his back, broke his spine and split his head open. The buffalo pinned a second man to the grass and, with a sweeping motion of his horns, tore the man's ribcage out. He trampled the first man with his flesh-chopping hooves, not knowing the man was already dead, like the second man whose ribcage, organs and blood were spread all over his mutilated corpse.

The other men doubled back south to seize their rifles in one last vain attempt to shoot the elephant and the buffalo. But the elephant plunged his enormous tusks into a third poacher, hurling him three hundred feet into the air whilst trampling and crushing two other criminals under his club-like hooves.

The tigers and leopards hurtled towards the last seven men and viciously savaged the brutes. The tigers' scimitar-like claws ripped and shredded the legs, shoulders and chests of five men as the leopard and the black panther used all their claws to tear, disembowel, and shred the chests and shoulders of two other men, tearing their scalps from their heads, exposing their brains. The tigers' fangs strangled their victims or crushed their skulls as the leopards' fangs throttled their victims. All seven men were dead in twelve or thirteen seconds.

The elephant and the buffalo welcomed each other, but both giant herbivores, the tigers and leopards were very badly traumatised by the slaughter of the nine informants, first by the poachers and then by the sharks and ocean killers. The elephant's gang saw no further sign of the sharks and ocean killers who had swum back towards the Gulf, leaving the informants horribly mutilated and bleeding profusely in the river.

***

The Lin Wu Beasts continued their journey northwards to locate the jaguar and the apes. The tigers, the leopard and the black panther killed and ate eight rabbits and seven hares as the elephant and the buffalo chomped on the corn and wheat, and then guzzled down water from the river. The tigers' senses told them to head east to find the apes. The tigers and leopards followed this direction with the elephant and the buffalo walking behind. Hurrying down the trunks of twenty trees ahead came the chimpanzees and orang-utans, who recognised and greeted the elephant's gang with high-pitched screaming, snorting and grunting.

The elephant and the buffalo trumpeted, roared and screamed back, followed by the tigers' roaring and the sawing and screaming noises of the leopard and the black panther. The elephant asked the chimpanzees for the location of the three gorillas and the jaguar, and the chimpanzees and orang-utans informed the elephant that these four deadly beasts were being pursued by another gang of poachers. The elephant ordered the twenty apes to join the five cheetahs at the hippo's former lair, which was on the river's east side, three miles from where the river flowed out into the Gulf. The apes evaporated into the mist and, a few seconds later, greeted the cheetahs at the hippo's lair.

The tigers and leopards were worried sick that the jaguar and the three gorillas were being pursued by the second gang of poachers. Had these beasts ended up dead, full of gunshot wounds? The giant herbivores and big cats quickened their pace until they saw a gang of poachers surrounding a desolate house with no people inside. Six men entered the building whilst the rest waited outside. The jaguar and the gorillas were hiding inside the house.

The six men disappeared into two rooms, and the gorillas and the jaguar attacked the three men in the first room with vicious savagery. Two gorillas threw three blows from their fists, dispatching two men, felling the brutes to the floor with fractured skulls. The jaguar accounted for the third man, his awesome strength and devilish ferocity being equal to that of any tiger, leopard or black panther. His claws raked through the poacher's legs, chest and shoulders whilst his powerful fangs crushed the man's skull.

The three men from the second room charged across the corridor into the first room, but the three enormous gorillas were ready for them. Flailing fists the size of footballs broke the men's arms and ribs and then bludgeoned their heads. The men lay in heaps beside the first three.

The poachers outside the house were becoming more nervous that the men inside had not returned from the building. Then the giant herbivores and big cats charged out of the thickets surrounding the house with awesome power, spitfire speed and vicious fury. The elephant used his tusks and hooves to destroy nine men whilst the buffalo used his horns and hooves to pulverise three others, goring, tossing and crushing the evil brutes. Leaping onto the backs of seven men, the tigers used all their paws, claws and fangs to rip five poachers apart and break their necks. In the same fifteen seconds, the leopard and the black panther used their claws and fangs to fracture the necks of the last two gunmen, tearing them to ribbons.

The tigers, the leopard and the black panther roared and screamed to the gorillas and the jaguar inside the building, telling them it was safe to come out. The four formidable beasts emerged from the building, walking in single file through the front door. The jaguar greeted the big cats as the gorillas welcomed the elephant and the buffalo. Using mind signals, the gorillas asked the elephant the whereabouts of the cheetahs, chimpanzees and orang-utans. The elephant replied that they were at the hippo's lair near where the Mississippi opened out into the Gulf. But before returning to the lair, the Lin Wu Beasts needed to eat some food from a nearby ranch.

They soon found a ranch, and the tigers, the leopard, the black panther and the jaguar killed eight sheep and dined on the carcases. The elephant, the buffalo and the gorillas consumed fruits and leaves from the nearby trees before eating grass. Dozens of farmers were drawn by the noises of the sheep being killed, and saw them being devoured. The tigers bellowed and roared at the men whilst the leopard, the black panther and the jaguar roared, screamed and hissed with savage fury. The elephant and the buffalo bellowed and roared like an avalanche whilst the gorillas beat their chests and screamed like thunder.

The petrified men ran away with terror and panic, and the Lin Wu Beasts made their escape. Having journeyed north, the giant herbivores, apes and big cats doubled back south towards the hippo's lair. The white rhino and the black rhino sent mind signals to the elephant and the buffalo to say that, having left the hippo at a river in the Congo, the rhinos had returned to Louisiana and reunited with the cheetahs, chimpanzees and orang-utans at the hippo's lair. The elephant was grateful and told them that the giant herbivores and big cats had found the gorillas and the jaguar and would return to the lair shortly.

The elephant and the buffalo spotted two gangs of poachers closing in on the Lin Wu Beasts from the fields and forests to the east and the river to the west. The farmers from the ranch were pursuing the Lin Wu Beasts from the north. The beasts' walking became faster and then they were sprinting through the fields of corn and wheat. They avoided the poachers and farmers, who gave up their search as night approached.

During the night, the giant herbivores, apes and big cats finally returned to the hippo's lair. The elephant, the buffalo and the rhinos greeted each other as the cheetahs welcomed the tigers, the leopard, the black panther and the jaguar. The chimpanzees and orang-utans reunited with the gorillas. The elephant told the chimpanzees and orang-utans of their hostile encounter with the farmers at the ranch, and that the farmers had spread the word, which had reached two gangs of poachers.

***

Word of the elephant's gang's presence in Louisiana also reached the Li Hei Beasts in the Mississippi itself, namely an alligator local to Louisiana, a crocodile warped over from Kenya by Li Hei, and the two sharks from the Gulf of Mexico. The sharks were backed up by the barracuda, the conger eel and the moray eel, together with the octopus, the giant squid and the cuttlefish. The crocodile, the alligator and the sharks and ocean killers again were different individuals from the two gangs of killer reptiles, sharks and ocean killers who had terrorised divers, swimmers and Lin Wu sorcerers off California and Florida.

The crocodile and the alligator agreed with the sharks that these Li Hei Beasts must double-cross the poachers and kill any poachers who'd survived or devour any who'd died in the final battle against the Lin Wu Beasts. For the Lin Wu Beasts were not stupid enough to enter the river when they knew the sharks, ocean killers and killer reptiles lurked in the murky depths of the brown and green water.

***

Two gangs of poachers closed in on the hippo's lair during the third hour, early in the evening, the darkness hiding the poachers' movements. One gang crossed the Mississippi River in a large boat whilst the other gang advanced down the pathway flanking the river.

But the sharks, ocean killers and killer reptiles foiled the men's plans. Crunching open the boat with their enormous jaws and razor-sharp teeth, the sharks, the barracuda, the conger eel and the moray eel ripped the vessel to pieces before they ruthlessly savaged the crew. The crocodile twisted off one man's arm before the crocodile and the alligator wrenched off the legs of another two men and three poachers were ripped apart and dismembered by the great white and the tiger shark. The barracuda, the conger eel and the moray eel viciously mauled three other crewmen while the octopus, the giant squid and the cuttlefish tore apart and mutilated the last three.

The men's screams as they were savaged to death alerted the giant herbivores, apes and big cats hiding in the cornfield surrounding the hippo's lair, overlooking the pathway and the river. They sprayed magical spells, which caused the second gang's rifles to explode in their arms. Then the elephant, the white rhino, the black rhino and the buffalo led the other Lin Wu Beasts in a highly violent and ferocious attack. In the same minute that the elephant's tusks and hooves destroyed eight poachers, the rhinos pulverised five huntsmen, and another two gunmen had their pelvises and ribcages ripped out by the buffalo's horns. The tigers leapt towards four men as the cheetahs lunged at three others, but the men dodged out of the way and jumped into the river. The leopard, the black panther and the jaguar used their flailing front claws to slash at another three men. The gorillas bashed their barrel-shaped chests and chased three poachers while the chimpanzees and orang-utans darted after the last ten—two chimpanzees or two orang-utans to each man. But, like the men set upon by the tigers and cheetahs, these terrified gunmen escaped into the river. All these evil brutes swam back upstream in shallow water to avoid being savagely mauled by the sharks, ocean killers and killer reptiles.

The three hours the Lin Wu Beasts had had in Louisiana were nearly over, and they needed to return to Florida's Everglades Zoo. At that moment, Marion's dream was over.

***

Marion awoke, and climbed to her feet. The Lin Wu Beasts surrounded her. In her psychic mind, she sensed a gang of poachers advancing through Florida with hunting dogs to confront her and the Lin Wu Beasts at the Everglades Zoo. Marion and her formidable beasts had to ambush the men and dogs.

Waiting behind the trees and thickets flanking a pathway that overlooked the Everglades' mangrove swamps, Marion had no intention of murdering the poachers. She would only massacre the hunting dogs, using the smaller deadly creatures, whilst the giant herbivores would intimidate the men into surrendering.

Then she heard the men and dogs approaching. The men strolled down the pathway overlooking the swamps. Their dogs ran on ahead and stopped at the trees. Within the next two or three seconds, the five tigers and five cheetahs leapt down from the branches upon ten dogs whilst the leopard, the black panther and the jaguar dropped down onto another three hounds. The three gorillas, ten chimpanzees and orang-utans hurtled down towards thirteen dogs. All these canine beasts were torn to shreds and massacred in the next twelve or thirteen seconds. The poachers aimed their rifles, but Marion and the giant herbivores fired bolts of lightning, which scalded the men's hands. The men screamed with agony. The elephant bellowed and roared at six Mexicans as the rhinos roared and screamed at three Colombians and three Venezuelans, and the buffalo snorted and grunted with fury at two Brazilians. The men fell on their fronts on the ground, crying with terror, horror and panic.

"Don't kill these men," Marion ordered the giant herbivores. "I must interrogate them."

She addressed the men. "Do you speak German? Or English?"

"Yes, we do, señorita," one of the Brazilians cried. "I'm the leader of this poaching gang.

Us two men are from Brazil. The rest are from Colombia, Venezuela and Mexico. We've shot and killed many wild animals in these four countries."

"You're very quick to confess to your guilt," Marion commented.

"If we don't confess, these four giant beasts will kill us," the gang leader said.

"Have you heard of Li Hei?" Marion asked.

"Yes, we have," the leader replied. "His family are immigrants from China and Japan. They moved over to America twenty years ago. They are good, noble people. Only Li Hei is a bad apple in a barrel of good apples."

"Where in America do they live?" Marion wanted to know.

"We don't know," the leader cried. "We first met him in Brazil and broke off contact with him in Mexico."

"Okay, that's all," Marion finished off. "Which prison do you want me to warp you to by magic? A prison in Brazil or a prison in Mexico? Or a jail in the United States, Canada or Alaska?"

"They'll respect our human rights in Canada or Alaska, but not in the United States, Mexico or Brazil," the leader insisted. "Warp us to a prison somewhere in Canada."

"I'll warp you to a jail in the capital city, Ottawa," Marion decided. With a spell, the men evaporated and ended up in a secure prison in Ottawa. Marion turned towards the dangerous beasts. "I'll warp you giant herbivores and apes back to the rainforests and mountain forests in the dreamworld joining the Congo with Nepal. But Lin Wu is contacting me by mind signals. He wants me to warp you big cats to a farmhouse on a deserted ranch in British Colombia, where Canada borders with Alaska—a farmstead three miles north of Vancouver. It's called the Grizzly Ranch, named after Canada's grizzly bears. He's warped a grizzly bear and black bear to this ranch from Yellowstone, plus a male American bison and a bull moose. The other two bears are staying in Yellowstone for another task. Also being sent over from Wyoming are a puma, a lynx and a bobcat, together with a wolf, a coyote and a fox. But Lin Wu does not want me at the ranch yet. He has left another clue for me at the Everglades Zoo. I must make my way back there. But first, I'll warp all of you to the Congo, Nepal or British Colombia."

With her proficiency in witchcraft, she transported the elephant, the rhinos, the buffalo and the apes to the dreamworld border between the Congo and Nepal. The big cats were sent by magic to British Colombia.

At the Everglades Zoo, Marion located the next clue and read it loudly.

"To Lake Geneva in western Switzerland," she announced. "I must make my way there now."

***

Marion met up with Lin Wu in Switzerland's

rugged, spectacular Alpine Mountains overlooking Lake Geneva. They shook hands, and then lowered themselves into a row of seats facing the mass of water.

"We meet again," Marion began.

"It gives me great pleasure," Lin Wu continued. "But I have disturbing news about pollution incidents in parts of Europe and North America reported to me by gangs of weasels or mustelids of different species local to these countries or states. Animals cannot talk like us humans, but with their powers of sorcery, they psychically showed me images of dead animals who had died from drinking polluted water. And I'll show these images in my mind to prove I'm not making this up."

The first picture emerged from Lin Wu's mind, showing an acid rain problem on the border between Norway and Sweden. Dead fishes floated on the lakes, and the coniferous and evergreen trees had lost their foliage due to being eaten away by sulphuric acid, which had poured down over Norway and Sweden as acid rain. Two common badgers, two weasels and two stoats, along with two polecats and two pine martens, one of each mustelid species being local to Norway or Sweden, saw the dead fishes. Then, two brown bears, two wolves and two lynxes on both sides of the border were about to drink from a lake. The badgers' gang of mustelids warned the larger predators not to drink this polluted water.

The second picture was of Denmark, where

a badger, a weasel and a stoat saw birds lying dead in a forest after falling from the sky due to being poisoned by gas pollution. This was followed by a scene in eastern Poland's Bialowieza Forest National Park, concerning oil pollution seeping from cars into a river. A bear, a wolf and a lynx were about to drink from this river but were prevented from doing this by a wild boar, a red deer and a roe deer.

The next scene happened in southern Germany's Bavarian Forest, where rabbits, hares and rats died after eating vegetables poisoned by pesticides and herbicides. A badger, a weasel and a stoat failed to save a wolf, a lynx, a wild cat and a mountain fox from eating the rabbits, hares and rats. The three mustelids watched with horror as the four large predators collapsed and died.

The next scene occurred on the border between Holland and Belgium. A river running between both countries was poisoned by chemicals and industrial effluence. A weasel and a stoat, together with a polecat, a ferret, a pine marten and a beech marten from Holland, as well as six mustelids of the same six species from Belgium, began to drink the water. Two badgers from both countries indicated to the twelve mustelids the dead fishes and ducks floating on the water, which proved the water was contaminated.

This was followed by a picture of a forest in Burgundy in north-eastern France, where rabbits, hares and rats had died from eating grass contaminated by manmade poisons and weed-killers. A badger, a weasel and a stoat were about to consume these dead beasts, but a wild boar, a red deer and a roe deer showed the three mustelids the corroded grass, weeds and flowers, proving that poisons and weed-killers had killed this vegetation and then the rabbits, hares and rats who had eaten the plants. The badger's gang were grateful to the wild boar's gang for preventing them from being the next victims.

The next scene showed Alberta's Wood Buffalo National Park in Canada. Fishes, frogs and toads had died when their river was contaminated by sewage pollution after a sewage treatment plant had a leakage of human waste. The American badger and the mink—who had previously escaped from the tundra where the five bison, five polar bears and nine large predators had been massacred by Li Hei's poachers—were very hungry. The badger and the mink ate the fishes and amphibians, and then died of food poisoning. The bison or wood buffaloes and moose used their sorcery to photograph the dead bodies in their psychic minds and, like the large herbivores and mustelids in Europe, passed these photographic visions to Lin Wu.

The last vision took place at Wyoming's Yellowstone National Park in the United States. Of the two male grizzlies and two male black bears local to Wyoming, a grizzly bear and a black bear had been warped by Lin Wu over to British Colombia with a male bison and a bull moose to join the big cats from the

Congo, Nepal and Brazil. Going with them were a puma, a lynx and a bobcat, together with a wolf, a coyote and a mountain fox led by Klaus Weisberg. Klaus would join Marion and Lin Wu at the ranch three miles north of Vancouver. The other two bears of both species stayed behind at Yellowstone with the three dogs, two feral cats, five rabbits and four hares, backed up by an American badger, a mink and a fisher. They witnessed the problem of visitors and tourists to Yellowstone dropping garbage and litter everywhere, including food packets and open bottles. The rabbits and hares were about to climb into these bottles, where they would be trapped and die, whilst the cats and dogs would feed on packets that smelt of food, but the badger, the mink and the fisher prevented them. This saved the beasts' lives.

At that moment, Lin Wu's visions were withdrawn back into his brain. He faced Marion.

"Those were many cases of pollution fed into your psychic brain from large herbivores and mustelids all over Europe, Alberta and Wyoming," Marion indicated. "Apart from showing me you have animal friends with magical powers in all these countries and states, what was the main purpose of showing me so many traumatic cases? One or two cases of animals being poisoned is traumatic enough, but several cases?"

"Each of these pollution cases was different," Lin Wu pointed out. "One of the main problems of pollution, global warming and climate change is that there are so many different forms of pollution, in the air, the sea, the rivers and lakes and on land. From acid rain, gas, coal and oil pollution to pesticides, herbicides, manmade poisons and weed-killers, and then to pollution from chemicals, industrial effluence and liquid metals. Not to mention rubbish and litter pollution, sewage pollution, and smoke pollution from forests being burned by humans to make way for farms, towns and roads. Most countries— including even the biggest polluters, China, India and the United States—are passing government legislation to curb their greenhouse emissions, but the vast scale of different forms of pollution will take many years to eradicate completely."

"About these clues you've left me every time I've completed a dangerous mission," Marion said. "Only you could've left these clues, because the only other people who know of my involvement in your war are Li Hei and my husband Klaus. These clues are designed to guide me to the whereabouts of the magic gold that feeds the Men and Beasts of Li Hei their magical powers. Which means you know where the gold is and you haven't told me. An evil criminal like Li Hei would not deliberately leave clues leading me to his secret weapon."

"I left these clues," Lin Wu admitted. "But I have no knowledge of where this gold is and nor does your husband. Klaus and I have been using our magical powers to execute our own missions, mostly to detect potential environmental disasters like those throughout Europe, Alberta and Wyoming. And also to trace your movements. Klaus and I know you have been fighting the Men and Beasts of Li Hei in California and Florida. My psychic mind detected your three previous dreams, one set in the waters off California, the second in the dreamworld joining the Congo and China with Colombia and Venezuela, and the third around the Mississippi River in Louisiana. Then I had two visions of wildlife parks, one on the border between Mexico and California, the other on the border between Canada and Alaska. This exposes a more sinister side to the magic gold the Li Hei Men buried in these wildlife parks. These men deliberately committed mass suicide by allowing lions, tigers, bears, bison and moose to kill them so evil spirits would pass from the gold into the deadly creatures, and that's how the beasts died. After the deaths of the Li Hei Men and the dangerous beasts inside the two wildlife parks, Li Hei's remaining men moved the gold from Canada's border with Alaska to another location. The only way to find out exactly where the gold was moved to is to interrogate the poachers who stayed behind in British Colombia. That's why Klaus and I warped ourselves—and the dangerous beasts of Wyoming and the big cats of the Congo, Nepal and Brazil—over to British Colombia.

"A bison, a moose, a grizzly bear and a

black bear joined an Alaskan Kodiak bear, the largest of all bears, at the Grizzly Ranch three miles north of Vancouver and two miles south of the second wildlife park bordering Alaska and the Pacific Ocean, where lions, bears, bison and moose died after killing Li Hei's men, due to the magic gold. Klaus and the dangerous creatures from Wyoming are setting a trap for the poachers who complied with Li Hei's men in removing the gold, and he will send mind signals to me in half an hour's time asking us two to join him in British Colombia. But we and the dangerous beasts will not kill the poachers. We will interrogate them as the dangerous beasts corner them, and the men may or may not know where the magic gold is. Then we'll warp the poachers to the jail cells at Vancouver Police Department with their rifles immobilised, ready to await trial for poaching and murder."

"That sounds like a watertight plan," Marion said. "But these dogs, cats, rabbits and hares running towards us—are they your allies, and are they local to Switzerland?"

"The answer to both questions is yes," was Lin Wu's reply. "And they're drawing our attention to another tragedy."

The two dogs, three cats, three rabbits and two hares local to Switzerland were barking, caterwauling, squealing and squeaking with panic. The dogs tugged at Lin Wu's denim jeans. Lin Wu and Marion followed his animal friends along the pathway and into a copse of spruce, pine and fir trees. And what they saw turned their stomachs.

Three ruthless industrialists from Great Britain, Poland and Alberta in Canada had been mauled to death by a bear, a lynx, a wolf and a mountain fox native to Switzerland, the wolf and the fox cooperating to kill the man from Alberta. All four large predators were dead nearby, and Marion immediately pointed her finger at magic gold. The two mass suicides combined with animal massacres, which had happened in two wildlife parks in California and British Colombia, had occurred again, here in Switzerland.

"This is awful," Marion sobbed, unable to control her tears. "But again, I know these three men committed suicide by allowing the four predators to murder them so the predators would die from being poisoned by the evil spirits coming from the magic gold."

"You're right," Lin Wu said.

The dogs, cats, rabbits and hares dug up the snow-covered soil to find the gold, but it was gone.

"But this may be different gold to the deadly gold in British Colombia," Lin Wu said.

"Why do you say that?" Marion wanted to know.

"My two visions of the deaths of Li Hei's men and the dangerous beasts in California and British Colombia due to the magic gold happened only two hours ago," Lin Wu said. "British Colombia is thousands of miles away from this copse of trees in Switzerland, and gold weighs a ton. There's no way Li Hei's men could've transported the same gold thousands of miles and buried it at this copse and, at the same time, arrange for the three industrialists to commit suicide whilst laying a trap for the four predators in only two hours. It is possible Li Hei's men used their sorcery to bring the gold from Canada to Switzerland in only a few seconds using a warping spell, but it's highly unlikely. Arranging for the industrialists to fly over here from Great Britain, Poland and Alberta, then the men setting themselves up as bait, as well as burying the gold and then removing the gold somewhere else would take several days of planning. The gold buried here—and then removed to another location, probably somewhere else in Europe—was definitely not the same gold as the gold that killed those deadly beasts in California and then British Colombia."

"And there's another thought in my mind," Marion said. "About the three industrialists from Great Britain, Poland and Alberta. Look at their Identity and Work Permit Cards."

"I'm looking," Lin Wu told her.

"The British man worked for an industry called Dalseo Factories in Newcastle in northern England bordering Scotland," Marion said. "Dalseo Factories are notorious for sending sulphur dioxide emissions into the atmosphere, and the sulphur dioxide was carried by heavy winds to Norway and Sweden before it condensed into sulphuric acid in liquid form and fell over Scandinavia's forests, rivers and lakes as acid rain. Then arsonists burned his factories to the ground, and he was bankrupt. That's why he came over to Switzerland to end his life.

"The Polish man was an oil tycoon working for a car company near Bialowieza Forest National Park in Poland. He manufactured gas-guzzling cars and vehicles, which sent smoke and gas emissions from oil or petrol into the atmosphere and also sent petrol, diesel and anti-freeze seeping from the cars into the soil and rivers at Bialowieza Forest. Then, due to a case of sexual harassment against a female colleague, he was sacked, stripped of all his money and ended his life here in this copse.

"The man from Alberta in Canada worked for a sewage treatment company near Wood Buffalo National Park. When there was an enormous leakage of raw sewage from the treatment plant, it was closed down for polluting Alberta's water supplies, and this man and his employees lost their jobs. He lost all his money, came over here to Switzerland and set himself up to be killed by the wolf and the fox, just as the bear and the lynx savaged the British man and the Pole.

"The acid rain from the sulphur dioxide emissions coming from Dalseo Factories in Newcastle destroyed the lakes in Norway and

Sweden and nearly poisoned the two bears, two wolves and two lynxes on both sides of the Norwegian-Swedish border, but these six predators were saved by the two badgers, two weasels and two stoats, together with the two polecats and two pine martens. They fed visions of this near-tragedy into your mind here in Switzerland. The petrol, diesel and anti-freeze spilling from cars outside Bialowieza Forest in Poland seeped into the forest's river, and a bear, a wolf and a lynx who nearly drank the water were saved by a wild boar, a red deer and a roe deer. The wild boar and the two deer sent visions over towards your brain here in Switzerland.

"At Alberta's Wood Buffalo National Park, the sewage leaking into the area's water supplies from the sewage treatment plant caused the deaths of the American badger and the mink native to Alberta. Again, the local bison and moose sent visions of their dead bodies and the polluted river to your mind while you were over here near Geneva. I know these three industrialists, after losing their jobs, got involved with Li Hei's gang. They wanted to commit suicide, and this was Li Hei's opportunity to bury more magic gold underneath this copse and lure the bear, the lynx, the wolf and the fox into a trap, using the three men as bait. He knew these four predators were your allies, and he wanted to get back at you by killing these predators. The men were poisoned by the magic gold, the predators savagely mauled them until they died, and then the predators were poisoned themselves by the gold and perished. This must have happened four or five hours ago, because the blood on the men's injuries is still fresh and liquid, and also because this gave Li Hei's men time to warp the gold by sorcery to another location somewhere else in the world."

"All this makes sense," Lin Wu pointed out. "Of all the industrialists responsible for the different forms of pollution passed to my psychic mind from the animals' visions, three men from Great Britain, Poland and Canada are now dead. But there are still the industrialists behind the pollution the local animals and I detected in Denmark, Germany, Holland, Belgium and France, as well as Wyoming in America. They are still at large, and probably working for Li Hei. And now, Klaus is contacting me by mind signals from the Grizzly Ranch in British Colombia. What is that, Klaus? You, the big cats and the dangerous beasts from Wyoming are hiding in the Grizzly Ranch's farmhouse three miles north of Vancouver. The Kodiak bear from Alaska has joined the grizzly bear and the black bear. The poachers know about the magic gold Li Hei's men took from that wildlife park near Alaska; they know you are with a gang of lethal beasts at the ranch and want to kill you and the beasts. They are big game hunters as well as poachers, and the deadly beasts will be prized trophies. They know they have to murder you and are closing in on the ranch now. You want me and Marion to warp ourselves from Lake Geneva in Switzerland to British Colombia now. We're coming over."

Lin Wu and Marion bade farewell to the dogs, cats, rabbits and hares, and then disappeared into the air.

***

They found themselves at the ranch near Canada's border with Alaska, rejoining Klaus.

"Marion!" Klaus exclaimed. "Long time no see! What war have we been caught up in?"

"A war between humankind and Nature!" Marion cried. "But I'm happy to see you again! How was Wyoming?"

"Yellowstone in Wyoming is as untameable as northern Alberta's tundra and these Coastal Mountains of British Colombia, and more wild than Lake Geneva in Switzerland," Klaus said.

"You've been to Alberta as well as Wyoming!" Marion exclaimed. She was excited. "How did you end up there?"

"It's a long story," Lin Wu explained. "But the dangerous animals are coming out to greet you."

From the right of the farmhouse came the male bison, the bull moose and the five cheetahs. From the left came the five massive tigers, leading the Kodiak bear, the grizzly bear and the black bear. And from behind a former cattle barn emerged the leopard, the black panther and the jaguar, leading the puma, the lynx and the bobcat as well as the wolf, the coyote and the mountain fox. The big cats reunited as the cheetahs headed inside the kitchen area with the wolf, the coyote and the fox. The kitchen faced southwest. The puma, the lynx and the bobcat made their way through the front door into the farmhouse's hallway, facing northwest. The bears and tigers gathered inside the lounge and the library with the leopard, the black panther and the jaguar. The lounge overlooked the Coastal Mountains to the east.

And then Klaus spotted the poachers, armed with rifles, coming from three directions.

"The poachers are closing in from the east, southwest and northwest," Klaus said. "Get inside the farmhouse."

Klaus, Marion and Lin Wu hurried inside and closed and locked all the doors.

"We must not use the animals to massacre the poachers," Lin Wu ordered. "Only to terrify and intimidate the men and manipulate confessions out of them through their petrified terror of these beasts. And then we'll warp them into prison cells at Vancouver Police Department."

"What questions do we fire at them?" Klaus asked.

"You and Marion don't ask any questions," Lin Wu told them. "I'll do all the talking. If we keep these men alive and have them detained at Vancouver PD, the Canadian police may gather more evidence and more confessions from these men. More information gives us a better chance at smashing Li Hei's criminal organisations. And now, the poachers are firing at the doors and windows. Get down."

A ferocious hail of fierce gunshots shattered all the windows as the poachers blazed with their high-velocity rifles, the bullets ricocheting around the rooms and ripping gaping holes through the woodwork and furniture.

With their witchcraft, Marion, Klaus and Lin Wu sprayed a bombardment of lightning bolts towards the next barrage of bullets, melting the rounds in mid-air before burning the powerful hunting rifles in the poachers' hands. The firearms burst into flames as the men screamed with agony and dropped the weaponry.

"We'll confront them now!" Lin Wu shouted.

"Their guns are harmless!" Klaus said.

"Release the dangerous creatures from this place!" Marion cried.

Opening the doors of the kitchen, the hallway, the lounge and the library, they released the beasts. Too enormous to fit inside the farmhouse with the three bears and all the big cats, the bison and the moose had been hiding inside the warehouse lying north of the farmhouse. They charged out into the farmstead, ramming into two armed men from behind. They sent the men flying through the air to land on their shoulders, shattering the bone and breaking their arms. The bison winded another man before he and the moose used their horns and antlers to pinion two other men against the farmhouse's north wall, beside the hallway door. The puma, the lynx and the bobcat slammed against the chests of three men after leaping through the hallway door, knocking the wind out of them so they hurtled to the snow. The three feline beasts fastened all their four sets of claws into the men's thighs, stomachs, chests and shoulders, and their killer fangs were close to the brutes' faces.

Leaping through the kitchen door, the wolf tackled another gunman, his jagged teeth seizing the man's arm as the coyote and the mountain fox, both sizeable beasts, dug their teeth into both hands of a fifth thug. All five crooks were petrified.

But the beasts knew they must not kill the men, only intimidate them with their ferocity. Also hurrying out of the kitchen, the cheetahs outnumbered two violent criminals, leaping towards them and throwing the men to the ground. The cheetahs restrained the men with all their sets of claws and fastened their fearsome fangs into the brutes' arms and hands.

Attacking from the lounge and the east-facing library were the bears and big cats. With crushing blows from their massive paws and tremendous claws, the Kodiak bear smashed the ribs of two criminals as the grizzly bear broke the arm of a third brute. The Kodiak bear, the grizzly bear and the black bear pinned three other crooks to the snow with their claws whilst their huge paws and terrifying fangs intimidated the petrified men.

At the same time, the tigers crunched their

fangs and claws into the legs of two poachers and the chests and stomachs of three more, threatening murder, but never crossing that line. The last three poachers had their brawny arms seized by the fangs and claws of the leopard, the black panther and the jaguar, who dealt severe injuries without tearing off the men's arms.

Klaus, Marion and Lin Wu faced the terrified men.

"You tried to kill Klaus, and then Marion and myself when we got in your way," Lin Wu growled. "Why is this?"

"I'll do all the talking!" the gang leader ordered his men.

"Then it is you I will interrogate!" Lin Wu told him. "What's your name?"

"Julio Sifuentez!" the gang leader cried, terrified, as one of the tigers fastened fangs and claws into his leg.

"I'll call you Julio," Lin Wu said. "Are you from Mexico, or were you born in the United States or even Canada or Alaska?"

"I'm from Sonora in north-western Mexico, bordering California," Julio replied.

"I know you are poachers," Lin Wu said. "Your rifles are high velocity or high calibre hunting rifles, fit to bring down an animal the size of a bison or a moose. You knew there were large, dangerous animals on this ranch classed as Big Game, and these would fetch you heavy prizes as trophies to sell on the Black Market. But you also tried to kill Klaus, and then all three of us. Why is this the case?"

"He knew too much about our poaching activities, señor," Julio snapped.

"There was more to it than just poaching," Lin Wu observed. "I'll tell you of three mass suicides, which resulted in the deaths of deadly beasts due to magic gold. Gold that protects evil men from animal attacks by passing evil spirits into the men. And if one or more animals kills any one or more of these men, the evil spirits pass from the human victims into the animals, poison the animals and kill them.

"You, Julio, are from Sonora on Mexico's border with Arizona and California, and all your men are either Mexicans or Americans. The two men being restrained by the wolf, the coyote and the fox are Japanese, whilst the three men being pinned down by the three bears are Chinese. Li Hei's family are immigrants from Japan and China, so the five Orientals have links to my arch enemy from China, Li Hei.

"Going back to you, Julio. You lived in Sonora and then California, where the first mass suicide happened in a wildlife park on the border with Mexico. Men loyal to Li Hei proved their loyalty by burying magic gold inside the premises of this wildlife park, and then committed mass suicide by allowing themselves to be savaged by lions, tigers and bears, both grizzlies and black bears from Montana, Wyoming and California. The evil spirits protecting the men passed into the lions, tigers and bears, and they all died.

Then you dug up the gold and, with Li Hei's magical powers, you warped yourselves and the gold to another wildlife park two miles from here, on Canada's border with Alaska. To prove their loyalty to Li Hei—like the men who died in California—a second group of men from India, China and Japan gained protection by burying the gold inside the wildlife park, then committed a second mass suicide by being gored or mauled by bison, moose, lions and bears, both grizzlies and black bears from southern Alaska and British Colombia and polar bears from northern Alaska and Canada's Arctic regions. After these dangerous beasts murdered the men, the gold's evil spirits poisoned the beasts, and the beasts perished.

"The third mass suicide happened near Lake Geneva in western Switzerland, involving three ruthless industrialists from Great Britain, Poland and Alberta in Canada. They were behind pollution from acid rain in Norway and Sweden, petrol, diesel and anti-freeze in Poland and sewage pollution in Alberta. Due to three cases of arson, sexual harassment of a female worker, and criminal negligence, two men lost their businesses and the Polish man was sacked. They were bankrupt, got involved with Li Hei and then arranged with his gang to travel to Switzerland and end their lives. Li Hei's gang buried magic gold in the copse of trees and used the three men as bait to set a trap for four large predators local to Switzerland. Li Hei knew a bear, a lynx, a wolf and a fox were my allies in Switzerland and wanted to hurt me by harming these beasts. And he succeeded. The predators mauled the industrialists until they died, then they were poisoned by the magic gold, which dealt the same fatal consequences on these predators as it had upon those big cats, bears, bison and moose at those two wildlife parks in California and here in British Colombia—that park, two miles from the Grizzly Ranch. The three men from Great Britain, Poland and Alberta, responsible for three forms of pollution, are now dead. But other men behind other forms of pollution in Denmark, Germany, Holland, Belgium and France, as well as in Wyoming in America, are still walking alive and free and can commit more pollution offences. That is not the point."

"What is your point, señor?" Julio asked. "And please don't let this tiger or the other beasts kill me and my men. I'll tell you whatever you want to know."

"Am I right that you are connected to Li Hei?" Lin Wu said. His question was leading.

"We are connected to Li Hei," Julio told him.

"Were you behind the two mass suicides in California and here in British Colombia where you buried magic gold, and two groups of animals in both wildlife parks died as a consequence?" Lin Wu wanted to know.

"Yes, we were," Julio confirmed.

"Was the same magic gold used in both wildlife parks?" Lin Wu asked.

"Yes, it was, señor," Julio informed him.

"Was this the same gold that killed those four predators who massacred the three industrialists in Switzerland?" Lin Wu demanded.

"No, it wasn't," Julio told him. "It was a different batch of magic gold, probably used by Europeans. We never set foot in Europe, let alone Switzerland. And we had no knowledge of these industrialists until you told us just now. You must believe me."

"I know you're telling the truth," Lin Wu replied. "For certain reasons, including distance, time and planning, it couldn't be the same gold. Which means there were two or more batches of magic gold used by different gangs of poachers and criminal developers, all linked to Li Hei. The gold buried in Switzerland was dug up by the criminals before us three could find it and taken somewhere else in Europe. You poachers who buried and then dug up the magic gold in California, then buried and dug it up at that wildlife park two miles from here, must know where the gold is now. Where was it taken next?"

"Li Hei's men confiscated the gold from us and, with his sorcery, he evaporated the gold into the icy mist," Julio explained. "Li Hei has the gold. And we don't know where."

"I find it hard to believe you," Lin Wu said. "Do any of you men know where Li Hei took the gold? Or even if he really did take it?"

"It's the truth!" they cried out.

"They're telling the truth," Marion said.

"How do you know?" Klaus asked her.

"I just know," Marion replied. "Li Hei and his men are not stupid. They knew you had come up here from Wyoming with the dangerous beasts, and they would take precautions to prevent you confiscating the magic gold long before any confrontation between Julio's men and the three of us. As soon as Li Hei had the gold safely in his hands, he ordered Julio's men to kill you. Or kill all three of us and the dangerous beasts."

"What this lady says is true," Julio explained. "The two batches of magic gold that killed those two gangs of beasts in California and Canada and the four predators in Switzerland killed them instantly. But another type of magic gold kills dangerous animals slowly after corrupting them to kill their animal allies and also humans. Herbivores who murder men protected by the gold are corrupted by the noble spirits, which compel these herbivores to kill all predators on sight. And predators who murder men protected by the gold are led by evil spirits, which force them to murder all herbivores on sight. Herbivores and predators working for you will turn on each other as two gangs and also kill any humans who get in their way. Only your sorcery can destroy these noble and evil spirits and save the rival beasts."

"With bolts of fire reduced in temperature from our hands," Lin Wu called out. "Do you know where this gold is?"

"No, for the blessing of God, no," Julio cried.

"That's all," Lin Wu finished off. "Your rifles

are harmless. Rather than allow my dangerous beasts to kill you, I'll warp you to the prison cells at Vancouver PD with your rifles on you as evidence to incriminate you. I'll make a phone call to the Vancouver police to tell them what you told me. Then they'll interrogate you. If you lie to them, you will increase your prison sentences by many years. But if you tell them the truth, you may have your sentences reduced. Goodbye."

Lin Wu caused Julio's gang to disappear.

Marion addressed Lin Wu.

"Our trail of the magic gold has gone cold."

"How do we find new leads?" Klaus asked.

"I'll use my psychic mind to trace Li Hei's whereabouts," Lin Wu remarked. "Without knowing that I'm listening to his conversations thousands of miles away and watching all his movements, he may betray new leads that lead us to the gold."

"That's wishful thinking," Marion said, "thinking it will be that easy. Li Hei is not stupid, and he will probably know you're watching and listening to him."

"Which means he'll take special care not to do or say anything suspicious that would lead us to the gold," Klaus remarked.

"It's the only option we have," Lin Wu explained. "In the meantime, I will send Wyoming's dangerous beasts on a mission, warping them around Europe to investigate different cases of pollution. The big cats will be warped back to the dreamworld joining the Congo and Nepal with Brazil. Because the snowy wastes of Alaska and British Colombia are the only suitable environment for Kodiak bears, the Kodiak bear will remain here in British Colombia. The grizzly bear and the black bear will pass messages between the puma, the lynx and the bobcat in one team and the wolf, the coyote and the fox in the other. The bison and the moose will keep surveillance over the messenger bears and the two predator teams, and if any of these eight predators faces a gang of armed men, the bison and the moose will charge in to give assistance. The two teams of wild cats and wild dogs will use their psychic minds to interview the local predators in each European country, whilst the bison and the moose will interrogate any European herbivores. But whilst we're keeping a low profile, both of you need to get some sleep. We don't know how long tomorrow or the next day will be."

"In that case, we'll sleep inside the farmhouse of the Grizzly Ranch," Marion told Klaus.

"I'm all for it," Klaus agreed.

***

Marion and Klaus slept in two single beds for five hours. The last two hours of Marion's rest were taken over by a long dream, travelling around Europe. It began in the mountains of the Massif Central in southern France.

The wolf, the coyote and the fox killed and ate three rabbits and three hares as the puma, the lynx and the bobcat murdered and consumed five rabbits and four hares. At the same time, the two bears slaughtered a red deer and a roe deer, and after all these predators ate their prizes, they were approached by a common badger and a stoat, backed up by a polecat and a ferret. These mustelids ate four rabbits, and then asked who the large predators were. Here in France, they were not accustomed to bears, pumas and wolves competing with them for rabbits, hares and deer.

The grizzly bear and the black bear told the badger's gang of mustelids that the large predators were friendly and, through warping spells, had ended up in the Massif Central by accident. Then the bison and the moose took over the conversation. The herbivores asked the badger's gang whether they possessed psychic minds and magical powers cast into them by Lin Wu, to which the badger replied that they did. The bison explained about pollution incidents in Burgundy in northern France and other regions of western and northern Europe, and that the herbivores and predators would interview the countries' formidable beasts, asking them whether they could identify the industrialists behind these pollution incidents. The mustelids then told the bison and the moose of more pollution incidents in southern Europe, namely sewage pollution in northern Spain's Cantabrian Mountains, acid rain at Gran Paradiso National Park on north-western Italy's border with south-eastern France, and petrol and diesel pollution in Slovenia's forests in northern Yugoslavia—or the former Yugoslavia, before it broke up into many states including Slovenia, which borders Italy. The incidents of sewage pollution, acid rain and oil pollution that had happened in Alberta, Norway, Sweden and Poland were being repeated by different industries in Spain, Italy and Yugoslavia.

The badger, the stoat, the polecat and the ferret were rewarded by the bears with the two deer carcases to top up their meal of four rabbits.

To speed up the investigations, the bison and the moose ordered the wolf, the coyote and the fox to interview a bear, a wolf and a wild cat local to Spain at the same time as the puma, the lynx and the bobcat would question a bear, a wolf, a lynx and a wild cat native to Italy's Gran Paradiso National Park, and the two bears would interrogate a bear, a wolf, a lynx and a wild cat local to Slovenia. The bison and the moose would interview the ibexes, chamois and mouflons native to these three countries, these herbivores being wild goats and sheep. As the bison and the moose warped themselves into Spain, the bears, wild dogs and wild cats of Yellowstone used magical spells to split up into all three Mediterranean countries.

In Spain's Cantabrian Mountains, the herbivores of Wyoming talked to a Spanish ibex and a chamois, both wild goats. The bison found out that three Australian men owned the sewage treatment plant and, through their criminal negligence, an accident had caused a leakage of raw sewage into the local waterways. The ibex and the chamois could not drink the water from the nearby river.

At the same time, a bear, a wolf and a wild cat native to these mountains told the Wyoming wild dogs how they could not drink the water.

Then a gang of armed men working for the Australian industrialists fired at the Wyoming wild dogs and Spanish predators, who fled into the nearby forest. The bison, the moose, the ibex and the chamois ran away from another armed gang. The ibex and the chamois had to head deep into the mountains and leap across ledges to escape the armed men, and they bade farewell to the bison and the moose.

The Wyoming herbivores magically travelled from Spain to the Italian Alps around Gran Paradiso National Park in north-eastern Italy. The Wyoming wild dogs joined the puma, the lynx and the bobcat at Gran Paradiso as these wild cats interviewed a bear, a wolf, a lynx and a wild cat local to Gran Paradiso. Then the Wyoming wild dogs and wild cats reunited with the two Wyoming bears in Slovenia's mountain forests bordering north-eastern Italy's Dolomites Mountains. The bison and the moose interrogated an Alpine ibex, a chamois and a mouflon indigenous to the Italian Alps bordering France and asked them where the acid rain pouring down over the forests and rivers of Gran Paradiso came from. The ibex, the chamois and the mouflon told the bison it came from a factory five miles south of Gran Paradiso, a factory owned by four New Zealanders.

The bison realised that Li Hei had contacts from Australia and New Zealand who were ruthless industrialists. Maybe they had deliberately polluted forests and rivers to please Li Hei, the three Australians knowingly causing a mass leakage of sewage in Spain, and the four New Zealanders behind the sulphur dioxide emissions that poured acid rain over the mountains, forests and rivers in Italy.

Then the bear, the wolf, the lynx and the wild cat native to Gran Paradiso approached the bison and the moose. These predators told the bison that they, along with the ibex, the chamois and the mouflon, could not drink from the poisoned river, and that these Italian herbivores had to graze on mountain pastures across the French border and the predators had to prey on young cattle and sheep in France. The mountains, pastures and forests across the French border had escaped the acid rain pollution that fell upon Gran Paradiso.

The bison and the moose bade farewell to the park's seven beasts and warped themselves from Italy into Slovenia's Julian Alps.

The Julian Alps were teeming with mountains and forests, but the Wyoming herbivores had no time to admire Slovenia's picturesque beauty and splendour. They saw fishes, frogs and toads lying dead in a river from oil pollution, where either petrol and diesel had seeped into the river from gas-guzzling vehicles, or the owners of a fuel station were emptying surplus petrol and diesel, as well as chemicals, into the river.

The bison and the moose interviewed a chamois and a mouflon, together with a bear, a wolf, a lynx and a wild cat local to Slovenia, asking these six creatures who owned the vehicle company and the fuel station behind this oil pollution in the river. The chamois and the mouflon informed the bison that two Russians owned the vehicle company and were breaking Slovenia's laws by producing faulty cars and vehicles, which seeped petrol or diesel from their tanks. The predators told him two Japanese men owned the fuel station, and they emptied excess fuel into the river.

Then the six beasts heard gunfire, and the four predators had to escape along a mountain path from armed men working for the Russians and Japanese. The chamois and the mouflon would wait for the bison and the moose, who they knew must assist the Wyoming bears and large predators who were being fired at by the armed men.

After the bears, the wolf, the coyote and the fox each killed and ate a rabbit and a hare, and the puma, the lynx and the bobcat slaughtered and consumed a hazel grouse and two rabbits, they were shot at by the armed men. But the predators' spells melted the bullets and then burned the men's rifles red hot. The men screamed with pain and dropped the guns. Their weapons burning on the forest floor, the men were totally defenceless against the bears and predators, who outmatched them in strength, speed and ferocity.

The bison and the moose were also on the scene and attacked three men from behind. The bison's horns ripped one man's spine from his back. The second man turned around, and the bison tore out his ribcage. Both men perished in minutes. The moose plunged his antlers into a third man's back, then bashed him with his flailing front hooves, breaking his spine and smashing his skull.

Unprepared for this surprise attack from behind, the remaining criminals were attacked from the front by the predators. Three blows from the grizzly bear's paws and claws broke a man's left arm and all his ribs before the grizzly bear and the black bear horribly savaged two other crooks with claws and fangs. All three brutes died in minutes from agony and loss of blood.

The wolf ripped another crook's throat out as the coyote and the fox chewed and mangled the hands of two other crooks. The puma, the lynx and the bobcat tore the last three criminals to bits before their fangs strangled the brutes. The coyote and the fox released their bites on the hands of their two victims before the puma and the wolf took over the attack, the puma tearing one man to ribbons and killing him instantly whilst the wolf sank his teeth into the other man's throat until his victim lay on the forest floor with his throat dangling from his neck.

The bears were grateful to the bison and the moose for rescuing the eight predators, but more men were approaching the ten beasts.

The Wyoming herbivores ordered the bears, wild dogs and wild cats to return by sorcery to Yellowstone and allow the herbivores to continue the interviews in Europe alone. The bears and predators warped themselves back to Wyoming whilst the herbivores doubled back along the pathway and rejoined the chamois and the mouflon. All four herbivores sprinted towards the mountains and saw the Slovenian predators fleeing in the distance.

The second gang of armed men pursued the herbivores from behind, but they were able to outrun humans and left the men far behind. They were in the mountains. The bear, the wolf, the lynx and the wild cat joined the Slovenian herbivores and promised to protect them.

The bison and the moose bade farewell to Slovenia's creatures and, using a warping spell, travelled to eastern Poland's Bialowieza Forest National Park in only five seconds. The American bison and the moose heard the crunching of feet in the forest and thought it was more armed men, but the hooves belonged to the European bison and the elk. Bialowieza Forest in Poland is famous for Europe's last herds of European bison and elks; these bison also exist in Byelorussia and Russia and elks thrive in Norway, Sweden, Byelorussia and Russia. Although the European bison and the elk were enormous beasts closely related to the American bison and the bull moose from Wyoming, these two male herbivores were smaller in size and weight than the two Wyoming herbivores.

The American bison and the moose told the European bison they needed to meet up with the wild boar, the red deer and the roe deer local to Bialowieza Forest. The two bison, the moose and the elk headed through this primeval forest until they met up with the wild boar's gang of three. The American bison explained to the five Polish herbivores how Lin Wu had told the American bison and the moose about petrol and diesel pollution from vehicles seeping into the nearby river. The European bison and the elk informed the American bison of how a bear, a wolf and a lynx native to Bialowieza Forest were about to drink water from the poisoned river. The wild boar, the red deer and the roe deer prevented the three predators from consuming the polluted liquid. Then the bear, the wolf and the lynx arrived and told the Wyoming herbivores how they were grateful to the wild boar's gang for saving their lives. They also told them how Lin Wu had united the herbivores and predators of Bialowieza Forest by sorcery, just as he had united herbivores and predators in other regions of Europe and North America. Then the Wyoming herbivores told the Polish beasts how the Polish industrialist behind the oil pollution was one of three men slaughtered near Lake Geneva in Switzerland by a bear, a lynx, a wolf and a fox. The Wyoming herbivores saw smiles of joy lighting up the faces of the Polish herbivores and predators, and told the wild boar, the red deer and the roe deer how the Wyoming herbivores needed to visit the two bears, two wolves and two lynxes in Norway and Sweden to inform them of the British industrialist's murder in Switzerland.

Once the bison and the moose were on the border between Norway and Sweden, they met up with the bear, the wolf and the lynx from Norway and the three predators of the same three species from Sweden. After the bison told the bears, wolves and lynxes how the British industrialist behind the acid rain pollution in Norway and Sweden had been with a Pole and a Canadian in Switzerland and that all three industrialists had been massacred by a bear, a lynx, a wolf and a fox near Lake Geneva, the six predators rejoiced. The five mustelids of Norway and five mustelids of Sweden were also relieved, but faced another pollution problem—people throwing rubbish in the lake.

The two badgers, two weasels and two stoats, together with the two polecats and two pine martens, decided they had to spy on the lake at night to discover the identities of the men littering the lake with paper wrappers, drink cans and plastic bottles. The bison and the moose wished the mustelids all the luck in the world before disappearing into the snowy mist.

Back in Yellowstone, they met up with the American badger, the mink and the fisher. These mustelids told the herbivores how they had saved the five rabbits and four hares from climbing into large open bottles, which would have trapped and suffocated them, and prevented the two cats and three dogs eating food packets and wrappers that tasted of food and would have choked the cats and dogs.

There was a problem of garbage and litter pollution in Wyoming. The badger, the mink and the fisher backed up the bison, the moose, the two grizzlies and two black bears in spying on men who abandoned paper or plastic bags, plastic or glass bottles, drink cans, paper wrappers and packets in the forests that were hazardous to wild animals. The puma, the lynx and the bobcat focused on men fly-tipping—dumping garbage and useless equipment on the roadsides. The wolf, the coyote and the fox spied on humans killing rats, mice and voles with poisons and weed-killers. These rodents were then eaten by birds of prey, who either died or failed to produce fertile eggs or live chicks through their reproductive systems being damaged. The same effect was caused on birds of prey and mammals by pesticides, herbicides and acid rain.

The bison and the moose bade farewell to the mustelids, and then set off in search of the puma, the lynx and the bobcat. But if the wild cats were hunting for vehicles guilty of fly-tipping, the herbivores had no intention of exposing their position behind trees and thickets on the opposite side of the highway. The bison and the moose reached the highway and spotted six men abandoning garbage and litter on both sides of the wide road. Across the road and behind the trees, the puma, the lynx and the bobcat watched three men in a truck fly-tip their garbage by the roadside and then drive off. The herbivores and wild cats knew these nine men had committed these two offences before. The next time they caught both gangs in the act, they would use their sorcery to warp the men into the hands of Lin Wu as kidnap victims.

The puma's gang saw the herbivores retreating away from the highway and mistook them for rabbits, hares or deer. They pursued the two herbivores, who then ran into the wolf, the coyote and the fox. The bison, the moose and the wild dogs bellowed, roared and barked at each other. This sent the message to the wild cats that the bison and the moose were not rabbits, hares or deer.

Once the bison and the moose were joined by the puma, the lynx and the bobcat, together with the wolf, the coyote and the fox, the bison told them all that they must continue their interviews in Europe. In his mind, he had visions of evil sewer rats threatening the dogs, cats, rabbits and hares in Switzerland— rats sent by Li Hei's sorcerers to infect and kill these beasts with their poisonous bites. Another horde of sewer rats backing up Li Hei's men were threatening the mustelids on both sides of the border between Holland and Belgium. The Wyoming herbivores knew how Li Hei's men, having discovered how the herbivores and predators had incriminated the three Australians, four New Zealanders, two Russians and two Japanese in Spain, Italy and Slovenia, were determined to prevent the mustelids who had informed them of which industrialists were behind the leakage of chemicals and industrial effluence into the river running between Belgium and Holland. The Wyoming beasts would have to travel by witchcraft to Switzerland's Lake Geneva, gather together the two dogs, three cats, three rabbits and two hares and warp these beasts over to Holland and Belgium to assist the fourteen mustelids in combating the sewer rats, whilst the Wyoming beasts would murder Li Hei's men. Two of the bears and all six predators agreed to make their way to Holland and Belgium, whilst the other two bears would stay in Wyoming in case the dogs, cats, rabbits and hares of Yellowstone came up against the Li Hei Men and rats of Wyoming.

The wild dogs and wild cats arranged to meet the two herbivores and two bears at the Coyote Ranch on Wyoming's state border with Idaho and Montana, for the herbivores' psychic minds had detected the rabbits, hares and fierce rodents of Wyoming being menaced by birds of prey. The herbivores and bears darted through the forest until they spotted the five rabbits and four hares, backed up by a porcupine, a beaver and a muskrat together with a marmot, a woodchuck and a prairie dog, fighting with their chisel-like teeth and formidable claws against an eagle, a hawk, a harrier and a falcon as well as a kestrel, a buzzard and an owl. These seven raptors had been hired by Li Hei to massacre the rabbits, hares and fierce rodents, but these smaller mammals had fighting experience from fending off attacks by foxes, cats, weasels, stoats and rattlesnakes. The porcupine fired his barbed quills into the eagle. The beaver and the muskrat broke the legs of the hawk and the harrier a few seconds before the marmot, the woodchuck and the prairie dog fractured the legs of the falcon and the kestrel. The rabbits and hares outnumbered, bit and clawed at the buzzard and the owl before the three dogs and two cats along with the American badger, the mink and the fisher rescued the smaller mammals. The bison, the moose and the two bears arrived in the last few seconds as the dogs ripped apart the eagle, the hawk and the harrier, and the cats tore and strangled the owl. The badger, the mink and the fisher clawed the falcon, the kestrel and the buzzard, biting them to death, before the dogs, cats and mustelids ripped the feathers away and dined on the birds of prey.

The large herbivores showed their regret to the rabbits, hares and fierce rodents. The dogs, cats, rabbits, hares and mustelids were also remorseful of how the birds of prey had been corrupted by Li Hei's dark sorcery, and that it had been necessary to kill the predatory birds. The two herbivores and two bears promised the smaller beasts that the other two bears would support and assist the dogs, cats and mustelids in protecting the rabbits, hares and fierce rodents of Yellowstone.

The bison, the moose and the first two bears rejoined the wild dogs and wild cats at the Coyote Ranch before all ten Wyoming beasts warped themselves over to Lake Geneva. On arriving inside the copse of spruces, pines and firs, they saw the Swiss rabbits, hares and fierce rodents being savagely attacked by a horde of sewer rats. The three rabbits and two hares, together with a beaver, a muskrat and a marmot, took a terrible toll on the rats, but twenty of the evil vermin tore apart and devoured the beaver, the muskrat and the marmot. The rabbits and hares retreated, and then the three cats and two dogs local to Switzerland lunged into action, the cats clawing and biting to death eight rats as the dogs took gnashing bites which crushed to death the last twelve.

Whilst grieving over the deaths of the beaver, the muskrat and the marmot, the rabbits and hares were thankful to the cats and dogs for rescuing them. The bison and the moose offered their sympathies to the Swiss beasts for their loss. The Wyoming herbivores explained the situation, that the Swiss beasts were in mortal danger from more sewer rats roaming Lake Geneva, and that the herbivores and predators would have to warp the Swiss beasts over to the border between Holland and Belgium to help the fourteen mustelids on both sides of the border to fight another horde of sewer rats. The two herbivores and eight predators would protect the mustelids from Li Hei's men.

Upon arriving on the border between Holland and Belgium, the herbivores, predators and Swiss beasts received psychic mind signals from the common badger, the weasel and the stoat in Burgundy, and the other three mustelids of the same three species in southern Germany's Bavarian Forest. The two badgers, two weasels and two stoats told the herbivores and predators how their two forests were threatened by two other swarms of sewer rats sent by Li Hei to kill the mustelids. The bison promised the French mustelids that he would hire the wild boar, the red deer and the roe deer native to Burgundy to protect them from the horde of rats. Then he told the German mustelids he would send the lynx and the bobcat to the Bavarian Forest. The bison knew how Li Hei wanted to silence the herbivores and mustelids in France and Germany about the pollution incidents there.

On the Belgian side of the border, the Wyoming and Swiss beasts met up with the common badger, the weasel and the stoat, backed up by the polecat, the ferret, the pine marten and the beech marten of Belgium, together with the seven mustelids of the same seven species of Holland. All fourteen mustelids promised to protect the Swiss rabbits and hares inside the badger's sett in Belgium whilst the dogs and cats crossed the border into Holland to keep watch for Li Hei's sorcerers and sewer rats. The wolf, the coyote and the fox stood guard with the moose outside the sett whilst the bison, the bears and the puma received information from the two badgers, two weasels and two stoats about the spillage in the river of chemicals and industrial effluence from a nearby chemical plant in Holland. The interview was held at a bridge crossing the river from Holland into Belgium, and the badgers explained to the bison, the grizzly bear and the black bear how the other twelve mustelids had been about to drink the river's water when the badgers had spotted dead fish and ducks floating on it. The badgers had saved the other mustelids' lives by preventing them drinking the poisoned water. When the bison asked the badgers, weasels and stoats to identify the men running the chemicals plant, the mustelids told the bison, the bears and the puma that they knew the owners of this plant were British men because they spoke no Dutch, but fluent English. The bison asked the badgers, weasels and stoats to join the polecats, ferrets, pine martens and beech martens inside the badger sett.

As the mustelids joined their cousins in the sett, the rabbits and hares emerged from the entrance and asked the cats and dogs if they had spotted any sewer rats. Communicating with mind signals, the cats and dogs reported no sightings of these evil vermin. As the moose and the wild dogs guarded the badger sett, the rabbits and hares asserted to the bison that the bison, the rabbits and hares would have to cross the bridge into Holland and spy on the chemicals plant. They would listen to the conversations of the British men who ran the plant in case the men told each other incriminating information about their negligence or deliberate foul play regarding the spillage of the chemicals and industrial effluence. The bears and the puma would stay in Belgium with the moose and the wild dogs to watch out for men or rats in Belgium coming to attack the badger sett.

Near the chemical plant, the bison, the rabbits and hares overheard the British men boasting about how they had deliberately weakened the equipment, which led to the leakage of chemicals and industrial effluence. These industrialists had formed a destructive pact with the industrialists and polluters in several European countries to defy Lin Wu and the Green campaigners by destroying the forests and rivers and killing Lin Wu's animal allies. Their influence spread from Spain, Italy and Slovenia to Burgundy, Holland and the Bavarian Forest, and then to Norway, Sweden and Denmark.

The bison, the rabbits and hares had to make their way back across the bridge into Belgium to inform the other beasts.

Advancing towards the dogs and cats on Holland's side of the river was a swarm of sewer rats, but the dogs and cats were ready for them. Aiming their rifles at the moose and the wild dogs, a large gang of armed men were flanked by another horde of sewer rats on the Belgian side.

The moose bellowed and roared as the four beasts hurled magical spells that burned up the rifles. The men screamed with agony, and the guns fell from their hands to the ground. On hearing the moose's roars and the men's screams, the bears and the puma raced to the aid of the moose, the wolf, the coyote and the fox. At the same time, the fourteen mustelids sprinted out of the badger's sett and attacked the sewer rats, while the dogs and cats defended themselves against the rats in Holland.

The armed men ran away, but humans cannot outrun moose, bears or wild dogs. On catching up with the men, the moose ploughed his tough, velvet antlers into a gunman, pinned him down and then kicked him with his front hooves. Trying to defend his accomplice, another man threw soil into the bull moose's eyes, but the moose felled this man with five lethal kicks before dropping his first victim with another six blows.

The grizzly bear swiped crushing blows that broke the necks of two men and smashed another's skull. Within the same thirteen seconds, the black bear repeated these slashing blows against another two riflemen, splitting their heads open.

The wolf lunged towards another gunman from behind and ripped flesh from his arm at the same time as the coyote and the fox fractured both hands of a slightly-built man. The puma was upon the last man's back, his hind and front claws raking down the man's thighs, back and shoulders before his dagger-like fangs broke the man's neck. The wolf tore mercilessly through his victim's arm, rupturing arteries and blood vessels. Blood sprayed and gushed from this limb, and then he released his hold, knowing the man would bleed to death within minutes. Assisting the coyote and the fox, who had mangled their victim's hands, the wolf leapt at the man's throat, fastened his jagged teeth in and strangled the man in ten seconds.

The dogs, cats and mustelids on both sides of the river used slashing blows from their claws and gnashing bites from their fangs to slaughter the rats. The remaining rats doubled back and fled.

At that moment, the bison, the rabbits and hares returned. On seeing the carnage, the bison ordered the rabbits and hares to cross the bridge and seek safety amongst the mustelids in the badger sett. The bison informed the puma and the wild dogs of the men's conversation at the chemical plant, where they had gossiped about Li Hei's conspiracy to pollute forests and rivers throughout Europe. Then he explained this to the moose.

The bison and the moose decided to follow the trail of the armed men and rats back to their vehicles to see if they could find any evidence linking the riflemen to the British men at the chemical plant in Holland. After tracing the gunmen's boot prints through the grass, they located their truck. The herbivores also discovered traces of chemicals and industrial effluence on the truck's wheels and the same traces on the boot prints in the mud. The bison also saw the name 'Dalseo Factories, Newcastle, UK'. The truck was from England, and the armed men—together with the men who owned the chemical plant in Holland—were British. The same nationality as the manager in Switzerland who had died alongside two men from Poland and Canada after being mauled by a bear, a lynx, a wolf and a fox. Dalseo Factories were behind the sulphur dioxide emissions from Newcastle, which were carried by heavy winds towards Norway and Sweden and then fell over the countries' forests as acid rain. They were not only behind acid rain pollution, but also chemical and industrial effluence pollution in Europe, including Holland and Belgium. The bison was thinking, *What other pollution are they responsible for?*

Although the factories in Newcastle had been burned down in an arson attack, this truck was from Newcastle and had been to other Dalseo factories and plants all over

England and even Europe. The bison and the moose needed to return to the river to inform the bears and the puma.

The rabbits and hares ventured outside the badger sett again, bade farewell to the bears, the wolf, the coyote and the fox, and made their way through the grass to seek out the bison and the moose. But a horde of sewer rats pounced on the rabbits and hares, not to kill them but to kidnap them. The rats warped themselves and the rabbits and hares into the murky haze. The bison and the moose witnessed this upon returning.

The bison and the moose were joined by the puma, and all three beasts were enraged that the bears, the wolf, the coyote and the fox had allowed the rabbits and hares to leave the safety of the badger sett. The bison informed the five predators about the armed men and their truck being linked to Dalseo Factories, formerly based in Newcastle, and the British-owned chemical plant in Holland.

While the bears, the puma and the wild dogs remained with the mustelids in Belgium, the two herbivores needed to cross the bridge into Holland and question the dogs and cats as to whether they smelled chemicals and industrial effluence on the rats they had massacred when the armed British men and two hordes of rats attacked the Lin Wu Beasts. Then the herbivores would use their psychic minds to detect where the rats were holding the rabbits and hares captive.

Heading into Holland, the Wyoming

herbivores rejoined the dogs and cats before interrogating them. The dogs and cats told the bison there were no traces of chemicals and industrial effluence on the dead rats. If there had been, the rats would have died of contamination long before the dogs and cats had killed them in self-defence. The bison ordered the dogs and cats to relieve themselves of guard duty, cross the bridge back into Belgium and help the Dutch and Belgian mustelids to guard the badger sett against more rats whilst the bears, the puma and the wild dogs kept watch for another gang of armed men.

Then the bison had psychic visions of the rabbits and hares being held captive at that forest in Burgundy in France. He knew the rats' underground warren was in France because the rabbits and hares were calling the wild boar, the red deer and the roe deer for help as the French herbivores walked past the warren. The herbivores failed to hear the rabbits and hares, and the rats shut them up by threatening to kill them if they continued calling.

The bison told the puma and the wild dogs that he and the moose would travel by sorcery to that forest in France. The moose agreed to assist the bison.

Once they reappeared at that forest in Burgundy, the bison and the moose sought out the wild boar, the red deer and the roe deer, and eventually found them. The three French herbivores led the Wyoming herbivores to the rats' warren, hoping to rescue the rabbits and hares. They were joined by the badger, the weasel and the stoat local to France. The three mustelids charged through the burrows into the warren but found no sign of the rats or the captive rabbits and hares. The mustelids came out of the burrows and told the French herbivores that the rats had taken the rabbits and hares, possibly to Switzerland or Germany's Bavarian Forest. The Wyoming herbivores knew the lynx and the bobcat from Yellowstone were in the Bavarian Forest with the German mustelids. The French mustelids sent psychic mind signals to the German mustelids telling them to get back-up from the lynx and the bobcat in attacking the rat warren in this forest. The Wyoming herbivores would join the lynx and the bobcat, together with the three mustelids in the Bavarian Forest. Bidding farewell to the French mustelids—and then the wild boar, the red deer and the roe deer—the bison and the moose disappeared into the murky mist and travelled from France into Germany.

Once inside the Bavarian Forest, the herbivores encountered the badger, the weasel and the stoat local to this forest. They were as handsome, fierce and brave as the badger, the weasel and the stoat in France. The German mustelids led the Wyoming herbivores to the lynx and the bobcat, and then left the four beasts alone. The Wyoming wild cats told the herbivores about how the German mustelids had been badly traumatised by the pollution from pesticides and herbicides, which had poisoned vegetables and vegetation. Rabbits, hares and rats had died from consuming these plants, and a wolf, a lynx, a wild cat and a mountain fox had perished after eating the small vegetarian beasts. The wild cats told of how the badger, the weasel and the stoat had failed to save the larger predators' lives by preventing them from eating the small mammals.

The Wyoming beasts grieved over the deaths of the Bavarian Forest predators, before the lynx and the bobcat asked the bison and the moose what had brought them to Germany. They all agreed that the Dutch, Belgian and French rats had probably joined up with the German rats in this forest and were holding the rabbits and hares captive here.

But then, the Bavarian Forest mustelids entered the hideout and told the bison that the badger, the weasel and the stoat from a forest in Denmark had sent mind signals to them. The Danish mustelids explained how the four hordes of rats had joined the Danish rats and were holding captive three rabbits and two hares from Switzerland. The German mustelids were no longer at risk from the German rats, who were now with the French, Belgian and Dutch rats in Denmark. Bidding farewell to the lynx, the bobcat and the German mustelids, the bison and the moose warped themselves out of Germany and joined the three mustelids in Denmark.

In this Danish forest, the badger, the

weasel and the stoat pointed out how the five hordes of rats had warped themselves and the captive rabbits and hares across the Baltic Sea to the border between Norway and Sweden. The bison and the moose said goodbye to the mustelids and travelled by sorcery into Norway. They met up with the badger, the weasel and the stoat, together with the polecat and the pine marten from Norway, flanked by the five mustelids of the same five species from Sweden. The ten mustelids told the Wyoming herbivores how the German, Dutch, Belgian and French hordes of rats had united with the Danish rats, then the Norwegian and Swedish rats, so the mustelids of Norway and Sweden were heavily outnumbered. But with assistance from the two bears, two wolves and two lynxes local to both countries, they would massacre the rats.

Backed up by two wolverines from Norway and Sweden, the bears, wolves and lynxes joined the ten mustelids, who led them and the Wyoming herbivores to a rats' warren on Norway's side of the border. The mustelids disappeared into the three burrows leading inside the warren and slaughtered dozens of rats. The badgers, polecats and pine martens killed more vermin than the weasels and stoats. The three rabbits and two hares attacked five rats from behind and tore them to pieces before joining the badgers' gang of mustelids. The dozens of rats left alive fled outside the warren, where they were ruthlessly massacred by the bears, wolves, lynxes and wolverines.

But armed men hired to protect the rats aimed their rifles at the large predators and Wyoming herbivores. They were also British men working for Dalseo Factories, for the truck behind them gave the name 'Dalseo Factories, Manchester, UK'. With the armed men were a gang who had thrown rubbish into the lake. Both gangs had conspired with the British owners of the Dutch chemical plant, and other industrialists and polluters all over Europe, to deliberately poison forests and rivers. All three gangs and other mobs in Europe had been corrupted by Li Hei. Being cowards with no rifles, the British men who had thrown garbage and litter into the lake doubled back and ran towards their motorboats. They pulled the engines, and the boats sped across the lake into Sweden.

Being the most vicious and savage of the eight large predators and the most ferocious of all weasels or mustelids, the two wolverines sprang towards two riflemen and ripped them to shreds with their claws before their razor-sharp teeth strangled the men. The other gunmen blazed at the wolverines with several gunshots, and the wolverines perished in fifteen seconds. But as the savage, devilish beasts died, the bison, the moose, the bears, wolves and lynxes fired lightning spells at the gunmen. The men eventually dropped their rifles and hurried inside their truck. Two armed men failed to escape and were gored, kicked and trampled to death by the bison and the moose. The bears, wolves and lynxes chased the truck as it sped away, but they failed to massacre the remaining men.

The ten mustelids thanked the larger predators for assisting them and the three rabbits and two hares rejoined the bison and the moose. The herbivores and predators exchanged praise and gratitude for the rescue, before the bison and the moose warped themselves, together with the rabbits and hares, back to the river bordering Holland and Belgium.

In Belgium, the five rabbits and hares joined the cats and dogs, whilst the lynx and the bobcat from Wyoming had returned to renew their alliance with the puma, the wolf, the coyote and the fox. The grizzly bear and the black bear greeted the bison and the moose. Then the five hours the Wyoming beasts had had in Europe were almost over. They had to warp themselves back to British Colombia in Canada, encounter the Kodiak bear again, and return to the company of Marion, Klaus and Lin Wu.

***

In one of the two single beds in a room at the Grizzly Ranch, Marion suddenly awoke. The Wyoming beasts had been investigating pollution and interviewing herbivores and mustelids throughout Europe for five hours as Marion slept. She climbed out of bed, headed for the window and saw all the deadly creatures positioned beside the Kodiak bear, the grizzly bear and the black bear in the farmyard outside. And then Klaus woke up.

"Good morning, Klaus," Marion said.

"Good morning," he said.

"The beasts are back from Europe," she told him.

Lin Wu was sleeping in a separate room, and the last ten minutes of his rest were occupied by two dreams involving magic gold. Unlike the batches of gold buried in California, British Colombia and Switzerland, the evil spirits in this gold corrupted allied groups of predators and herbivores into killing each other rather than killing these beasts instantly.

The first dream occurred on the dreamworld border between Kenya, the Indian Ocean, north-eastern India and Brazil. Where the beaches of Kenya and India met the ocean, magic gold was buried. Ivory poachers approached an African elephant and a hippo, together with a white rhino, a black rhino and an African buffalo. Five armed men waited for the poachers in a get-away boat. But the boat was capsized by a Komodo dragon and a crocodile. The killer reptiles ripped apart two men, and a bull shark, a blue shark and a hammerhead shark savaged and tore apart the other three.

Taking the poachers on the beach by surprise were two tigers, a leopard, a black panther and a jaguar from India, Kenya and

Brazil. The tigers' flailing front claws ripped open the throats of two men, and the razor-sharp claws of the leopard, the black panther and the jaguar slashed the throats of three other men. The elephant, the hippo, the rhinos and the buffalo savagely gored the last five poachers.

Immediately, noble spirits passed from the gold into the giant herbivores, and evil spirits travelled into the sharks, killer reptiles and big cats. The giant herbivores brutally stabbed and trampled the big cats before engaging in a battle royal with the sharks and killer reptiles. After goring the sharks and killer reptiles to death, the elephant, the hippo, the rhinos and the buffalo were ruthlessly savaged by three great whites and two tiger sharks until they died.

The second dream showed the dreamworld border between the Congo, northern India's Himalayas, Brazil and British Colombia overlooking the Pacific Ocean. Magic gold was buried underneath the rainforests of the Congo and India. Criminal developers were felling the rainforests and Canada's evergreen forests when five men in a motorboat had their speedboat capsized by five enormous sharks. A great white and a tiger shark dismembered two men, while a bull shark, a blue shark and a hammerhead tore the other three to pieces.

An African elephant and an African buffalo brutally gored two developers, and the remaining men were cornered against trees by four male lions, five cheetahs and five tigers as well as the leopard, the black panther and the jaguar. The developers destroying the evergreen forests were surrounded by the Kodiak bear, the grizzly bear, the black bear and the three polar bears, together with the puma, the wolf, the coyote, the mountain fox and two dogs. But having heard from Julio at the Grizzly Ranch about the magic gold, the big cats, bears, wild dogs and the puma only intimidated rather than attacked the men.

Petrified with terror and horror, the developers hurried into their two trucks and drove away from the three forests. Noble spirits corrupted the elephant and the buffalo as evil spirits manipulated the sharks, and the giant herbivores charged into the Pacific to attack the sharks. But ten killer whales brutally savaged the five sharks, just as another African elephant and an Indian elephant stabbed and bashed to death the duped elephant and a white rhino, a black rhino and another African buffalo fatally gored the corrupted buffalo. These four African giant herbivores were the same ones that had been up against poachers and criminal developers in the Congo and China, poachers in Louisiana and evil sorcerers in Florida, and they were joined by the Indian elephant from the Himalayan Mountains.

At that point, the dream was over.

Marion spent an hour telling Klaus and Lin Wu about her dream involving Wyoming's deadly beasts journeying around Europe and mentioned how Dalseo Factories were responsible for acid rain in Norway and Sweden. Armed men from Dalseo were conspiring with human polluters throwing rubbish and litter into Norway's lakes, and were also behind chemical and industrial effluence pollution from a chemical plant on Holland's border with Belgium. Marion told them how sewer rats – who were the armed men's savage pets – roaming Europe from Switzerland, Burgundy in France, and Germany's Bavarian Forest, to the coniferous forests of Norway and Sweden, were a threat to the dogs, cats and mustelids. The rats had kidnapped the rabbits and hares and were finally all massacred by large predators and mustelids in Norway. But there might be more rats in Norway, Sweden and western Europe.

Then Lin Wu used ten minutes to explain his two dreams, in which dangerous beasts had been corrupted by magic gold into killing each other. In the second dream, the big cats, bears and wild dogs had learned from Julio's testimony not to kill the criminal developers, and they had escaped corruption. What Julio had told Lin Wu about magic gold corrupting animal allies into fighting each other rather than killing them instantly really was true.

"I have two clues for you," Lin Wu explained, addressing Marion.

"Two more clues," Marion said. "I'll read them." She took a glance at both clues. "'To eastern Kenya, north-western India and the Indian Ocean in between' is the first clue," she read. "'To the eastern Congo and northern

Michael Elia

India's Himalayan Mountains' is the second clue."

"Do you want us to come with you?" Klaus asked his wife.

"No, I'll go alone," Marion told him. "First stop, the Congo and northern India's Himalayan Mountains, to gather the giant herbivores, apes and big cats together. Then I'll head for Kenya, the Indian Ocean and western India before returning to the Congo and the Himalayas. Wish me luck."

Marion evaporated in the light of the farmhouse's lounge.

***

Where the Congo met northern India's border with Nepal, Marion reappeared at a farm where two packs of banded mongooses and Indian mongooses were cornered by a horde of Indian marsh crocodiles. Banded mongooses are indigenous to Africa, whilst Indian mongooses are native to India and the Far East. Both species are fierce and fearless killers of snakes, rats and mice. But the mongooses, even together with both continents' fiercest wild cats, were no match against large, ferocious crocodiles, who could maim or kill even a lion or a tiger with a crushing bite.

Protecting the mongooses were the five male tigers, the leopard and the black panther together with a snow leopard, a clouded leopard, an Asian golden cat and a jungle cat from Nepal, as well as a lynx-like caracal and a serval native to the Congo, all wild cats. Even the tigers and leopards cowered before the bone-chilling savagery of the crocodiles as they lunged with their powerful jaws and vice-like teeth and backed the big cats and smaller wild cats into a corner.

Marion sprayed lightning at the killer reptiles, but they were immune to this electricity. Then an Indian elephant charged through the wooden fence into the farmstead and crushed several crocodiles with his club-like hooves. The remaining crocodiles warped themselves out of danger, and the big cats and smaller wild cats growled and hissed their gratitude to the elephant.

"Thank you, oh elephant of India," Marion stammered. She was shaken by the sheer ferocity of the crocodiles, and then the elephant killing the devilish beasts.

She sensed, in her psychic mind, a similar peril on the dreamworld border between Kenya, India and the Indian Ocean. The Lin Wu Beasts were in danger from crocodiles in Kenya, Komodo dragons brought into India from Indonesia, and hyenas and wild dogs in Kenya. As well as savage hyenas, there were African hunting dogs and jackals, who rivalled the hyenas in ferocity.

"As for you smaller wild cats, I want you to head into Nepal," Marion addressed the snow leopard's gang of six. "I don't want you or the Indian and banded mongooses to get killed in any fights you can't handle. The tigers, the leopard and the black panther will come with me to eastern Kenya and western India, but for their safety, they must wait up in the trees until I need them. You, the Indian elephant, will be more effective against the killer reptiles and wild dogs, but first I must call the African giant herbivores and apes to come over to this farm before warping all of you into Kenya. I have visions of your friends—an Indian rhino, a Sumatran rhino and a Javan rhino together with five Himalayan black bears, four sloth bears and five sun bears local to Nepal. I have quite an army on my side. Whilst all you beasts are playing cat and mouse with the killer reptiles and dog-like beasts, I must find the magic gold buried in Kenya or western India. And then, I must find the magic gold buried somewhere in northern India."

Before the apes left the Congo and Nepal, they faced hostility from the warthogs, bush pigs and giant forest hogs, together with the baboons, drills and mandrills. The wild pigs screamed and squealed with devilish ferocity at the three male gorillas and ten chimpanzees, just as the baboons and their cousins screamed, howled and barked with vicious savagery at the orang-utans. Knowing five zebras, four giraffes and five ostriches along with five cassowaries and four kangaroos native to Uganda and Australia were here in the Congo, the wild pigs blamed these large herbivores and big flightless birds for the deaths of the peccaries, giant anteaters and giant pandas in the battle against the criminal developers. The large herbivores and flightless birds had failed to assist the giant herbivores, apes, baboons and wild pigs in that last battle in the Congo, and the wild pigs believed this was why the giant pandas, giant anteaters and peccaries had died. The baboons and their cousins blamed the apes for allowing the giant pandas, giant anteaters and peccaries to draw the developers' gunfire towards them and sacrifice their own lives, whilst the gorillas, chimpanzees and orang-utans failed to carry out a second attack soon enough, hesitating with the baboons in the trees. The warthogs, bush pigs and giant forest hogs wandered away, swearing revenge against the herbivores and flightless birds, whilst the baboons, drills and mandrills hurried away, deciding retribution against the male gorillas, chimpanzees and orang-utans.

The three gorillas knew a civil war between the Lin Wu Beasts was imminent in the Congo. Then the three troops of apes heard Marion calling them in their minds to join the two elephants, five rhinos and the African buffalo, together with the fourteen Asian bears, outside the farm in northern India.

Once the giant herbivores, apes and bears were warped with Marion from the farm to western India and Kenya, Marion was using her psychic mind to find the magic gold. The African elephant, the white rhino, the black rhino and the African buffalo encountered a horde of Nile crocodiles and Indian marsh crocodiles, whilst the Indian elephant, the

Indian rhino, the Sumatran rhino and the Javan rhino faced a gang of five Komodo dragons. Forming a circle and lowering their enormous heads, huge tusks and massive horns, the giant herbivores deterred the crocodiles and Komodo dragons, who made a hasty retreat.

Wandering into the rainforest, the Indian rhino, the Sumatran rhino and the Javan rhino were again attacked by the Komodo dragons. They fought the killer reptiles with extreme savagery. But three giant Komodo dragons overpowered and killed the Indian rhino, just as the other two awesome beasts murdered the Sumatran rhino and the Javan rhino.

On hearing the Asian rhinos' fierce cries, the two elephants, two African rhinos and the buffalo charged in to assist the Asian rhinos, and they attacked the five Komodo dragons.

Their massive heads, tusks and horns smashing with ruthless brutality into the killer reptiles, the elephants, the rhinos and the buffalo fractured the beasts' ribs and spines and broke their legs. Fatally injured, the Komodo dragons collapsed and died in agony.

The African elephant, the white rhino and the black rhino offered the Indian elephant their sympathy for his loss of the three Asian rhinos, but life was cheap for the wild beasts of the rainforests. The Indian elephant snorted and grunted his gratitude towards the four African giant herbivores.

Further east in the rainforest, the four sloth bears were surrounded and outnumbered by two packs of wild dogs, namely dholes or

Asian wild dogs local to India and dingoes introduced by Li Hei from Australia. The sloth bears fought with evil savagery and brute strength, their long claws slashing at the dholes and dingoes, who dealt bite wounds with their wolf-like teeth. But the five Himalayan black bears and five sun bears charged to the sloth bears' rescue. Even sun bears, the smallest of all bears, were as ferocious as Himalayan black bears, and a sun bear could maim or kill a fully-grown man with its long claws and brutal teeth. The black bears massacred eight dholes with fearsome blows from their powerful paws and claws before jumping upon five dholes and ripping them apart with claws and fangs. The sun bears slashed the necks of three dholes before hurling themselves at five other dholes, their fangs and claws tearing the wild dogs to pieces. The sloth bears swiped the necks of five dingoes before leaping at the last four, the shaggy beasts savagely mauling the dingoes until the wild dogs perished.

The black bears, sloth bears and sun bears stood over the wild dogs' corpses, the sloth bears thanking the black bears and sun bears for the rescue.

Then, from Kenya, the bears saw hyenas, African hunting dogs and jackals approaching—dog-like beasts as ferocious as wolves and coyotes and more savage than dholes and dingoes. The bears fled from the scene to find the apes, knowing Kenya's hyenas and wild dogs were more than a match for sloth bears and sun bears.

The gorillas, chimpanzees and orangutans offered the African elephant and the Indian elephant their sympathies over the deaths of the Indian rhino's gang of three, before empathising with the bears over that horrific fight with the dholes and dingoes. The black bear and sun bear leaders decided that the black bears, sloth bears and sun bears would back up the apes in another potential battle in a nearby Indian village overlooking the Indian Ocean. The apes knew killer reptiles, wild dogs and ocean killers would target the people in this village or swimming in the ocean, so the apes and bears swore to protect the men, women and children in this village. Before setting off, the gorillas asked the two elephants, two rhinos and the African buffalo to find the big cats hiding in trees in the forest. The tigers, the leopard, the black panther and the jaguar of Nepal and Brazil would assist the African elephant, the white rhino, the black rhino and the African buffalo in fighting the crocodiles, whilst the Indian elephant faced any Komodo dragons. The five cheetahs would assist the bears and apes in fighting the hyenas and wild dogs.

Marion's psychic mind traced the magic gold to the village overlooking the ocean. She was getting closer to finding it buried somewhere on the beach. Only the weight and strength of an elephant's hooves could break this gold and destroy its deadly magical powers. The killer reptiles, hyenas and wild dogs, together with the sharks and ocean killers who had fought for Li Hei, had been corrupted by batches of magic gold. If the gold was destroyed, maybe this would stop these Li Hei Beasts from attacking humans and Lin Wu's men and beasts. Maybe the sharks and ocean killers in the waters off this beach would refrain from attacking the Indian elephant who was destined to defend the beach against possible Komodo dragons.

Marion was in the village and heard a titanic battle. She was petrified with terror but hurried over to the church where the battle was being fought. The five black bears, four sloth bears and five sun bears had ripped twenty jackals to pieces. The ten chimpanzees had viciously savaged ten dingoes whilst the ten orang-utans savagely mauled and bashed thirteen dholes to death. The three enormous gorillas hurled rocks towards eight Komodo dragons. The heavy boulders smashed the reptiles' foreheads open, killing the Komodo dragons instantly.

Marion knew that, with all the Komodo dragons, dholes, jackals and dingoes slaughtered, only the crocodiles, hyenas and African hunting dogs threatened the men and women in the village. Three great whites, two tiger sharks, a barracuda, a stingray and a manta ray were extremely dangerous to men swimming or fishing in the sea. These great whites and tiger sharks were the same five sharks that had mauled to death an elephant, a hippo, two rhinos and a buffalo, who had been corrupted by noble spirits into killing big cats, two killer reptiles and three smaller sharks turned by evil spirits in Lin Wu's dream. Now the Indian elephant would be alone defending people in the ocean against these enormous sharks, a barracuda, a stingray and manta ray. Unless the elephant destroyed their evil spirits by smashing the gold with his hooves. And Marion knew the gold was buried under the sandy beach.

Marion approached the bears and apes by the church.

"I've found the magic gold," she announced.

The two elephants, two rhinos and the buffalo returned to the village with the big cats, and all the deadly beasts took up their positions. On the village's southwest side, overlooking the Indian Ocean, was the Indian elephant. On the northwest side, the African elephant, the two rhinos and the African buffalo were situated near the church with the five tigers, the leopard, the black panther and the jaguar. Positioned on the east side were the twenty-three apes, fourteen bears and five cheetahs. But to avoid a battle which would be costly in animal lives, Marion wasted no time locating and digging up the magic gold. Then the Indian elephant threw a massive and terrifying kick with one of his front hooves, and the gold shattered into dozens of pieces.

Men swimming in the sea were menaced by the sharks, the barracuda, the stingray and the manta ray, but with their evil spirits destroyed, the savage ocean killers swam away and left the men alone. The elephant snorted and grunted with relief that he would not have to risk his life fighting the sharks and ocean killers. The men swam back to shore, climbed out of the water and thanked Marion and the Indian elephant for smashing the deadly magic gold.

On the village's northwest side, where the dreamworld joined India with Kenya, the African elephant, the white rhino, the black rhino and the African buffalo, together with the tigers, the leopard, the black panther and the jaguar, faced two hordes of Nile crocodiles and Indian marsh crocodiles. But with the magic gold destroyed, the evil spirits in the crocodiles evaporated into nothing and the killer reptiles ran away from the giant herbivores.

On the east side, the gorillas, chimpanzees and orang-utans, backed up by the black bears, sloth bears, sun bears and cheetahs, confronted two vast packs of hyenas and African hunting dogs.

A savage battle had been about to ensue, but with the magic gold pulverised by the Indian elephant's hooves, the hyenas and hunting dogs were free of their evil spirits and retreated into the undergrowth. They would return to Kenya across the border. The apes, bears and cheetahs grunted, snarled and growled with relief. The people in the village were safe from the crocodiles, hyenas and hunting dogs.

Marion warped the African giant herbivores, big cats and bears back to the dreamworld border between the Congo, Nepal and Brazil.

But she still had to find the magic gold buried near the farm on northern India's border with Nepal, and also protect the mongooses. She would need the three gorillas, ten chimpanzees and ten orang-utans to help her protect the mongooses and the Indian elephant against a vast gang of poachers operating in this region of India. The elephant had to accompany her in order to break the magic gold and prevent evil or noble spirits passing into the elephant and the apes when they massacred the poachers.

In the space of three seconds, Marion, together with the elephant and the apes, found themselves on northern India's border with Nepal, but they were not at the farm. They were on a rainforest road leading towards the farm, which was four or five miles away.

"We'd better start walking," Marion told the formidable beasts.

When they had travelled about two or three miles down the rocky, muddy road, Marion saw ahead of her three hyenas, five African hunting dogs and five jackals devouring the corpses of six men that the hyenas and wild dogs had murdered. These beasts had crossed into India from the Congo, and now they were possessed by evil spirits due to the magic gold.

Enraged, the apes charged the savage canine beasts. It was the work of two or three minutes for the larger, more powerful gorillas to tear apart the hyenas and bite them to death in a highly ferocious attack, the same period of time it took the chimpanzees to tear the

hunting dogs limb from limb and the orang-
utans to outnumber the jackals and rip them
apart.

Marion screamed with horror, her heart
dropping to her stomach and nausea
tormenting her throat. With the thirteen dog-
like beasts horribly mutilated, the apes hurried
back towards Marion and the elephant. Marion
examined the six men savaged to death by the
hyenas and wild dogs. Their graphic injuries
tortured Marion, but she knew she and the Lin
Wu Beasts could have done nothing to save
the men.

With tears flowing down her face, Marion
fought back her shock, horror and grief over
the men's deaths as she entered the farm.
The Indian and banded mongooses had
returned to the farm and were eating a cobra,
a mamba, a viper and a krait they had killed
in four separate fights with these venomous
snakes. They welcomed the return of the
Indian elephant and the apes who would be
their protectors against crocodiles, hyenas and
wild dogs. But Marion required the elephant
to help her find the magic gold and destroy
this deadly weapon with his lethal hooves.
Trusting the elephant's powerful sense of
smell, as sharp as a dog's, she followed the
elephant through the forest of pipal, hardwood
and rhododendron trees and into the foothills
of the Himalayas.

After walking three miles, they discovered
a patch of loose soil surrounded by miles of
hard earth. It had been dug up by men with

shovels and then thrown back into the same hole.

"You'd better dig," Marion told the elephant.

In only a minute, his hooves made short work of the soil, and they located the batch of magic gold.

"Destroy this lethal weapon now," Marion ordered. "And then we must return to the farm before the poachers arrive."

With a highly brutal and devastating kick of his heavy right hoof, the elephant pulverised the strong, solid piece of metal, which shattered like glass.

"Let's head back."

On approaching the farm, Marion saw a vast gang of poachers closing in on the apes and mongooses with crocodile-like stealth. Without hesitation, she ejected bolts of lightning towards the men's rifles, which burst into flames. The terrified men threw their guns to the soil. Alerted by the men's screams, the apes and mongooses attacked with savage fury and murderous violence. Charging up the legs of two men, the Indian mongooses used their razor-sharp teeth to sever all of a man's fingers whilst the banded mongooses chewed off the second man's fingers.

Another man was bashed repeatedly by a gorilla, suffering a broken arm and broken ribs, as the other two gorillas savaged two other men with several crushing bites, smashing in their ribs and breaking their right legs. All three gorillas bludgeoned the men to death with blows to the head.

The chimpanzees outnumbered and mauled the arms and faces of five men just as the orang-utans viciously bit the arms, faces and necks of another four. The last five huntsmen fled away from the farm, but the elephant stabbed two gunmen with his tusks, then used his violently strong front hooves to kick the last three. The men died in a matter of minutes. With eight men massacred by the elephant and the gorillas, the eleven poachers mutilated by the chimpanzees, orang-utans and mongooses sprinted back through the jungle. The apes and mongooses had finished their deadly work.

There were too many poachers for Marion to capture and detain, but she knew the Indian and Nepalese police would identify the men later from their horrific injuries consistent with the teeth of apes and mongooses.

"Now the magic gold is no more," Marion said. "You predatory mongooses don't look possessed by evil spirits, or the elephant and the apes possessed by noble spirits. Nor have you taken your aggression out on me. But you apes want to tell me something."

From their photographic memories, visions came from the gorillas' heads of the battle against criminal developers and armed men out to destroy the Congo's rainforests. These pictures reflected exactly the end of Marion's second dream set on the dreamworld border between the Congo, China, Colombia and Venezuela. Again, she saw the giant pandas, giant anteaters and peccaries sacrificing their own lives by mauling, biting and chopping twelve men to death before they were gunned down with no mercy by another fourteen men. Up in the trees, the three gorillas had hesitated to give the order to the chimpanzees, orang-utans and baboons to drop down from the trees and attack alongside the wild pigs. As the silverback male gorilla gave the order, the gorillas, chimpanzees and orang-utans hurtled down and savaged twenty-three men whilst the baboons, drills and mandrills mauled a dozen more and the warthogs, bush pigs and giant forest hogs gored and ripped open another fourteen. The African elephant, the two rhinos and the African buffalo also took terrible toll of the criminal developers. The rainforest had been saved.

But another vision came from the gorillas' brains, one where the wild pigs threatened the gorillas and chimpanzees with screams and squeals, and the baboons intimidated the orang-utans with screaming, howling and barking.

A third vision emerged from the gorillas' minds of five zebras, four giraffes and five ostriches from neighbouring Uganda, and five cassowaries and four kangaroos from Australia, warping into the Congo. The baboons blamed the apes for causing the deaths of the giant pandas, giant anteaters and peccaries by not ordering the apes, baboons and wild pigs to attack the developers sooner. The wild pigs blamed the herbivores and flightless birds of Uganda and Australia for not assisting the giant herbivores, apes and wild pigs in that battle, their apparent cowardice being a deciding factor that led to the deaths of the giant pandas, giant anteaters and peccaries.

"So the baboons blame you apes for the beasts' massacre?" Marion asked. "And the wild pigs blame the zebras, giraffes and ostriches for not fighting alongside you beasts. Not to mention the cassowaries and kangaroos from Australia. My psychic brain senses that these herbivores and flightless birds are in the Congo, with only the African giant herbivores to protect them. You apes will need protection too.

"Right, I want you, the Indian elephant and the mongooses, to stay here in India. I must warp the Asian bears over to this farm and together the bears and apes will travel with me to the Congo, where we'll assist the herbivores and flightless birds against the baboons and wild pigs. I fear it may come to a battle where we have to kill the baboons and wild pigs, which for me is breaking a moral rule to respect Nature. But the baboons and wild pigs are blinded by their grudge against the apes and herbivores. This is the worst day of my life."

On the dreamworld border between India and the Congo, the twenty-three apes and fourteen Asian bears welcomed the arrival of the zebras, giraffes and ostriches along with the cassowaries and kangaroos. Despite their reputation for being powerful and fierce fighters against predators, the herbivores and flightless birds were friendly to the apes and bears. Marion was not so positive when she saw twenty wild pigs and fifteen baboons closing in on the beasts—namely eight warthogs, seven bush pigs and five giant forest hogs, together with four baboons, five drills and six mandrills. The Himalayan black bears, sloth bears and sun bears stood their ground alongside the large herbivores, flightless birds and apes, all of whom turned their terror into fury and aggression. But Marion knew that any fruitless violence and fighting would cost lives or result in crippling injuries to the beasts, and Li Hei's gangs would win the final victory.

After a stand-off lasting five minutes, in which Marion gagged and gulped with nausea and petrified fear, dogs belonging to criminal developers and their armed men attacked the wild pigs and baboons. Marion sprayed a hail of lightning bolts towards the men's rifles, which became red-hot pieces of metal, flaming and smoking in the men's hands. The men dropped their fearsome weapons, and Marion fired lightning at their legs and feet, burning their feet severely so they would struggle to run away.

The dogs were viciously gored and ripped open or savagely torn apart by the wild pigs and baboons. The armed men, despite their horrific agony, grabbed rocks and stones and bludgeoned the ugly beasts, fatally injuring them. The wild pigs and baboons lay in heaps from the bites and blows, their skulls badly fractured, but the giant herbivores led the opposing Lin Wu Beasts in a ferocious and brutal counterattack to rescue the hogs and primates. To prove their alliance to their opponents, the herbivores, flightless birds and apes hurled themselves towards the men throwing stones and rocks, like lions leaping at prey. Flailing with their front hooves, the zebras bashed five men senseless, and then their hind hooves kicked backwards at another five men who had sneaked behind them. Kicking forwards, backwards, left and right with all four hooves, the giraffes attacked sixteen men, disembowelling them or breaking their legs, pelvises and ribs. The ostriches and cassowaries used their clawed feet to drop-kick and rip open fifteen men, and the kangaroos leapt upwards, kicking with powerful hind feet to rupture the stomachs of another four.

Attacking thirteen other men who had fatally wounded the baboons, drills and mandrills, the male gorillas rained fearsome blows with their huge fists, fracturing the spines, ribs and shoulders of three developers, before killing the men by breaking their necks or smashing their skulls.

Outnumbering the other ten brutes, the chimpanzees and orang-utans dealt multiple bite wounds to the crooks' arms, shoulders and upper bodies before their lethal fangs split the men's heads open or strangled them. Fourteen men sustained claw and puncture wounds on their arms, bodies and faces from the black bears, sloth bears and sun bears until these bears slaughtered them. In the same five minutes of terrifying, brutal slaughter and carnage, the elephant, the two rhinos and the buffalo horribly gored and massacred thirteen criminals. Marion threw up vomit and bile at witnessing this ruthless slaughter, but she told herself the armed men and their dogs had seriously wounded the wild pigs and baboons.

After the brutal carnage, the fatally injured warthogs, bush pigs and giant forest hogs were no longer hostile to the large herbivores and flightless birds, and the dying baboons, drills and mandrills were no longer furious and deadly to the gorillas, chimpanzees and orang-utans. Their faces conveyed forgiveness and loyalty towards the Lin Wu Beasts that they had been about to fight. Marion gasped with relief, her stomach painful from vomiting on the grass, for she knew a fruitless and costly battle between the Lin Wu Beasts had been avoided by the criminal developers and their hunting dogs fatally injuring the wild pigs and baboons before the remaining herbivores, bears and apes fought another battle to save these wild swine and primates. But after forgiving the herbivores and apes, the wild swine and primates passed away. Marion wept and sobbed at this tragedy.

***

When Lin Wu had those two dreams about four gangs of giant herbivores and predators being corrupted by noble or evil spirits through killing two gangs of criminals, the second dream involved Vancouver Zoo's four male lions backing up the big cats from the Congo, Nepal and Brazil.

Three male polar bears and two male dogs supported the North American bears, as well as the puma, the wolf, the coyote and the fox. The lions were different individuals from the male lions and lionesses shot to death at Malibu Beach in California and the polar bears were not the ones shot dead with the five bison and the large predators on northern Alberta's tundra. All these big cats, bears and wild dogs had avoided being corrupted simply by not killing the criminal developers.

Lin Wu and Klaus had created another dreamworld linking British Colombia with Nepal in order to recruit five giant male yetis from Nepal's Himalayas and four enormous male bigfoot creatures from the forests outside Vancouver, all massive apes larger than gorillas. The yetis were the most ferocious of all apes that Lin Wu had worked with. From Vancouver Zoo, two African elephants, a white rhino, a black rhino and three African buffaloes, along with ten male gorillas, joined the yetis and bigfoot creatures, whilst the zoo's male lions were backed up by three male Bengal tigers, a leopard and a black panther, together with two jaguars and three male cheetahs who were released from the zoo. These big cats were different individuals from the tigers, the leopards and the jaguar operating with Marion in Nepal and Brazil. The three polar bears and two dogs took their place alongside the Kodiak bear, the grizzly bear and the black bear, backed up by the puma, the lynx and the bobcat, together with the wolf, the coyote and the fox. Standing alongside them were the bison and the moose from Yellowstone National Park.

"Why have we created another dreamworld joining Canada with Nepal?" Klaus wanted to know. "And why have we recruited giant herbivores, gorillas and large predators from Vancouver Zoo to back up the bison, the moose and the predators of Wyoming? Are poachers or criminal developers about to make another attempt on our lives?"

"No, Klaus," Lin Wu said. "The mustelids in Wyoming and northern and western Europe have identified the men behind the pollution after spying on these crooks, both the bosses and their armed men. From American badgers and common badgers to weasels, stoats, polecats and martens, all mustelids can attack a man and fracture his hand or sever his fingers with their razor-sharp teeth, but they cannot kill a man. Not even mink and fishers as large and fierce as house cats can kill a man. Only the wolverine is large, powerful and ferocious enough to take a man's life. So the mustelids of Europe and Wyoming must freeze the men with their witchcraft and warp them over to British Colombia."

"You won't allow these large, savage beasts we have here to massacre the industrialists and polluters," Klaus objected. "That's another mass murder."

"The giant herbivores, apes and large predators will refrain from such a gruesome massacre," Lin Wu promised. "I'll interrogate these men whilst using the threat of animal violence, but I will not use any violence. We'll see what incriminating information comes out of their mouths, both about themselves and other polluting industries. I am especially targeting the British men working for Dalseo Factories in Great Britain, Holland, Belgium and Italy, among many other countries. But the Australians, New Zealanders, Russians and Japanese in Spain, Italy and Slovenia really are about to die. The predators protecting the local ibexes, chamois and mouflons are stalking these men. I'll show you the visions from my psychic mind."

"Here we go," Klaus said.

Three visions rose from Lin Wu's head. The first vision showed Spain's Cantabrian Mountains, where the three Australians behind sewage pollution were lying dead in a forest with the bear, the wolf and the wild cat eating their victims from Down Under. The second image showed Gran Paradiso National Park in Italy where the four New Zealanders working for Dalseo Factories, which was behind acid rain pollution, were savaged to death by the bear, the wolf, the lynx and the wild cat.

In the third vision, which happened in Slovenia, the same gruesome end befell the two Russians and two Japanese men behind oil and exhaust pollutions from cars and petrol cans. These men were brutally mauled by the bear, the wolf, the lynx and the wild cat, different beasts from the predators in Spain and Italy.

Then the visions withdrew back inside Lin Wu's head.

"The industrialists and polluters we interrogate will be warped by sorcery to Vancouver Police Department's prison cells to await extradition, trial and detention in their own countries," Lin Wu explained. "I'll make a phone call to Vancouver PD to tell the police chief what these men told me. And now, I sense the mustelids about to arrive in this forest with the men they've captured with their sorcery."

"What do I ask them?" Klaus inquired.

"I'll ask all the questions," Lin Wu explained. "Here we go."

In the next five seconds, the badgers, weasels and stoats, alongside the polecats and pine martens from Norway and Sweden, reappeared out of the forest mist. They delivered twenty-two British men working for Dalseo Factories to the ten male gorillas, five yetis and four bigfoot creatures. The British men from Dalseo, whose industries were behind acid rain and rubbish pollution, were petrified of the three gangs of giant apes. A few seconds later, the badger, the weasel and the stoat from a forest in Denmark arrived with twelve German men and dumped them in front of the two African elephants, the white rhino, the black rhino and the three African buffaloes. These men ran heavy industries in northern Germany, sending out poisonous gas emissions, which killed birds in the skies over Germany and Denmark and contributed to climate change. With the elephants preparing to stab and crush five men, the rhinos about to gore and trample four more and the buffaloes ready to impale three crooks, these men were rooted to the spot by a crippling terror and horror.

Next came the badger, the weasel and the stoat from Germany's Bavarian Forest, delivering to the three tigers three farmers responsible for pollution from pesticides and herbicides. The brutes were petrified of the massive tigers, who were larger and more ferocious than the four male lions.

Then, from the border between Holland and Belgium, the badgers, weasels and stoats together with polecats, ferrets, pine martens and beech martens dropped off four British men from Holland's chemical plant in front of the leopard, the black panther and the two jaguars. They left three British bosses from Dalseo Factories in Belgium at the teeth and claws of the three cheetahs. These seven men were behind pollution from chemicals and industrial effluence from the plants seeping into the river dividing Holland and Belgium, and they were not petrified with terror of the leopards, jaguars and cheetahs.

In the short period of two or three seconds,

the badger, the weasel and the stoat from that forest in Burgundy arrived with four criminals and left them at the mercy of the four lions. The brutes had deliberately contaminated grass, vegetation and rivers in France with poisons and weed-killers, destroying the plants and poisoning rabbits, hares and rats, which had nearly been eaten by the badger, the weasel and the stoat. These men were now crippled with horror and blind fear that they would be mauled to death by these huge male lions almost as massive as the tigers.

Lastly, a vast gang of men behind rubbish, litter and fly-tipping pollution at Yellowstone were delivered by the American badger, the mink and the fisher to the beasts of Wyoming and Alaska. Six men and their two gang bosses, whom the bison and the moose had witnessed dumping garbage and litter on both sides of the highway in Yellowstone, were now petrified with a paralysing terror of the bison, the moose and the three polar bears backing up the Kodiak bear, the grizzly bear and the black bear. Three men that the puma, the lynx and the bobcat had watched fly-tipping their garbage from a truck onto the wild cats' side of the road were highly fearful of being ripped to pieces and strangled by the puma, the lynx and the bobcat. And the last four men guilty of dropping poisons and weed-killers were scared of the wolf, the coyote, the fox and the two dogs.

"You ruthless industrialists and polluters of the natural environment had better not lie to me or twist the truth to your own advantage after I've shown you these visions passed from the mustelids' psychic minds to my psychic brain when I was in Switzerland," Lin Wu began. "Or the visions passed to me here in Canada, proving you polluted the forests and rivers in Europe and Wyoming and killed wild animals. One lie and all these dangerous creatures will massacre you in a ferocious and brutal manner. And if you lie to the police at Vancouver PD, you will increase your prison sentences. If you all tell me the truth and then tell the truth to the police, you'll prevent these creatures from killing you and you'll reduce your prison sentences."

"We'll tell you the truth," they all cried.

The men's testimonies took an hour, and Lin Wu used his mobile phone to film and record what the men told him. He then used sorcery to warp the men to Vancouver PD's prison cells before calling the department's police chief and passing on mobile phone footage of the men's testimonies. The Vancouver police had enough evidence to show the police in western Europe and in Wyoming, to extradite the industrialists and polluters back to these countries or to Wyoming and have them tried, convicted and imprisoned over there.

"Do we still need the giant herbivores, big cats and gorillas from Vancouver Zoo?" Klaus wanted to know. "Or the yetis and bigfoot creatures?"

"No, Klaus," Lin Wu said. "I'll warp the lions, big cats and polar bears along with the giant herbivores and gorillas back to Vancouver Zoo. But I'll create another dreamworld between Nepal and Louisiana. I'll warp the yetis and bigfoot creatures over there, for there is magic gold buried near the Mississippi River. My psychic mind has just detected Li Hei and his men burying the gold. I'll warp the African elephant's gang of four giant herbivores over there from the Congo, for only the elephant's hooves can break this gold. But first, the two elephants must smash magic gold at two locations, Florida and the dreamworld joining Florida with the Congo and Nepal. I must send psychic mind signals to Marion in the Congo."

Klaus and Lin Wu waited in anticipation.

***

On the dreamworld border between the Congo, Nepal and Brazil, three groups of smaller predators, led by the big cats, approached the African elephant, the rhinos and the African buffalo. Among these predators were the Indian and banded mongooses who had bid farewell to the Indian elephant in Nepal, and a ratel, or honey badger, local to the Congo. The honey badger walked alongside the lynx-like caracal, the serval and the African wild cat, led by the five cheetahs, also native to the Congo. The five tigers, the leopard and the black panther walked alongside the snow leopard, the clouded leopard, the Asian golden cat and the jungle cat of

Nepal. From Brazil came the jaguar, the ocelot, the jaguarundi and the margay.

The honey badger, the snow leopard and these smaller wild cats were ferocious killers, fit to injure or kill a man in self-defence, and the mongooses could take on venomous snakes or savage rats. In the nearby river was the hippo, who would guard Marion's underground hideout.

The tigers' psychic minds produced a vision of Uganda and India. Hyenas and wild dogs, namely African hunting dogs, jackals and feral dogs, were ruthlessly mauling and eating men and women on the savannas and rainforests joined by the dreamworld. Using growls and grunts, the tigers told the African elephant that these beasts must be stopped. The elephant agreed and called over the Asian bears to protect and assist the cheetahs in one group. The elephant, the rhinos and the buffalo would form a second group, and the tigers would unite again with the leopard, the black panther and the jaguar. The hippo and the smaller predators would stay in the Congo and Nepal to protect Marion.

Marion was exhausted. She climbed down through a hole in the ground, laid a large stone by the hole and fell asleep on a bed of thick grass. This would be the perfect hiding place against poachers and criminal developers, and the hippo and the smaller predators were a fearsome and deadly army of bodyguards with their vicious savagery and magical powers.

Marion slept for four hours, and during the

last hour, she had a dream of the dreamworld border between Uganda's grasslands and plains and India's rainforests. There was a war against the hyenas and wild dogs who had been corrupted into killing humans by magic gold. In the first scene, hyenas and wild dogs brutally mauled and dismembered or severed the hands of thirty men and women. The hyenas, African hunting dogs and jackals were backed up by dholes in India and dingoes warped into Uganda from Australia. The elephant, the white rhino, the black rhino and the buffalo charged in and crushed all the dholes and dingoes as the tigers, cheetahs and bears mauled and tore apart twenty-five feral dogs. The hyenas, hunting dogs and jackals cantered away down the savanna whilst the men left alive thanked the elephant's gang, the tigers and bears for saving them from further attack.

The Himalayan black bears, sloth bears and sun bears, together with the tigers and cheetahs, asked the elephant, the rhinos and the buffalo to keep a low profile whilst the bears and big cats used their smaller size, cunning and stealth to observe the movements of the dog-like beasts. The giant herbivores agreed to this. Then the tigers set off to scout out the land.

The hyenas were spying on the giant herbivores, bears and cheetahs as they drank at Lake Victoria. Wanting revenge on the bears and big cats, the hyenas made their way back through the savanna. They would return to their gang of hunting dogs, jackals and feral dogs.

There were two attacks on tribesmen committed by the wild dogs. The first attack involved the hunting dogs severing the hands and biting the arms and legs of six men with their shark-like teeth, so the men bled to death. The second attack involved the jackals and feral dogs chewing off the hands and viciously mauling the arms and bodies of nine men, so they died from excessive loss of blood. Then the wild dogs reunited with the hyenas. A third attack on game wardens was led by the hyenas. As the hyenas broke the arms and legs of eight men, the hunting dogs fractured the hands of five men and the jackals and feral dogs repeated this attack against another seven. The game wardens bled to death.

On witnessing this gruesome massacre, the bears and cheetahs were outnumbered and outmatched by the dog-like beasts and fled as fast as possible. The hyenas and wild dogs chased them, but the bears and cheetahs leapt into Lake Victoria, disappeared underwater and reappeared in another area of Uganda overlooking the lake.

The leopard, the black panther and the jaguar reported the three wild dog attacks to the elephant, the rhinos and the buffalo. They also told them how the bears and cheetahs had narrowly escaped the hyenas and wild dogs. The elephant decided that he, the rhinos and the buffalo would use their powerful senses of smell to seek out the magic gold that had corrupted the wild dogs.

The four giant herbivores split up in two directions to find the gold, the elephant assisted by the tigers. The elephant spotted feral dogs eating the corpses of five men that the dogs had savaged to death. The tigers charged five dogs whilst the elephant bounded towards another eight, but the dogs ran away. The elephant and the tigers sensed that the rhinos, the buffalo and the other big cats were in danger from the hyenas and another gang of feral dogs.

The rhinos and the buffalo, along with the leopard, the black panther and the jaguar, were cornered by the hyenas and feral dogs, who had savaged and dismembered another ten men, but one final charge by the rhinos and the buffalo drove the hyenas and dogs away. The elephant and the tigers arrived ten minutes later.

The elephant was relieved that the rhinos and the buffalo were all right. The leopard, the black panther and the jaguar comforted them. The bears and cheetahs also returned and offered their praise to the giant herbivores and tigers.

The elephant and the tigers renewed their search for the magic gold by heading north, whilst the leopards and the jaguar made their way west, and the rhinos and the buffalo went east.

The bears and cheetahs attacked and massacred a pack of feral dogs before sending psychic mind signals to the elephant and the tigers. The bears and cheetahs had no luck in finding the magic gold.

The leopard, the black panther and the jaguar sent mind signals to the tigers and the elephant, telling them the big cats, with their sharp senses of smell, had found no trace of the gold. The elephant and the tigers found no trace either. The elephant rejoined the rhinos and the buffalo, and then picked up mind signals from the cheetahs and bears.

The black bears, sloth bears and sun bears, together with the cheetahs, chased another pack of feral dogs, but the dogs reached the hyenas, hunting dogs and jackals. The bears and cheetahs turned tail and fled into a river, but this time, the hyenas and wild dogs leapt in after them. The dogs and jackals reached the shore first and were viciously savaged by the bears and cheetahs until they died. The cheetahs ran to bring over the other big cats and giant herbivores whilst the bears climbed trees for safety.

The elephant, the rhinos and the buffalo arrived on the scene with the tigers, the leopards and the jaguar, backed up by the cheetahs. In a titanic battle, the elephant, the rhinos and the buffalo destroyed twenty-five hyenas whilst the tigers savagely mauled eight hyenas, and the leopard, the black panther, the jaguar and the cheetahs ripped nine hunting dogs to pieces. The black bears, sloth bears and sun bears hurried down the trees and tore apart the last fourteen hunting dogs.

The elephant knew they had to renew their search for the magic gold. The bears told the elephant, the tigers and the leopards they would renew their search in Nepal and headed for the Himalayas. The jaguar and the cheetahs would warp themselves from Uganda to the Congo and continue their search there.

The elephant, the rhinos and the buffalo, together with the tigers and leopards, ran into crocodiles and Komodo dragons who had savaged, dismembered and devoured thirteen game wardens. The giant herbivores bellowed, roared and screamed at the killer reptiles. Combined with the roaring and screaming of the tigers and leopards, the crocodiles and Komodo dragons hurried into the river.

But the elephant spotted traces of gold dust on the crocodiles' bodies and thrashing tails, and he realised that the killer reptiles would lead the beasts to the gold.

The tigers, the leopard and the black panther sent mind signals to the jaguar and the cheetahs in the Congo, telling the big cats they were getting closer to finding the magic gold.

The river that the giant herbivores, tigers and leopards followed narrowed into a stream, underneath which the gold was buried. The giant herbivores dug with their hooves until they exposed the gold, and with one mighty kick of his front hoof, the elephant smashed the gold to smithereens.

At that moment, hyenas, hunting dogs and jackals who had killed and eaten twelve poachers, together with crocodiles and Komodo dragons who had savaged and devoured seventeen armed men, suddenly charged the giant herbivores and big cats. The elephant and the buffalo ploughed into seven Komodo dragons, breaking their legs, ribs and spines, whilst the rhinos crushed eight crocodiles. The killer reptiles were no more.

With crushing blows from their bear-like paws and rapier claws, the tigers destroyed all eight hyenas and five jackals as the leopard and the black panther slashed at the ten hunting dogs. The buffalo gored and trampled all these hunting dogs until they perished.

With the gold destroyed, there would be no more attacks on humans by killer reptiles, hyenas and wild dogs. The elephant and the tigers knew the giant herbivores and big cats had to return by sorcery to the dreamworld joining the Congo with Nepal and Brazil.

In the next few seconds, Marion's dream ended, and she awoke in her underground hideout. But she did not feel at ease, for she was tormented by the stench of dead bodies of both animals and humans. She had to remove the rock at the entrance, climb out of the hideout and see what had happened. She had her feet and hands flexed in combat style, preparing to fire lightning at poachers or criminal developers and dogs who challenged her.

On walking outside, Marion was shocked and appalled to see the dead bodies of fifteen criminal developers and their pet rats, who had been savagely massacred by the hippo, the honey badger, the smaller wild cats and the mongooses. The Indian and banded mongooses had slaughtered all the rats whilst the honey badger had disembowelled and ripped the chest and arms of the leading criminal developers. The caracal, the serval and the African wild cat had torn the legs of three developers so the men bled to death. The ocelot, the jaguarundi and the margay had shredded the legs of three men, and the golden cat and the jungle cat had ripped the legs of two others, puncturing arteries and blood vessels so these eight men all died from excessive loss of blood. The snow leopard and clouded leopard had ripped the upper bodies and arms of two developers before their lethal fangs strangled the men, the snow leopard being as savage and deadly as any leopard or black panther. The last four criminal developers had been fiercely gored, impaled and crushed to death by the hippo. Their mutilated bodies lay in the river. But the hippo, the honey badger, the mongooses and the wild cats were also dead.

There were no gunshot wounds on these beasts.

"There is magic gold buried here," Marion

pointed out. Then she heard mind signals from Lin Wu.

"Hello there, Marion," Lin Wu said.

"Hello, Lin Wu. I have some tragic news," Marion informed him.

"What is this tragic news?" he asked.

"The hippo, the honey badger, the mongooses and the smaller wild cats have died by killing fifteen criminal developers and a horde of rats," she told him. "I know there is magic gold buried here in the Congo or Nepal. As I slept in an underground hideout, I had another dream set in Uganda and India. The giant herbivores and big cats eventually found another batch of magic gold buried near a stream, which had corrupted killer reptiles, hyenas and wild dogs into killing humans. And now, there is magic gold buried here in the Congo."

"That's not the worst of it," Lin Wu added.

"I'll bet it's not," Marion commented.

"There are three batches of magic gold, including yours buried in the Congo or Nepal," Lin Wu explained. "There is a batch buried in Florida, which has corrupted alligators, sharks and ocean killers into attacking only game wardens and park rangers in the Everglades. There is that batch in the Congo or Nepal. And a third batch buried near the Mississippi River in Louisiana. I will create another dreamworld joining Louisiana with Nepal in order to involve four bigfoot creatures that I'll warp down from British Colombia and five yetis local to Nepal. To save you the trouble of joining the Congo and Nepal to Florida, I have joined the three states. The Indian elephant in Nepal will join the jaguar, the cassowaries and kangaroos from Brazil and Australia in your first mission in Florida. The four African giant herbivores, the big cats and apes, together with the zebras, giraffes and ostriches, will execute the second mission in the Congo and Nepal. Any questions?"

"There are no questions," Marion said.

***

Drenched in warm rivers of sweat from the boiling sunshine in Florida's Everglades, a group of game wardens and park rangers paddled in the river leading out into the Gulf of Mexico. Suddenly, five alligators seized five men and, with their dreaded death rolls, wrenched the men's legs off. The men screamed in appalling agony and horror before the alligators clamped their jaws around the men's bodies and crushed in their ribs.

At the same time, a barracuda, a conger eel, a sawfish and a swordfish, together with a giant grouper, four hagfishes and five lampreys, savagely mauled seven game wardens. The sawfish and the swordfish used their saw-like jaw and sharp snout to slash open and stab two men, whilst the giant grouper, the barracuda and the conger eel bit large chunks out of three other men. The parasitic hagfishes and lampreys sucked flesh and blood from the last two.

The alligators and ocean killers finished the men in minutes. All, except the fish-eating swordfish, the hagfishes and lampreys, devoured the men. The giant sawfish ate his own victim before consuming the swordfish's impaled victim, whilst the conger eel and the giant grouper dined on the two men who had bled to death after being mauled by the blood-sucking hagfishes and lampreys.

Five feral dogs approached the alligators. The dogs told the killer reptiles how Marion and the Lin Wu Beasts were in Florida, hunting for the magic gold, the dogs barking and growling their message to the reptiles. The alligators and dogs decided to hunt down and kill Marion before she found the gold.

***

Marion was with the jaguar, the five cassowaries and four kangaroos in the undergrowth when she spotted ten dark sorcerers talking to a great white shark, a tiger shark, an octopus and a giant squid. The sorcerers told the sharks and ocean killers they had hidden a batch of magic gold in a church west of Miami.

With an explosion of roaring, screaming and hissing, the jaguar sped towards one of the men. The cassowaries darted and lunged with their clawed feet at five other men and the kangaroos hopped towards and dropkicked the last four.

Taken by surprise and terrified, the men leapt into the river, hoping the sharks and ocean killers would protect them, but these savage beasts decided the men knew too much and had to die. The sharks severed the legs of three men and crushed the ribs and spines of two others whilst the octopus and the giant squid ripped open three sorcerers with their slashing tentacles and shredded the last two to pieces. The jaguar, the cassowaries and kangaroos withdrew from the riverbank as Marion sprayed lightning at the ocean killers. The sharks and ocean killers sped out into the river estuary leading into the Gulf of Mexico.

"The magic gold is in a church west of Miami," Marion said. "We had better warp ourselves there now."

Then the Indian elephant joined with her team.

***

Two sorcerers guarded the church. Marion and the Lin Wu Beasts emerged from behind the trees. Marion fired lightning to disable the men, and then the elephant and the jaguar charged. The elephant gored one guard to death as the jaguar used hind and front claws and bone-crushing fangs to rip apart the second and bite into his skull. Both men died instantly.

The elephant was too enormous to fit through the church door, and Marion would have to warp the giant beast inside so he could break the gold. The jaguar, the cassowaries and kangaroos hurried inside to confront the five alligators and five feral dogs. In Australia, the cassowaries had killed crocodiles and dingoes whilst kangaroos had injured dingoes, so the five cassowaries and four kangaroos had no problem with the slower alligators and dogs. The jaguar lunged towards one dog and ripped him to pieces whilst the kangaroos dropkicked the other four and broke their ribs. The dogs died of their injuries.

The alligators hurled themselves at the cassowaries, who leapt upwards, slashing with their deadly clawed feet, and tore open the alligators from stem to stern. Fatally wounded, the alligators slunk away in horrific, terrifying agony.

Marion warped herself and the elephant inside the church, and the woman opened a hole in the floor where the magic gold was. With a brutal kick of his right front hoof, the elephant smashed the gold into splintered metal. He did this just in time to save himself and the jaguar from being corrupted by noble or evil spirits for killing those two guards outside the church door.

With a warping spell, Marion transported the elephant and the Lin Wu Beasts outside the church, towards the Everglades forest facing the mangrove swamps to the west.

Her next task was to find the magic gold buried in the Congo or Nepal.

***

In the Congo, three packs of hyenas, African hunting dogs and jackals dismembered seventeen game wardens, severing some of their hands. The ten victims of the wild dogs bled to death from their mutilated hands but were not eaten like the seven men crunched and torn apart by the seven hyenas.

When the hyenas had consumed their human victims, the dog-like beasts were approached by three crocodiles from the Congo and five Komodo dragons warped from Indonesia into Nepal by Li Hei's sorcerers. The crocodiles told the hyenas and wild dogs that Marion was on the dreamworld border between Florida, the Congo and Nepal, hunting for the magic gold. The killer reptiles decided the Li Hei Beasts must murder Marion and massacre the Lin Wu Beasts before they located the gold.

***

Marion was accompanied by the African elephant, the rhinos and the African Buffalo, backed up by the five zebras, four giraffes and five ostriches, along with the three gorillas, ten chimpanzees and ten orang-utans. Also supporting the herbivores, flightless birds and apes were the five tigers, the leopard, the black panther and the five cheetahs.

Stalking through the trees and thickets, Marion and the Lin Wu Beasts overheard a large mass of dark sorcerers talking at the river. The men told each other that the magic gold was buried at a mountain in the Congo positioned south of two mountains in Nepal.

The Lin Wu Beasts forgot that if they killed the men, the gold would corrupt them. Charging from the undergrowth, the elephant, the white rhino, the black rhino and the buffalo were hell-bent on thrusting their tusks and horns into four men, whilst the zebras, giraffes and ostriches would kick to death fourteen men, and the gorillas, chimpanzees and orang-utans would viciously maul thirteen more. The tigers were prepared to rip apart five riflemen whilst the leopard and the black panther would tear two gunmen to pieces. The last three men would be shredded to ribbons by the cheetahs.

Marion had to react within a few seconds to save the fearsome beasts.

She fired lightning over their heads, burning the dark sorcerers as well as disabling their rifles. Petrified with a nerve-shredding fear and cowering in terrible agony, the men plunged into the river, which led from Florida's Everglades into the

Congo and Nepal. In a matter of seconds, the three crocodiles, five Komodo dragons and two massive sharks led the other ocean killers coming back from the Gulf of Mexico in a horrific attack executed with extreme savagery. Within the same few minutes that the crocodiles twisted off the legs of three men, the Komodo dragons crushed the spines and ribs of five men and the sharks chopped with their enormous jaws and huge teeth at the legs and bodies of six others. The octopus and the giant squid slashed with their tentacles, ripping open six other men as the barracuda and the conger eel bit and chopped the legs and bodies of three sorcerers. The giant grouper horribly savaged two armed men at the same time as the sawfish tore open another two gunmen and another man was stabbed and impaled by the swordfish.

Of the forty-one men attacked by the savage beasts, thirteen tried to swim towards the other riverbank, but the four hagfishes and five lampreys sucked and drained the blood from nine of them, who bled to death in the water in a matter of minutes. Four men who made it to the riverbank were brutally savaged and torn to pieces by the hyenas, African hunting dogs and jackals.

The Lin Wu Beasts withdrew their deadly attack by retreating away from the river, determined not to be savagely mauled and eaten by the killer reptiles, sharks and ocean killers. The dangerous herbivores, apes and big cats fired lightning into the water, and

Marion sprayed a bolt of electricity. The Li Hei Beasts disappeared back downstream whilst the hyenas and wild dogs dragged their four victims into the rainforest to devour them.

"Next time, don't try to kill any men until I've destroyed the magic gold," Marion said. Her voice was calm but firm. "You could've been turned by noble or evil spirits. Or you could've been savagely mauled by the killer reptiles and ocean killers. I overheard the dark sorcerers saying that the magic gold is buried in a mountain in the Congo facing two mountains in Nepal. The mountain in the Congo is south of the other two mountains, which must face the northeast and northwest. The crocodiles and Komodo dragons have warped themselves to the south mountain. The hyenas, hunting dogs and jackals are guarding the northwest and northeast mountains. I must warp you fearsome beasts in three groups, to draw the Li Hei Beasts away from the three mountains before you massacre them. There are likely to be armed men guarding the south mountain, just like there were two men guarding the church outside Miami. There will be ten seconds between the time you slaughter the men and the moment the elephant destroys the magic gold. Whilst you're massacring these guys, I'll be digging up the gold ready for the elephant to destroy. I'll warp you Lin Wu Beasts in three gangs now."

***

Once the large herbivores and big flightless birds were hidden behind a mass of trees and thickets a hundred yards from the base of the south mountain, the killer reptiles were hidden away from the armed men and charged for the trees. With the element of surprise on their side, the African elephant used his formidable tusks and front hooves to rip open two Komodo dragons, smashing their bones, as the two rhinos and the African buffalo tore open the other three and bashed their bones. The zebras, giraffes and ostriches, with sledgehammer hooves and clawed feet, outnumbered the three crocodiles and kicked them until they were dead from shattered bones.

At the northeast mountain, the gorillas bashed to death five hunting dogs and eight jackals, whilst the chimpanzees viciously savaged ten hunting dogs and seven jackals, and the orang-utans savagely bit to death ten hunting dogs. The last five hunting dogs were clawed and strangled by the cheetahs.

At the northwest mountain, the seven hyenas were drawn towards the undergrowth lying to the west, when the tigers and leopards pounced. They wrestled the hyenas to the ground. The tigers brutally mauled and strangled five hyenas just as the leopard and the black panther clawed the last two to death and bit into their heads.

Upon hearing the awful screams of the killer reptiles, hyenas and wild dogs being gored, kicked and torn to pieces, the armed men at the south mountain were petrified with a stomach-churning terror. They raised their rifles, their blood-curdling fear equal to the terror a rabbit would feel when being attacked by a fox or a cat.

After the two gangs of Lin Wu Beasts in Nepal rejoined the first gang of large herbivores and flightless birds behind the trees and thickets in the Congo due to Marion's magical spell, Marion fired lightning at the men's rifles, burning them red-hot. Flames leapt up above the fearsome guns. The men's voices exploded with gut-wrenching screams of agony and fear before the men threw the weapons to the ground. The Lin Wu Beasts thundered with heavy hooves, silent paws and formidable hands at ferocious power and speed towards the men. Marion warped herself behind the men and started digging frantically for the magic gold. The elephant, the rhinos and the buffalo violently gored four burly men as fourteen great big brutes were kicked, disembowelled and torn open by the zebras, giraffes and ostriches. The men died from broken legs, pelvises, ribs and spines. The three gorillas bashed to death two gunmen whilst the chimpanzees and orangutans outnumbered and savaged six riflemen. Within the same fifteen seconds, the cheetahs mauled two gunmen until they died. In this same space of time, the tigers tore the legs, chests and arms of five armed men before strangling them or crushing their skulls. The last two men were ripped, disembowelled, clawed on their chests and shoulders, scalped and strangled by the hind and front claws and dagger-like fangs of the leopard and the black panther.

The giant herbivores only took eight seconds to gore their four victims, during which time Marion exposed the buried gold. Only two seconds remained before noble or evil spirits would pass from the gold into the herbivores and predators. It was the work of two seconds for the elephant to kick at the gold with his left front hoof, splintering the rock-hard metal to smithereens.

Two batches of magic gold in Florida and the Congo had been destroyed, but there was still the third batch buried somewhere in Louisiana, not necessarily near the Mississippi River. And although the killer reptiles, hyenas and wild dogs had been massacred, the sharks and ocean killers still roamed the Gulf of Mexico and the deep rivers and swamps of Florida's Everglades. Not to mention the two enormous sharks, six ocean killers and two killer reptiles in the Mississippi River. These were the Li Hei Beasts Marion had dreamt of in her third dream whilst sleeping in Florida, the beasts the giant herbivores, apes and big cats were in danger from whilst operating in and around the hippo's lair. Would destroying the magic gold in Louisiana cure the sharks, ocean killers and killer reptiles of wanting to murder and devour humans or intending to massacre the Lin Wu Beasts? This question ground at Marion's mind. For although she had once been petrified of sharks, crocodiles and alligators, she now had respect and sympathy for the misunderstood ocean and river beasts. She harboured no enjoyment or sense of victory when killing sharks and ocean killers or crocodiles, alligators and Komodo dragons, who were essential in the chain of life of the oceans and rivers.

Fatigue overcame Marion and she had to rest. Protected by the Lin Wu Beasts, she gave in to sleep in eight or nine minutes.

***

Klaus and Lin Wu were back at Yellowstone National Park in Wyoming and were leaving pots of honey for the grizzly bear and the black bear, who had not joined the three bears in British Colombia. The bison, the moose, the three wild dogs and three wild cats of Wyoming were with these three bears, whilst the other two bears were protecting the rabbits and hares. The three dogs, two feral cats, five rabbits and four hares were consuming dog biscuits, grass and flowers.

Klaus and Lin Wu came out of the lodge they were staying in. Two or three seconds later, Lin Wu received a call on his mobile phone. He answered the call.

"Lin Wu here," he said. "Can I help you?"

"Hi, it's Chief Eddie Lomax of Vancouver Police Department calling," the police chief replied. "I'm afraid, Lin Wu, that I have some bad news."

"Some bad news?" Lin Wu said. "What is this bad news?"

"It's about Julio Sifuentez's gang of Mexicans, Chinese and Japanese, and the combined gangs of ruthless industrialists and polluters from Europe and Wyoming you two men captured," Chief Lomax said. "They've been released on a technicality."

"They've been released!" Lin Wu exclaimed. "What is this technicality?"

"They were forced to confess to their crimes under threat of violence," Lomax explained. "Julio's gang of poachers who removed the magic gold from two wildlife parks in California and British Colombia and then tried to kill you at the Grizzly Ranch were intimidated by dangerous beasts. A bison, a moose, three bears, six large predators and a gang of big cats. Confessions made under torture or the threat of violence are not considered reliable in a Court of Justice.

"But we know Julio's gang are guilty and are still at large in British Colombia, and police drones have traced their hideout to a former Canadian Army fortress east of the Coastal Mountains. We also know Julio's gang are planning retribution against you, Klaus and Marion for foiling their poaching activities, using the dangerous animals to threaten them and then having them detained at Vancouver PD."

"What about the industrialists and

polluters from Europe and Wyoming?" Lin Wu asked. "Were they released due to the same technicality? That Klaus and I used dangerous beasts from Vancouver Zoo, British Colombia, Wyoming and Nepal to intimidate the men with their sheer ferocity?"

"The same technicality," Lomax confirmed. "Torture and the threat of violence won't stand up in a Court of Law. So we had to extradite the industrialists and polluters back to Europe and Wyoming, heavily guarded and handcuffed on private planes. Their polluting businesses, like Dalseo Factories in Great Britain, Holland, Belgium and Italy, have been closed down. But like Julio's gang of poachers, these industrialists and polluters are extremely dangerous men and will plan revenge against you and Klaus. You'd better lie low for a while until Europe and Wyoming's police forces capture them."

"Lie low?" Lin Wu growled. "You've got to be kidding! Goodbye, Lomax!"

"Goodbye," Lomax finished off.

The contact ended; Lin Wu slipped his mobile back inside the pocket of his leather jacket.

"What's going on?" Klaus wanted to know.

"Julio Sifuentez and his poaching gang have been released on a technicality," Lin Wu told Klaus. "The industrialists and polluters, including the men from Dalseo Factories, have been extradited back to

Europe and Wyoming, and then released on the same technicality."

Klaus's face was numb with shock, horror and cold anger. "What is this technicality?" he asked.

"When we captured Julio's poaching gang and the combined gangs of industrialists, we used dangerous beasts to intimidate them and coerce guilty confessions out of them," Lin Wu said.

"But we had no choice," Klaus said.

"A Court of Justice won't see it that way," Lin Wu said. "Confessions obtained through torture and the threat of violence are considered unreliable.

"According to Chief Lomax, police drones have traced the hideout of Julio's gang to a former Canadian Army fortress east of the Coastal Mountains in British Colombia. Julio's gang are planning to kill us. We must kill them first, and then worry about the industrialists and polluters. To massacre Julio's gang, we'll need the bison, the moose, the three bears, the wild dogs and wild cats of Wyoming. We'll also need the big cats from the Congo, Nepal and Brazil to back us up. Marion is asleep in Nepal, so rather than wake her, I'll warp the big cats over to the forest outside Vancouver to join Wyoming's beasts. Then we'll warp ourselves there."

***

The Kodiak bear, the grizzly bear and the

black bear in the forest near Vancouver were the first beasts to meet up with the tigers, the leopards, the jaguar and the cheetahs. The tigers, the leopard and the black panther had learned not to be intimidated by the enormous bears, for they knew all these rival predators were on the same side. They were also working shoulder to shoulder with the bison and the moose.

Lin Wu and Klaus appeared out of the snowy mist four or five seconds later and greeted the big cats and bears.

"I'll send mind signals to the bison, the moose and the six large predators, ordering them to make their way towards this spot," Lin Wu began. "The fortress is on the other side of the Coastal Mountains. As soon as the eight formidable beasts arrive, we'll warp ourselves to the pathway leading to this fortress."

"How do you know exactly where this fortress is?" Klaus asked.

"It's the only Canadian Army fortress within a few miles of the Coastal Mountains," Lin Wu explained. "For the moment, we'll just lie low until the bison, the moose and the predators arrive. And then, we'll make our move."

Klaus, Lin Wu and the fearsome herbivores and predators waited behind trees and thickets flanking the pathway that led to the fortress. Both men were scared to the point of being petrified with terror, due to there being only the two of them and the Lin Wu Beasts against a massive gang of men with rifles, but their fear became indomitable courage. They had to lure all of Julio Sifuentez's gang out of the fortress using noise and then warp themselves and the dangerous beasts inside, ready to take Julio's mob by surprise.

They saw cars on the opposite side of the pathway, belonging to Julio and his gang.

"Those cars over there," Klaus said. "I have an idea. We'll fire lightning at the cars' windows, which will set off the car alarms, and that will draw the gang outside the fortress. Then we'll warp ourselves and the beasts inside."

"I like surprises," Lin Wu agreed.

Aiming their hands, they blazed lightning and electricity towards the cars' windows. The electricity ricocheted between the vehicles, smashing the windows and activating the alarms.

High-pitched piercing noises charged up and echoed through the atmosphere. Within seconds, Julio Sifuentez and a gang of men brandishing powerful, high-calibre rifles opened the fortress's gates and sprinted outside like greyhounds. They noticed the cars' broken windows.

"We must all head inside," Klaus told Lin Wu.

The two men and their gang of formidable beasts disappeared into the atmosphere and then reappeared inside the fortress. It was a vast, open area like a prison yard, with offices and apartments on the opposite side from the gates.

"We must hide against the wall left of the

gates," Lin Wu said.

"And then we'll take the poachers by surprise," Klaus agreed.

They took positions against the wall to the left. Joining them were the tigers, the leopard, the black panther, the jaguar and the cheetahs, in front of the Kodiak bear, the grizzly bear and the black bear. Situated against the wall to the right, positioned in single file, were the bison and the moose in front of the puma, the lynx and the bobcat, together with the wolf, the coyote and the fox.

Julio's men stormed back through the gates, and Klaus and Lin Wu ejected lightning towards their arms and hands. Screaming and crying with terrifying agony, the men threw their rifles to the ground, and the Lin Wu Beasts closed in upon them from the left and right walls. Lunging with brute power and lightning speed, the big cats and bears were upon one group of men. The tigers ruthlessly savaged and strangled five men as the leopard, the black panther and the jaguar mauled and throttled three men with brutal savagery. The cheetahs outnumbered, strangled and ripped to shreds two criminals.

Swiping with bone-breaking blows from his huge paws and scimitar-like claws, the Kodiak bear dispatched three thugs. Within the same twenty seconds, the grizzly bear accounted for another three brutes and the black bear brought down two more. All eight criminals died from broken backs, broken necks or fractured skulls.

From the right wall, the Wyoming beasts lunged with nightmarish ferocity. The bison and the moose each stabbed, gored and kicked three men and killed them instantly, fracturing their spines or smashing in their ribs. The moose bludgeoned the sixth brute's head and face with flailing kicks from his rock-hard hooves. The wolf, the coyote and the fox lunged for two crooks, the smaller wild dogs' victim being Julio Sifuentez. They mangled his hands with their vice-like teeth as the wolf savagely tore the other victim's arm, then groped for his throat and strangled him.

The puma, the lynx and the bobcat used all their sets of claws to rip and shred the legs, stomachs, chests and shoulders of three gunmen. These sizeable wild cats outmatched the men in strength, speed and unrestrained ferocity. Their brutal fangs lunged for the poachers' necks and finished them with fearsome bites to the carotid arteries and jugular veins. The puma switched his attack with spitfire speed towards Julio, who screamed hysterically as he fought with the coyote and the fox.

Pouncing like lightning, the puma leapt for Julio. He raked his hind and front claws down Julio's legs, shoulders and chest, and then dug his killer fangs into Julio's throat, strangling him until he perished.

"Our work is done," Klaus said.

"We must warp the big cats down towards Louisiana," Lin Wu explained. "The bears will remain in British Colombia with the wild dogs and wild cats. We'll rejoin the other two bears protecting the dogs, cats, rabbits and hares in Wyoming. I sense in my psychic mind that the wild boar, the red deer and the roe deer of Burgundy in France have used their sorcery to link France to Wyoming. Warping themselves over to France are three wild boars from Spain, Italy and Slovenia in Yugoslavia, and three red deer and three roe deer from Spain, Italy and Yugoslavia, each of these three countries producing a red deer and a roe deer. They've joined the large herbivores in Burgundy. We must make our way to Wyoming and discover why."

With a warping spell, the big cats were sent to Louisiana before Klaus and Lin Wu headed for Wyoming.

***

On France's border with Wyoming, the wild boars, red deer and roe deer from France, Spain, Italy and Slovenia had joined the dogs, cats, rabbits and hares, together with the grizzly bear and the black bear who had stayed in Wyoming. The bears had finished their pots of honey. Fifteen men behind garbage pollution and a horde of rats lay horribly mutilated or gored to death by the beasts. The two gang bosses, six men who had dropped garbage and four men who had dumped poisons and weed-killers had been ripped open or impaled and kicked to death by the tusks, antlers and hooves of the wild boars, red deer and roe deer. The last three men, who had been guilty of fly-tipping garbage from their truck, had been killed instantly by crushing blows from the paws and claws of the grizzly bear and the black bear. All the rats had been massacred by the three dogs, two cats, five rabbits and four hares, the rabbits and hares attacking as fiercely as the dogs and cats.

"The men behind rubbish pollution, fly-tipping and poisoning the vegetation have finally met their demise," Lin Wu observed.

"Julio's gang of poachers are out of the way, and the rubbish polluters have met their demise, but there are still the industrialists in Europe," Klaus said. "But why did these wild boars, red deer and roe deer come all the way here from Mediterranean Europe and France?"

"It was loyalty to the Wyoming beasts and to me," Lin Wu pointed out. "They saw the fifteen rubbish polluters as a threat to the two bears and decided to support and help the bears in murdering them. We must use sorcery to warp the wild boars and deer back to France, Spain, Italy and Slovenia to help the bears, wolves and lynxes in these countries protect the ibexes, chamois and mouflons. Then we must act as bait in order to trap the industrialists and armed men."

"Won't that take planning?" Klaus asked.

"Yes, Klaus," Lin Wu said. "The men's

hideouts are in Poland's Bialowieza Forest National Park, British Colombia and here in Wyoming."

The bears, dogs and cats roared or growled their gratitude to Europe's large herbivores, whilst the rabbits and hares gnawed on the grass and flowers surrounding the lodge.

***

In the dreamworld joining the Congo and Nepal with Florida, Marion slept for five hours. The last two hours were occupied by a dream of Florida. In the first scene, the gorillas, chimpanzees, orang-utans and Asian bears grieved the dead primates and wild pigs, alongside the zebras, giraffes and ostriches, together with the cassowaries and kangaroos. The baboons, drills and mandrills lay alongside the warthogs, bush pigs and giant forest hogs as the herbivores, flightless birds and apes were in mourning.

Once their grieving was done, the beasts were joined by the Indian elephant before warping themselves to Florida's Everglades Zoo to team up with five llamas, four alpacas, three guanacos and five vicunas from the Andean Mountains in Chile and Peru. These llamas and their cousins were strong, fierce fighters when attacked by pumas, dogs or men. They would be fierce allies to the herbivores and flightless birds.

In the first battle in the mangrove swamp, the barracuda, the conger eel, the octopus and the giant squid ruthlessly savaged to death four male swimmers. The elephant, the zebras, giraffes and ostriches together with the cassowaries and kangaroos got to the men too late. Charging into the water, the elephant brutally gored the octopus and the giant squid as the zebras, giraffes and ostriches outnumbered the conger eel and kicked it senseless. The cassowaries dropkicked the barracuda and ripped it open. All four ocean killers died instantly. But the sawfish, the swordfish, the giant grouper, the hagfishes and lampreys were still roaming the Everglades, led by the two sharks.

The elephant sensed armed men attacking the Everglades Zoo.

In the battle at the Everglades Zoo, the llamas, alpacas, guanacos and vicunas kicked seventeen dark sorcerers to death before the three gorillas came on the scene with the herbivores and flightless birds. The gorillas viciously mauled three men, whilst the elephant trampled and crushed five more.

Aiming their hands, the sorcerers fired lightning at the llamas, alpacas, guanacos and vicunas, then the Indian elephant. Their lightning was too powerful for the beasts to survive. The elephant, together with the llamas and their cousins, was killed instantly and crashed to the ground whilst the gorillas retreated.

Attacking fiercely, the zebras, giraffes and ostriches took the men by surprise. They massacred fourteen criminals in the same few seconds that the cassowaries and kangaroos murdered nine brutes. The chimpanzees and orang-utans attacked the last nine men and brutally savaged them until they were dead.

The gorillas came out of hiding. The apes grieved the deaths of the elephant and the South American herbivores, whilst the herbivores and flightless birds from Uganda and Australia sought help from the Asian bears in Nepal.

The Himalayan black bears, sloth bears and sun bears told the zebras that Nepal would soon be joined by sorcery to Louisiana. The Asian bears and British Colombia's bigfoot creatures were needed to join Nepal's yetis and big cats for another mission in Louisiana. The bears could not help the herbivores.

The zebras left Nepal before Nepal's dreamworld with Florida ended, and Lin Wu formed another dreamworld between Nepal and Louisiana. The yetis and bigfoot creatures, as well as the bears, reunited with the African elephant, the white rhino, the black rhino and the African buffalo, along with the big cats in Louisiana, around what was the hippo's lair.

The herbivores and flightless birds saw twenty-one Li Hei sorcerers pushing five police informants into the swamps. The men were ripped open, stabbed or horribly savaged by the sawfish, the swordfish, the giant grouper, the hagfishes and lampreys. Attacking the sorcerers from behind, the zebras, giraffes and ostriches kicked and broke the backs of fourteen men. The cassowaries and kangaroos dropkicked seven men, fracturing their spines. The men drowned in the river whilst the zebras, giraffes and ostriches bashed and battered to death the giant grouper, the sawfish and the swordfish. The cassowaries and kangaroos kicked the hagfishes and lampreys senseless. The giant grouper's gang sank to the riverbed to die in horrific agony.

But the two sharks were still at large.

The herbivores and flightless birds rejoined the gorillas, chimpanzees and orang-utans on the beach overlooking the Gulf of Mexico. Advancing along the beach, they saw the great white and the tiger shark savagely mauling and murdering two male swimmers. The three gangs of apes fired lightning at the sharks. The dark sorcerers closed in on the apes. After the herbivores and flightless birds exchanged a crossfire of lightning with the brutes, the zebras, giraffes and ostriches fiercely kicked and ripped open seventeen crooks. The cassowaries tore open and disembowelled six criminals whilst the kangaroos ruptured the stomachs of four killers. After the apes' lightning attack, the sharks sank to the ocean bed and perished.

The gorillas then bashed three dark sorcerers until the brutes were dead. The last ten criminals were outnumbered and fatally mauled by the chimpanzees and orang-utans.

The black bears, sloth bears and sun bears reappeared on the beach. The Asian bears praised the herbivores and flightless birds for their fierce courage when fighting the sorcerers. The bears told the herbivores, flightless birds and apes that all four gangs of Lin Wu Beasts were needed in Louisiana. The zebras sent mind signals to Marion. Then the beasts warped themselves from Florida to Louisiana.

***

At that point, Marion awoke from her sleep. She had picked up the message from the herbivores. She had to leave the Congo and warp to the hippo's lair overlooking the Mississippi River. Marion rose to her feet, took one last look at the Congo's rainforests and Florida's swamps and then cast a spell.

Three seconds later, she was at the hippo's lair. Positioned in front of her was Lin Wu.

"Hello there, Lin Wu," Marion greeted him.

"Hello, Marion," Lin Wu replied.

"My husband is not with you," Marion said.

"Klaus is in British Colombia," Lin Wu told her. "He is okay."

"I must ask you a question," Marion said. "Why did you unite natural animal enemies into allies to kill men, even if these men were evil? I know you gave these beasts magical powers by feeding them magic bananas grown in India, just like you gave Klaus and myself powers of sorcery by feeding us three bananas each. But what was the reason for uniting animal enemies?"

"Two reasons," Lin Wu said. "Li Hei was using magic gold to corrupt sharks, ocean killers and killer reptiles into massacring humans, so I had to counter this by uniting other dangerous animals against these savage beasts and evil men. But gangs of beasts were already fighting each other over territory. The first feud was between the gorillas, chimpanzees and Asian bears on one side and the baboons, drills and mandrills on the other. I created the dreamworld joining the Congo with Nepal to unite the gorillas with the bears. I'll show you visions from my photographic memory."

In the vision, the gorillas were approached by the Himalayan black bears, sloth bears and sun bears in Nepal. The bears told the gorillas that they must deter the baboons and their cousins rather than fight them, for they could become powerful allies. The bears and gorillas then had to seek out the chimpanzees.

The chimpanzees of the Congo told the orang-utans from Indonesia to go into hiding in Nepal until the baboons, drills and mandrills became allies of the chimpanzees. Then the chimpanzees decided to locate the gorillas.

The bears and gorillas hid behind thickets as they watched a troop of baboons, drills and mandrills make their way past. The baboons and their cousins knew the gorillas had crossed the dreamworld border into Nepal. The baboons were hunting down the gorillas and bears, hell-bent on murdering them.

The bears and gorillas stayed in an enormous mountain cave massive enough to take all seventeen beasts. Then they heard the baboons, drills and mandrills approaching. The bears and gorillas fled out of the cave and made their way towards a river. The baboons and their cousins pursued them until the bears and gorillas jumped into the river and swam downstream. They climbed out of the water and shook themselves dry.

The gorillas sent mind signals to the chimpanzees in the Congo, telling them to meet the gorillas and bears on Nepal's border with India near the Gir Forest. The chimpanzees agreed and set off for the forest. The chimpanzees were forever vigilant of the baboons and their cousins.

The black bears, sloth bears and sun bears were hiding behind thickets, watching the baboons, when the gorillas came up behind them. The gorillas gave away the bears' position, and the beasts had to flee immediately. The baboons, drills and mandrills pursued them, but soon gave up the chase.

The black bears, sloth bears and sun bears took the three gorillas across the border into India, but they had gone east, away from the Gir Forest. They needed to head west for the Gir Forest.

The fourteen bears and three gorillas met up with the ten chimpanzees, and they planned a peace treaty with the baboons. The baboons, drills and mandrills closed in on the apes and bears, but the bears and apes had them outnumbered and outmatched. Then Lin Wu emerged out of the forest mist. He fed magic bananas to the baboons, drills and mandrills, and then to the bears, gorillas and chimpanzees. The sorcery from these bananas made both sides allies, and they ended their gang feud. The chimpanzees sent mind signals to the orang-utans, yetis and bigfoot creatures in Nepal and British Colombia. Lin Wu warped the orang-utans, yetis and bigfoot creatures over to the Gir Forest, fed them bananas, and they became allies of the gorillas, chimpanzees and baboons.

The visions withdrew back into Lin Wu's mind as he faced Marion in Louisiana.

"Do you see, Marion?" Lin Wu pointed out.

"Yes, I see," Marion said.

"The second gang feud took place in the dreamworld joining Uganda with Australia," Lin Wu said. "Between the zebras, giraffes and ostriches, backed up by the cassowaries and kangaroos, on one side, and the warthogs, bush pigs and giant forest hogs on the other. I'll release my photographic visions."

The next vision showed the zebras and giraffes finding the ostriches and cassowaries arguing about whether or not to make peace with the wild pigs. The zebras and giraffes backed up the ostriches, and the cassowaries were deterred from attacking the ostriches.

The herbivores and ostriches of Uganda decided to run rather than fight the wild pigs until Lin Wu allied the wild pigs with the herbivores and flightless birds. They encountered warthogs, bush pigs and giant forest hogs and decided to flee.

They outran the wild pigs, and then crossed

a giant pond almost as enormous as a lake. The zebras, giraffes and ostriches were in Australia, and they met the kangaroos.

The kangaroos had a conversation with the zebras. They persuaded the zebras not to negotiate from weakness and to be prepared to fight the wild pigs. The zebras knew the herbivores and flightless birds needed Lin Wu's help to achieve peace.

The beasts saw that the cassowaries were cornered and fighting with the wild pigs. Charging into the rescue, the zebras, giraffes and ostriches gently kicked the wild pigs with minimal force so as not to injure them. The cassowaries made their escape and greeted the ostriches and kangaroos. The herbivores and flightless birds headed towards the pond and crossed the mass of water, but the wild pigs ran around the water.

The zebras, giraffes and ostriches, together with the cassowaries and kangaroos, were joined by Lin Wu and the black bears, sloth bears and sun bears. The warthogs, bush pigs and giant forest hogs cornered the beasts, but Lin Wu fed them magic bananas. The wild pigs became friendly towards the herbivores and flightless birds and became allies. Lin Wu fed bananas to the herbivores and flightless birds, and they ended their feud with the wild pigs. The cassowaries and kangaroos thanked the zebras, giraffes and ostriches, and all these beasts were grateful to Lin Wu and the bears.

Lin Wu withdrew the visions back inside his head.

"I see now," Marion observed. "The two

feuds had been going on for a long time. There was more to it than the baboons and wild pigs blaming the apes, herbivores and flightless birds for the deaths of the giant pandas, giant anteaters and peccaries in that battle in the rainforest. Later, the baboons and wild pigs were massacred by criminal developers and their hunting dogs whilst the apes, herbivores and flightless birds tried to save them. Any other feuds I must know about?"

"There was one more feud," Lin Wu said. "But it was only brief, and it happened on the dreamworld border between the Congo, Nepal and Brazil. The lions and cheetahs, backed up by the tigers, the leopard, the black panther and the jaguar, allied themselves with the snow leopard, the clouded leopard, the Asian golden cat and the jungle cat, backed up by the caracal and the serval. They were cornered by the two elephants, the five rhinos and the buffalo, but again I fed all these giant herbivores and big cats magic bananas, and they became allies. These beasts would unite against Li Hei's men, together with the killer reptiles, hyenas and wild dogs. I united large herbivores, rabbits and hares in Wyoming and Europe with bears, wild dogs, wild cats and mustelids local to these areas. And dogs and cats would unite with the large predators and herbivores. Again, I fed all these beasts with magic bananas, which united them and granted them powers of sorcery."

"It was quite an achievement, Lin Wu," Marion gasped.

"It is nothing," Lin Wu added, his manner modest.

"What do you mean it's nothing?" Marion said.

"Us wise men of the Far East are modest and do not boast of great achievements," Lin Wu pointed out. "It is for Buddha to judge whether our achievements are great."

"And Germans like me are proud and arrogant," Marion commented.

"It is what you grew up with," Lin Wu said. "The Germans have achieved great things in their recent history since the Second World War ended. They have a right to be arrogant. But anyway, I must warp myself back to British Colombia to join Klaus. The beasts are coming back to you with food they have acquired. See you again."

"I'll see you again, Wise Man of the East," Marion finished.

The old man warped himself into the transparent haze, and Marion greeted the beasts. As the dreamworld joined Louisiana with Nepal, the yetis were carrying dead yaks they had killed in the Himalayas whilst the bigfoot creatures chomped on apples and the gorillas, chimpanzees and orang-utans consumed leaves from the nearby trees. The giraffes fed on leaves as the zebras dined on the wild grass. The ostriches, cassowaries and kangaroos consumed fruits and leaves different to those in Africa and Australia.

The elephant, the two rhinos and the buffalo ravenously chewed on the grasses, corn and wheat, whilst the Himalayan black bears, sloth bears and sun bears sucked on honey, ants and termites. The tigers, the leopard, the black panther, the jaguar and the cheetahs made easy meals of nine sheep and eight chickens they had stolen from a nearby ranch.

Without the means to cook meat or fish, Marion had nothing to eat but an apple and a pear from the nearby fruit trees. It had been days since she had eaten a proper meal, and she decided to buy herself a large pizza, a loaf of bread and a great big bottle of lemonade from a pizza parlour and a large bakery in New Orleans. Marion bade farewell to the Lin Wu Beasts, and ambled alongside the Mississippi River until she approached New Orleans.

A few hours later, Marion returned to the hippo's lair, having stuffed herself full of pizza and bread and guzzled down the bottle of lemonade. As the Lin Wu Beasts rested, night was approaching and she needed to sleep. She headed inside the hippo's lair, lay down on a bed of grass and faltered into a state of sleep in the short period of ten minutes.

Marion slept for nine hours until six in the morning. The last fifteen minutes of her rest were taken over by three dreams about three undercover operations where Klaus, Lin Wu and the Lin Wu Beasts of Wyoming and Europe acted as bait to trap three gangs of industrialists and polluters.

The first dream occurred in Yellowstone in

Wyoming. Three wolverines local to Wyoming were with the American badger, the mink and the fisher, along with the mustelids of Norway, Sweden and Denmark as well as the Bavarian Forest, Holland, Belgium and Burgundy. Also with these mustelids stood the three dogs, two cats, five rabbits and four hares, flanking two dogs, three cats, three rabbits and two hares that had warped over from the copse in Switzerland, and seven dogs, five cats, six rabbits and six hares that had transported by magic from that forest in France. The wild boar, the red deer and the roe deer from Burgundy had formed another dreamworld joining France with Wyoming and were positioned alongside the wolverines. The three wild boars of Spain's Cantabrian Mountains, Italy's Gran Paradiso National Park and Slovenia's Julian Alps together, with the countries' three red deer and three roe deer, were backing up the bears, wolves, lynxes and wild cats in Spain, Italy and Slovenia, protecting the local ibexes, chamois and mouflons. At the same time, the bears, wolves and lynxes of Norway and Sweden were on their guard against armed men who might seek revenge against these large predators and the ten mustelids of these two countries.

On the dreamworld border between France and Wyoming, nine British industrialists who had run Dalseo Factories, backed up by a horde of rats, sneaked up on the Lin Wu Beasts of Europe and Wyoming, armed with rifles. Surrounding the beasts, they aimed their weaponry and opened fire with evil ferocity and fury. The rifles exploded with stomach-wrenching blasts, pumping several rounds into many dogs, cats, rabbits and hares, including all those beasts from Wyoming and the badgers from Norway, Sweden, Denmark, Germany and France.

The evil swarm of rats savagely attacked the two weasels, two stoats, two polecats and two pine martens of Norway and Sweden, and the three weasels and three stoats of Denmark, Germany and France. The rats overwhelmed them, their gnawing teeth tearing apart the mustelids. The two ferrets from Holland and Belgium, and the Belgian stoat, were also ripped to pieces brutally fighting the rats, but the two badgers, two weasels and the Dutch stoat, together with the two polecats, two pine martens and two beech martens of Holland and Belgium, retaliated with savage fury, clawing and biting the vermin viciously. The American badger, the mink and the fisher also took terrible toll of the rats. The remaining five cats, eight rabbits and seven hares from France and Switzerland used needle-like fangs, gnawing teeth and fearsome claws to bite, rip apart, slash and kick at the rodents. In fourteen or fifteen seconds, the mustelids, cats, rabbits and hares had mutilated all the rats.

At the same time, the seven surviving dogs from Burgundy and Switzerland, the three wolverines and the wild boar, the red deer and the roe deer of Burgundy hurled lightning bolts at the nine armed men. Klaus and Lin Wu were on the scene and threw bolts, which caused the men's rifles to explode and burn the British brutes' hands. The industrialists from Dalseo Factories screamed with nerve-shredding agony, their arms and hands scalded. Their rifles dropped to the grass. The wolverines lunged towards three gunmen, clawing them to death. Within this same deadly interval, the dogs outnumbered and savagely mauled three riflemen, tearing at their arms, bodies and faces until the dogs' jagged teeth strangled the killers. The wild boar, the red deer and the roe deer plunged their scimitar-like tusks or tough velvet antlers into the last three gunmen, tearing open one man's stomach, rupturing a second's heart and lungs and puncturing a third's leg. The red deer took over from the roe deer in killing the third man by kicking him to death after the wild boar and the red deer had murdered the other two.

Once all nine British men had perished in this ferocious counter-attack, the wolverines and mustelids of Wyoming grieved the violent deaths of their fellow beasts from Wyoming and eight countries in western Europe, along with the dogs, cats, rabbits and hares of France and Switzerland and the mustelids of Belgium and Holland. The wild boar, the red deer and the roe deer mourned the loss of France's three mustelids.

After the grieving ended, Lin Wu told Klaus that the bison and the moose, together with the puma, the lynx and the bobcat, were at Poland's Bialowieza Forest, assisting the Polish herbivores and predators in trapping the second gang of thirteen British men. The wolverines had to stay in Wyoming to guard the lodge against armed men and rats, whilst the dogs, cats, rabbits and hares, together with the mustelids and the three French herbivores, would be sent by witchcraft to British Colombia. Lin Wu also explained how the two bears who had stayed behind in Wyoming had now been warped over to Canada's border with Alaska to rejoin the other three bears along with the wolf, the coyote and the fox. Klaus then informed Lin Wu that his psychic mind had detected thirteen British men in Poland burying magic gold in Bialowieza Forest, and the remaining thirty British, French and Germans burying gold in a forest in British Colombia.

With blind horror, they realised the herbivores and predators in Bialowieza and British Colombia could not massacre both gangs of armed men without being corrupted by noble or evil spirits. Both noble sorcerers and the dangerous beasts would have to use their lightning bolts to inflict enough agony on the criminals that the brutes would want to commit suicide to end the torture.

At that moment, Lin Wu sent mind signals to the formidable beasts in Bialowieza Forest and then British Colombia's Coastal Mountains, ordering them not to kill the men, but only to injure or torture them enough to force the men to take their own lives. Then Klaus and Lin Wu disappeared into the Wyoming forest haze.

They emerged two or three seconds later at the Coastal Mountains running along Canada's border with Alaska. Shortly, they reunited with the Kodiak bear, the two grizzlies and two black bears, together with the wolf, the coyote and the fox, not to mention the seven dogs, five cats, eight rabbits and seven hares from France and Switzerland who had survived the Wyoming battle. The fourteen mustelids from Wyoming, Holland and Belgium gave Lin Wu visions of the thirty British, French and German men advancing along a mountain ridge on the east side of the Coastal Mountains and closing in on the two noble sorcerers and the Lin Wu Beasts.

Once the puma, the lynx and the bobcat were in Poland with the bison and the moose, the wild cats were greeted by seven Polish mustelids. Again, these included a badger, a weasel and a stoat, along with a polecat, a ferret, a pine marten and a beech marten, who helped to protect the badger from rats that might invade his sett. The mustelids told the Wyoming wild cats that the wolf native to Bialowieza Forest was searching for the forest's common otters, the feral cat, the rabbits and hares in order to unite them with the mustelids in fighting the rats belonging to the armed men. These smaller predators, rabbits and hares would only disable rather than kill the rats to avoid being corrupted by the magic gold. The thirteen British men from Dalseo

Factories were determined to upset and annoy Lin Wu by massacring his animal allies, the seven Wyoming and Polish herbivores and five large predators of Bialowieza. In order to bring the larger beasts to the badger sett, the weasel and the stoat sent mind signals to the bear, the lynx, the sizeable mountain fox as big as a small Doberman, and the bull mastiff.

At the same time, the polecat, the pine marten and the beech marten repeated this message to the American bison, the European bison, the elk and the moose leading the wild boar, the red deer and the roe deer. In four or five seconds, all these beasts, except the wolf, joined up with the puma, the lynx and the bobcat. Led by the American bison and the moose, the European bison and the elk explained to the puma's gang and the mustelids how the armed British men and a pack of rats had gathered on the banks of a fast-flowing river to plan and rehearse their hunting operation against the Polish beasts.

The Wyoming and Polish beasts closed in on three groups of armed men and rogue rats from three directions. Four British men were confronted by the American bison, the European bison, the elk and the moose. They vomited several gunshots from their high-calibre rifles, but the enormous beasts sent lightning spells, which melted the bullets in mid-air, until the men ran out of ammunition. Charging like enraged elephants or man-eating lions in a fury, the large herbivores were more terrifying than lions. The men fled for the river, with the American bison and the European bison leading the elk and the moose in a powerful and fast-moving pursuit of the brutes.

The second gang of large predators—namely the puma, the two lynxes, the bobcat, the mountain fox and the dog—took the second group of five British men by surprise. They leapt at the criminals and pinned them down. Backing up the puma's gang were the mustelids, who immobilised eight savage rats. With slashing claws and gnashing teeth, the badger ripped the backs of two rats as the weasel and the stoat fractured the back legs of another two vermin. The polecat, the ferret, the pine marten and the beech marten broke the hind legs of four other rats without killing them. All the rats crawled away with crippling injuries.

The fox and the dog restrained the first of the five armed men by fastening their powerful teeth into his left hand and right arm, shredding flesh away so the man was in too much agony to use his rifle. The Polish lynx bit and clawed viciously at the second man's right arm, shoulder and chest whilst the puma, the Wyoming lynx and the bobcat raked their claws through the last three men. The talons sliced through legs, stomachs, chests and shoulders as killer fangs crunched through the men's left arms. The men screamed with horrible agony and panic, but to avoid ending the men's lives, the puma, the lynxes and the bobcat withdrew their savage attack. The fox and the dog also retreated, the killer beasts screaming, hissing, snarling and growling to deter the men from using their rifles. The gunmen scrambled to their feet and ran for the river, joined by the four riflemen being chased by the two bison, the moose and the elk. The large predators and mustelids joined the herbivores in chasing the nine gunmen towards the fast-flowing river.

The third gang, consisting of the bear, the wild boar, the red deer and the roe deer, attacked and injured the third group of four British men without taking their lives. The bear's bone-crushing fangs and scimitar-like claws broke the first man's left leg and raked through his right leg and stomach. The wild boar's razor-sharp tusks tore open the second man's right leg and broke his pelvis as the red deer and the roe deer brutally gored and bashed the other two brutes senseless with their antlers and front hooves. Unable to use their rifles, the crooks crawled away towards the river. They saw the other nine criminals diving into the water after being chased by the American bison's gang and the puma's gang. The last four British rolled from the riverbank into the water, but it was ice-cold and fast-flowing, freezing all thirteen men before the powerful currents dragged them underwater. The Wyoming and Polish beasts knew these men would die from their wounds, combined with drowning and hypothermia.

The American bison and the moose bade farewell to the elk and the European bison as the puma, the lynx and the bobcat repeated the gesture to the bear, the Polish lynx, the fox, the dog and the mustelids. In the next few seconds, the Wyoming herbivores and wild cats evaporated into thin air and travelled to British Colombia's Coastal Mountains. They joined the Kodiak bear, the two grizzlies and two black bears together, with the wild dogs and mustelids of Wyoming and Europe. With the five bears were Klaus and Lin Wu, who led the herbivores and wild cats towards a mountain's east side, where the enormous ledge overlooked a ravine.

The thirty gunmen came round the pathway. As the industrialists, farmers and criminals aimed their rifles, the noble sorcerers' lightning bolts ignited their rifles. The armed men dropped their weapons. The burly men were surrounded and cornered by the beasts with only the ravine as their escape—a sheer drop of three thousand feet that would kill all thirty.

With savage rage and fury, the bison and the moose bellowed and roared at six Germans. With unrestrained ferocity, the Kodiak bear bellowed at three German farmers just as the grizzlies roared at five men and the black bears screamed and growled at four more. The bison, the moose and the bears were awesome beasts, powerful and savage enough to massacre all eighteen gunmen in minutes.

The wolf, the coyote and the fox outnumbered and targeted a Frenchman, the wild dogs snarling and growling furiously, whilst the puma, the lynx and the bobcat screamed and hissed towards the other three Frenchmen. As the badgers, the weasels and the stoat outnumbered and threatened two British men with hissing snarls, the polecats, pine martens and beech martens ganged up against three British men, hissing. The last three Germans were growled at by the American badger, the mink and the fisher.

The thirty gunmen decided falling to their deaths in the deep ravine was a quicker and less painful way to die than being savagely gored, mauled and torn to pieces by these ferocious beasts, from the herbivores down to the mustelids. With gagging, choking mouths and their bodies sweating with insane fear, the gunmen all threw themselves over the cliff and hurtled with horrific speed into the ravine below.

Watching these men die was an appalling experience for Klaus and Lin Wu. Even though these industrialists, farmers and criminals had been behind poisonous gas emissions, chemical and industrial effluence pollution, and had dumped pesticides, herbicides, poisons and weed-killers, which destroyed the atmosphere or contaminated rivers, Klaus and Lin Wu wished taking the men's lives was not the only answer.

Back in Poland and here in British Colombia, two batches of magic gold were buried under patches of trees. Finding the exact locations of these trees would be no easy matter, and only the African elephant could break the gold with his hooves. And the elephant was tied up in another operation finding the magic gold buried in Louisiana.

Even though the thirteen British men had died in the river running through Bialowieza Forest, there was still a gang of poachers and their pet rats roaming the forest, and possibly more armed men and rats in British Colombia. The Lin Wu Beasts in Poland and British Colombia could not afford to risk being corrupted by the gold by killing these men and rats, not even in self-defence. And the demon lord of the gangs of industrialists, criminal developers and poachers by the name of Li Hei was still alive and dangerous.

At that moment, Marion's dream ended.

Marion woke up at the hippo's lair in Louisiana. She was relieved that the gangs of Germans, Frenchmen and British men who had destroyed Nature had committed suicide at Bialowieza in Poland and in British Colombia. But more problems entered her mind. She needed to find where Li Hei was located so that Lin Wu could rid the world of that ruthless gangster. And as well as the buried batches of magic gold that would corrupt the Lin Wu Beasts into killing each other and innocent humans, there were still those two batches of gold that already had killed dangerous animals instantly for attacking evil men and would do again. The first batch had been buried in two wildlife parks, first on the border between California and Mexico and then the border between Canada and Alaska. The second had been in Switzerland where a bear, a lynx, a wolf and a fox had died after killing those three industrialists.

Where are these deadly batches buried? Marion thought to herself.

The last problem Marion was thinking of was that she didn't know exactly where the magic gold in Louisiana was buried. Before she fell asleep, she had worked out the gold could not be buried near the Mississippi River, but was more likely far inland. When she'd had her third dream about the giant herbivores and big cats searching for the apes in Louisiana, the sharks, ocean killers and killer reptiles in the river delta had killed humans there and then been corrupted by the magic gold buried somewhere in the delta. This was why they continued to attack men in the Mississippi. But when the giant herbivores, apes and big cats had killed Li Hei's men in self-defence, they had not been corrupted. Which meant the gold had been removed from the delta by the dark sorcerers and buried several miles north of New Orleans and many miles east, away from the river.

Marion's logic behind this theory was that the dark sorcerers knew the Lin Wu Beasts would journey further away from the river and target these evil men, who were all positioned east of the river. The further north the gold was buried, the safer the Lin Wu Beasts were from being corrupted by its powers if they killed dark sorcerers, but as they ventured closer to its location, they would become more vulnerable to noble or evil spirits.

Marion rose up from the bed of grass and left the hippo's lair to greet the Lin Wu Beasts. Visions came up from their heads of different locations the gold might be buried. Marion had to separate the beasts into different groups in order for the beasts to warp themselves to these locations. Marion and the Lin Wu Beasts warped themselves into the warm mist.

Marion went to the first location, outside a remote fire department that was now derelict. With her were the five tigers, together with the zebras, giraffes and ostriches, backed up by the cassowaries and kangaroos. The herbivores and flightless birds used their front hooves or clawed feet to dig up a patch of loose soil on the lawn beside the fire department. They exposed fragments of gold dust, but this was not the magic gold. The magic gold was a large batch of solid metal, not powdery dust. Marion knew the Li Hei sorcerers had buried gold dust and other metals at different locations to draw the Lin Wu Beasts there and divert them away from where the real magic gold was. But any one of these locations could be the burial place of this gold.

A few miles away, west of the river, the African elephant, the white rhino, the black rhino and the African buffalo had discovered another burial underneath loose earth.

"You beasts stay here," Marion ordered. "I'll be back here soon."

Marion went to the giant herbivores and

assessed what they had dug up.

"Our last find was gold dust outside the fire department," Marion said. "But what you've found is not even gold dust, let alone magic gold. This is silver."

In her head, she picked up mind signals from a remote copse of trees lying east of the river again. They were coming from the leopard, the black panther and the jaguar.

"I must see what the leopards and the jaguar want," she said, and evaporated into the transparent air.

At the copse, Marion found the leopard, the black panther and the jaguar, who had dug up another find.

"The herbivores, flightless birds and tigers discovered gold," Marion said. "The elephant, the rhinos and the buffalo found silver. What have you big cats found?" She took a glance into the hole. "This is copper. It's no use to us." Then her mind detected a message being sent from outside a farmstead by the bears and cheetahs. "You, the leopard, the black panther and the jaguar, stay here. I must head for that farm, where the Asian bears and cheetahs have found something."

Marion met with the Himalayan black bears, sloth bears and sun bears, together with the cheetahs, who had discovered another find outside the farmstead.

"This is not gold, silver or copper," she pointed out. "This is iron. If Li Hei's men wanted to confuse us, they succeeded."

At that moment, her mind received signals

from the dreamworld border between Nepal and Louisiana to the west and north. The gorillas, chimpanzees and orang-utans, backed up by the yetis and bigfoot creatures, were calling her.

"You bears and cheetahs will remain here. I must find out what the apes have dug up."

Abandoning the bears and cheetahs outside the farmstead, she warped herself into the atmosphere.

At the border between Nepal and Louisiana, Marion discovered how the apes had used their enormous arms and strong hands to dig up another batch of metal near the river.

"This is not gold, silver, copper or iron," Marion explained. "This is aluminium. The only way I will find the magic gold is to do some searching of my own. You apes stay here. The gold is either north or east of here. I must set off now."

Marion spent the rest of the bright, sunny day and moonlit evening hunting for the gold until it was eleven p.m. She had no luck. She was overcome by fatigue.

"I must sleep," Marion decided. "Hopefully, another dream will give me more clues."

The German succumbed to sleep in a matter of minutes.

***

Marion slept for eleven hours until ten a.m. The last three hours were occupied by a dream, but there was no guarantee this dream would give away the exact location of the magic gold. The only thing guaranteed now was that the Lin Wu Beasts were more vulnerable, due to being in small groups at the burial sites they had warped to.

In the first scene, the herbivores, flightless birds and tigers were attacked by a vast gang of poachers. The armed men blazed with their rifles, but the magical spells from the beasts melted the bullets in mid-air. With flailing kicks, the zebras and giraffes smashed the bones of fifteen gunmen to pieces as the ostriches and cassowaries disembowelled and or shredded to ribbons thirteen riflemen, breaking their legs or ribs. Four gunmen had their bellies ruptured by the flying, kicking feet of the kangaroos. Leaping upon five poachers from behind, the tigers used all their claws to slice open the men's thighs, buttocks, shoulders and backs. Their bone-crushing fangs fractured the poachers' necks and skulls.

With mind signals, the tigers told the herbivores and flightless birds to abandon the gold dust and journey north to find the real magic gold. The tigers would warp themselves across the Mississippi River to find the elephant, the white rhino, the black rhino and the buffalo at the burial site where the silver was.

At the silver's burial site, the tigers found the elephant, the two rhinos and the buffalo using sorcery to burn up bullets being fired at them by another large gang of poachers, and then to set fire to the mens' rifles. The men ran, with the giant herbivores in dangerous pursuit. The tigers charged and cut off their escape route.

Men in boats on the ocean off Louisiana fired at the herbivores and tigers, but their boats were crunched open by the sharks and ocean killers. The two massive sharks severed the legs of three men and crushed the ribs and spines of two others as the barracuda, the conger eel and the moray eel shredded four men to ribbons. The octopus, the giant squid and the cuttlefish constricted and ripped to pieces another four. The conger eel and the giant squid each mutilated two boatmen.

The tigers knew the sharks, ocean killers and also the killer reptiles in the river had changed sides and saw the poachers and Li Hei sorcerers as their enemies. The elephant, the rhinos and the buffalo outran the poachers fleeing into the tigers' path. The elephant stabbed and crushed eight riflemen in the same two minutes that the buffalo gored and trampled two gunmen and the rhinos gored and crushed another five. The tigers lunged towards the last five men. The huge, striped felines ripped and tore the men's legs, shoulders and chests. Their powerful fangs, as strong as a bear's, crushed the men's skulls or strangled them in three seconds.

The elephant's gang informed the tigers there was only silver buried at this site. The tigers told the giant herbivores that, through savagely mauling and massacring the boats of poachers on the ocean, the sharks and ocean killers were now the Lin Wu Beasts' allies. Joined by a Komodo dragon that had been warped into Nepal and then Louisiana from Indonesia, the crocodile and the alligator were powerful allies in the fight against the Li Hei sorcerers. It was safe for the giant herbivores and tigers to swim across the Mississippi with no fear that the sharks, ocean killers and killer reptiles would attack them.

As the Lin Wu Beasts reached the Mississippi, they plunged into the river and swam across. Dark sorcerers in boats fired lightning spells at the beasts, but the tigers used their sorcery to beat off the spells. Then the sharks, ocean killers and killer reptiles violently bit open the boats so the sorcerers were stranded in the water. Chewing off the legs of three men and biting out the chests, stomachs and pelvises of another three, the sharks viciously savaged these six men, devouring them in plumes and clouds of blood. The barracuda savagely slaughtered another sorcerer as the conger eel and the moray eel bit another four male witches, chopping chunks of flesh and bones from them. All five bled to death in three minutes. The octopus constricted one man to death, and in the same two minutes, the giant squid and the cuttlefish shredded and ripped four sorcerers to pieces. All five brutes lay dismembered, with arms, legs and feet dangling in the water, which was churned red with flesh, blood and bones.

With spinning death-rolls, the crocodile and the alligator twisted off the legs of two thugs, who screamed as they bled to death in appalling agony. Within the three minutes of this savage massacre, the Komodo dragon used his razor-sharp claws to tear one brute to ribbons and crushed the last crook with his dreaded teeth. Both violent criminals died as horribly as the men were brutally mauled by the sharks and ocean killers.

With the sharks, ocean killers and killer reptiles paying them no attention, the herbivores and tigers climbed onto the riverbank and travelled eastwards.

The giant herbivores and tigers faced more dark sorcerers, but sprayed lightning at the men. The evil crooks fled southwards and northwards. The rhinos told the elephant they would pursue the three men heading south and would find the elephant and the buffalo later. The elephant, the buffalo and the tigers followed the other thirteen men, who were heading north.

The elephant and the buffalo caught up with the men. The buffalo killed three by tossing one into the air, stabbing a second and trampling a third with his sledgehammer hooves. The elephant used his ivory tusks and bone-crushing hooves to murder another five men, goring one of them savagely and crushing the other four into the ground. The tigers swiped a total of nine crushing blows from their enormous paws and slashing claws against the last five criminals. Two men had their throats gouged out and arms and shoulders broken, two died from broken necks, and the last man had his skull fractured.

The tigers sensed another gang of poachers coming from the north and east and decided to make their way south-east with the elephant and the buffalo to bypass the armed men and then head north.

After bypassing the gunmen, the giant herbivores and tigers watched the armed men approach the river and scream with horror at the mutilated corpses of the dark sorcerers in the river and on the riverbank. The Lin Wu Beasts were hiding in a copse of trees, and then decided to head north again to avoid the poachers. They made their way out of the copse.

The elephant, the buffalo and the tigers fed on apples and pears from fruit trees or on three rabbits and two hares the tigers had killed. Then thirteen of the poachers cornered the giant herbivores and tigers. They focused their rifles towards the huge beasts. These men were not all of the poaching gang that had closed in on the giant herbivores and tigers before the beasts had hidden in the copse lying south-east and then headed north. There were twenty poachers overall, but seven gunmen had journeyed east to locate the leopard, the black panther and the jaguar.

The armed men cornering the giant herbivores and tigers squeezed the triggers and blazed, but lightning spells destroyed the bullets before they hit the herbivores and tigers. The giant herbivores and tigers charged and attacked with awesome power, horrific speed and terrifying savagery. The elephant impaled, trampled and crushed six criminals as the buffalo tossed two gunmen into the air and crushed them under his hooves. They massacred all eight killers in the short period of a minute.

Kicking, ripping and tearing with all their claws, the tigers crippled the legs, chests and shoulders of the last five men before their bone-crushing fangs penetrated the brutes' heads or strangled them. The danger was over, and there were only the other seven poachers left alive.

The elephant and the buffalo picked up mind signals from the rhinos, who had pursued three dark sorcerers south whilst the elephant's gang chased the thirteen sorcerers fleeing north. The rhinos told the elephant and the buffalo how they had caught up with the sorcerers and murdered them outside New Orleans. They would meet the elephant and the buffalo at the copse of trees where the giant herbivores and tigers had hidden from the twenty poachers.

The elephant and the buffalo told the tigers this information and set off southeast towards the copse in order to join the rhinos. The tigers were alone. They would have to save the leopards and the jaguar from the seven armed men remaining. The tigers set off east across the field towards another copse where Marion had left the big cats, the burial site of the copper.

The tigers reached the copse where the copper was buried and located the seven men, who fired at the leopard and the black panther up in a tree. The leopards were beating off the gunshots with lightning spells, and then burned the men's rifles. The men screamed with excruciating agony, and then the tigers charged five riflemen from behind.

The gunmen spun round, but the tigers were upon them, all their sets of claws raking down the men's legs, chests, shoulders and arms. The tigers' fangs strangled the killers. The last two men faced the tigers with horror, and then the spotted leopard and the black panther hurtled from the tree towards the men. Pinning the men to the ground, their hind and front claws shredded the crooks' buttocks, thighs, backs and shoulders before their dagger-like fangs crunched through the brutes' necks. Both criminals were dead in seconds.

The leopard and the black panther abandoned the men and used mind signals to thank the tigers for saving their lives. They had to leave the buried copper and search out the jaguar.

After two hours, they located the jaguar. The tigers rebuked the jaguar for wandering off alone, but the jaguar told them he was eliminating the area south and east as the possible location of the magic gold. The tigers, the leopard and the black panther forgave the jaguar. There was no gold to the south, east or west of the river. The big cats made their way north.

The jaguar quarrelled with the leopard and the black panther about their plan to find the Asian bears and cheetahs at the farmstead where the iron was buried. The jaguar explained that finding the gold was more important, but the leopards told him they could not leave the bears and cheetahs vulnerable to the dark sorcerers. With the jaguar being arrogant, the leopard and the black panther lost their tempers and attacked the jaguar. A fight broke out. The tigers intervened and separated the leopard and the black panther from the jaguar.

The farmstead where the iron was buried was owned by dark sorcerers, and they surrounded the bears and cheetahs. Both sides exchanged a hail of deadly lightning spells before the bears and cheetahs began to weaken. Then the men heard bellowing and roaring from the farmstead's west side and devilish screaming coming from the east. Eight men made their way around the farmstead, whilst seven men headed east between the apple and pear trees. The leopard, the black panther and the jaguar took them by surprise, and their slashing front claws put four men out of action before they turned on the other three. With two slashing blows from his front paws and razor-sharp claws, the spotted leopard ripped out the throats of two men as the black panther gouged out the throat of a third. The jaguar tore the fourth man's throat clean away from his neck. The sorcerers were dead in a matter of seconds.

The spotted leopard, the black panther and the jaguar lunged towards the last three men and brutally savaged them with all their sets of claws and killer fangs. Attacking in true leopard style against human victims, the leopard and the black panther tore and disembowelled two of the killers, shredding their chests and shoulders and scalping their heads. Their fangs strangled the thugs. The jaguar ripped the third brute's legs and groin, as well as tearing his chest and shoulders, before his vice-like fangs penetrated the man's head. The man died instantly.

The three big cats charged towards the farmstead to rescue the bears and cheetahs.

On the west side, the five tigers took the other eight brutes by surprise. With crushing, slashing blows from their bear-like paws and razor-sharp claws, the tigers broke one man's neck and smashed the skulls of two other men. Leaping with lightning speed, the tigers used their claws to rip open the men's legs and groins, and tear open their chests, shoulders and arms. Then they fastened their fangs into the crooks' heads and necks. Two criminals had their skulls fractured whilst the other three men were throttled. It was all over in fifteen seconds.

The tigers charged to the rescue of the bears and cheetahs, and they encountered the leopard, the black panther and the jaguar from the copse of apple and pear trees.

The dark sorcerers cornering the bears and cheetahs panicked, and the beasts took the initiative. With slashing blows from their lethal paws and scimitar-like claws, the black bears mortally wounded six men. The sloth bears fatally wounded six more, and the sun bears crippled another five. The cheetahs darted towards the last five men, and all their sets of claws shredded the brutes' legs, chests and shoulders. Their needle-like fangs penetrated the crooks' throats, carotid arteries and jugular veins.

With all twenty-two men dead or fatally injured, the bears and cheetahs snarled and growled their gratitude to the tigers, the leopard, the black panther and the jaguar for saving their lives. The larger cats roared and screamed with pleasure.

The bears and big cats continued their journey north, and they reached the dreamworld joining Louisiana with Nepal. But there was no sign of the yetis from Nepal and the bigfoot creatures that had been warped to Louisiana from British Colombia. Instead, the big cats and bears encountered the zebras, giraffes and ostriches, backed up by the cassowaries and kangaroos. The tigers asked the herbivores and flightless birds about the whereabouts of the yetis and bigfoot creatures. The zebras and giraffes told the big cats that the yetis were hunting yaks and cattle in Nepal. The ostriches and cassowaries informed the tigers that the bigfoot creatures were searching for fruits from the trees, as well as stray sheep that these apes could kill and eat. The kangaroos told everybody that the gorillas, chimpanzees and orang-utans were drinking water from the river separating Nepal and Louisiana. The apes had dug up the aluminium in their search for the gold, and they would tell the tigers that this was not the gold.

The bears and tigers approached the gorillas, chimpanzees and orang-utans at the river, and the gorillas recounted their fruitless unearthing of the aluminium. The tigers explained Marion's unsuccessful journey north to find the magic gold and told the apes they must find the yetis and bigfoot creatures whilst the zebras, giraffes and ostriches, together with the cassowaries and kangaroos, focused their psychic minds for any possible location of the magic gold. The gorillas asked the tigers whether it was safe to swim across the Mississippi with the sharks, ocean killers and killer reptiles terrorising the river, but the tigers pointed out that these Li Hei Beasts had changed sides and were now allies of the Lin Wu Beasts. It was safe to swim across to locate the yetis.

The big cats and bears continued their journey north and were getting closer to finding the magic gold. They made their way east towards a forest. The tigers received mind signals from the gorillas, chimpanzees and orang-utans, telling them that they had located the yetis and bigfoot creatures. But the zebras, giraffes and ostriches, together with the cassowaries and kangaroos, had been unable to detect the magic gold, despite racking their psychic minds.

The black bears, sloth bears and sun bears, together with the leopard, the black panther and the jaguar, spotted dark sorcerers in the distance, advancing towards Marion's position in the nearby forest. The cheetahs told the tigers that there were too many Li Hei sorcerers for the predators to fight. The tigers would have to seek out the herbivores, flightless birds and apes. The big cats and bears lay crouched in the long grass, watching the men, whilst the tigers doubled back towards the pathway and hunted the herbivores and flightless birds.

After an hour's search, the tigers encountered the elephant, the white rhino, the black rhino and the buffalo, backed up by the five yetis and four bigfoot creatures. Also with the giant herbivores and apes stood the five zebras, four giraffes, five ostriches, five cassowaries and four kangaroos. They were shortly joined by the three gorillas, ten chimpanzees and ten orang-utans. The tigers addressed the elephant's gang and told them the other big cats and bears were an hour's walk away near a copse of trees and were getting closer to finding the magic gold.

The predators watched a vast force of Li Hei sorcerers making their way towards the copse. These men would probably capture and murder Marion if the Lin Wu Beasts did not reach her first.

After the conversation, the elephant, the rhinos and the buffalo led the herbivores, flightless birds and apes in following the tigers towards the position outside the copse where the other big cats and bears were waiting.

When they reached the big cats and bears, they encountered Klaus and Lin Wu, positioned alongside the leopard, the black panther, the jaguar and the cheetahs. The tigers took their position beside the other big cats, standing with the leopard and the black panther to their right and the bears to their left. The elephant's gang, the herbivores, flightless birds and apes stood behind Klaus and Lin Wu, and the big cats and bears faced both men.

In his psychic mind, Lin Wu sensed Marion lying fast asleep in a copse of trees, and the dark sorcerers closing in on her. He sent mind signals to the sharks, ocean killers and killer reptiles swimming in the Mississippi and commanded them to rendezvous with the Lin Wu Beasts, who would be positioned on the east bank of the Mississippi where pelicans gathered in their hundreds. This area of the river was three miles north of the position of the ocean killers and killer reptiles and two miles south of the Lin Wu Beasts' position. With his mind, Lin Wu then ordered the elephant's gang and the other herbivores, flightless birds and apes to meet up with the sharks, ocean killers and killer reptiles at the pelicans' breeding grounds. The tigers, the other big cats and bears would go with the elephant's gang and other vegetarian beasts. Lin Wu and Klaus had to locate Marion in the copse and rescue her from the Li Hei sorcerers.

In the next few seconds, Marion's dream ended.

***

Marion awoke to the sound of men talking and boots treading over mud and twigs. She rose to her feet, hidden behind a tree, and saw the men digging for the magic gold in an area of loose, disturbed soil surrounded by hard soil. But they failed to find the gold. These were Li Hei's sorcerers, and they told each other that Li Hei must have removed the gold. Then Li Hei appeared out of the mist.

"The gold is not here," he said.

"Then where did you take it?" one sorcerer asked.

"I warped the gold to the state border between Oregon and Washington State, to the Mule Deer Ranch three miles from America's Pacific coast," Li Hei said. "The sharks, ocean killers and killer reptiles have killed enough policemen, informants and Lin Wu sorcerers, and have now changed sides and joined the Lin Wu Beasts, for the gold is not here to corrupt them."

Hidden behind the tree, Marion knew that

what had happened in her dream made sense. She understood why the sharks, ocean killers and killer reptiles in the Mississippi had stopped attacking humans and changed sides to join the Lin Wu Beasts. And she also knew Li Hei's men had warped themselves to Louisiana to capture and murder her, but Klaus and Lin Wu were trying to find her.

Two of Li Hei's men sneaked up behind her with their hands raised, ready to fire lightning and kill her instantly if she turned round to fight them. Marion could feel their presence.

"Don't move!" one man cried. "Or you'll be fried with lightning!"

"I'm not moving," Marion said. Tension and fear resonated in her voice as she froze with terror. Her eyes were big and dilated. "What do you want?"

"We've been hunting for you," the man told her. "Li Hei will reward us handsomely for turning you in. Get moving, now." The men pushed Marion from behind the tree towards Li Hei and his vast gang of lethal brutes.

"We meet at last, lady from Bavaria," Li Hei addressed her.

"Go to hell!" Marion exclaimed.

"Are you talking to me?" he asked.

"No, I'm talking to a tree!" Marion snapped. "Of course I'm talking to you!"

"You know too much," Li Hei growled. "About my men throughout the world, who were behind poaching, pollution, acid rain, deforestation, and me hiring sharks, ocean killers and killer reptiles to massacre Lin Wu's men."

"And I know you were stupid enough to warp the magic gold from Louisiana to the Mule Deer Ranch on the state border between Washington State and Oregon," Marion announced. "That's why the sharks, ocean killers and killer reptiles changed sides and joined the Lin Wu Beasts. There was no longer any magic gold buried where you're standing to corrupt these Li Hei Beasts. You may as well kill me and destroy the evidence." Then she saw, in the long grass, Klaus and Lin Wu crawling towards Li Hei and his men from behind.

"You must've read my thoughts," Li Hei sneered.

"But before you put me in the ground," Marion asked. "Just one question. And your secret will die with me when I die, so you may as well lay your cards on the table."

"Ask me this question," Li Hei snarled.

"As well as the batches of gold that corrupted herbivores and predators into killing each other," Marion said. "There are two batches of magic gold that kill animals instantly after these animals kill evil men protected by the evil spirits in the gold. The first batch of gold massacred lions, tigers, bears, bison and moose in two wildlife parks. The first wildlife park was in the United States, on California's border with Mexico. After the animals there died through killing your men, this batch was warped over to a wildlife park in British Colombia, on Canada's border with Alaska. All the animals there died after murdering your men, and then, thanks to the late Julio Sifuentez and his poachers, the gold disappeared. The second batch of magic gold was buried in a forest near Lake Geneva in Switzerland. Three industrialists from Alberta in Canada, Great Britain and Poland committed suicide by setting themselves up as bait to be killed by the predators local to Switzerland. You cooperated with these men to upset and annoy Lin Wu by murdering these predators, and the plan worked. A bear, a lynx, a wolf and a fox massacred the three men and then died instantly due to the gold. Then you removed the gold before we could find it. Those were the two batches of gold.

"The question I want to ask is: where have you buried these two batches of gold now? The magic gold that will kill animals instantly. Are these batches of gold buried with the less lethal batches of deadly gold on the state border between Washington State and Oregon?"

"Your question deserves an answer," Li Hei growled. "Yes, they are buried there. At the Mule Deer Ranch, three miles from America's Pacific coast."

"That's all I need to know," Marion said.

And with great speed and the element of surprise, she dived for the ground, rolled between Li Hei's legs and ejected red-hot lightning at his groin. The lightning fried and burned his testicles severely, and he screamed like a hysterical woman in a blind panic. Appalling agony spread from his groin to his whole body so that his legs turned to jelly and gave way under him.

Li Hei's sorcerers fired lightning towards Marion, but Li Hei fell on top of her, his huge body crashing onto her diminutive body, so he took most of the barrage of lightning and electricity. Marion rolled clear of his body so as not to be electrocuted herself, and then sprayed lightning left, right and centre, throwing Li Hei's men backwards.

Klaus and Lin Wu had been crawling stealthily through the long grass. With a warping spell, Klaus evaporated the vast mass of men into the atmosphere. Lin Wu and Klaus then pressed home their deadly lightning attack towards Li Hei. Severely injured and in too much agony, Li Hei disappeared into the Louisiana mist.

"Li Hei's still dangerous!" Marion screamed.

"No, he's not," Lin Wu informed her. "He's too incapacitated by his injuries and the agony you inflicted on him. He's now badly injured at the Mule Deer Ranch in Washington State, but he will recover soon."

"That was a brave and vicious attack you executed, Marion," Klaus told her.

"You bet it was." Marion laughed. "Where do we head now?"

"To the breeding ground of the pelicans on the east bank of the river," Lin Wu decided. "That's where I warped Li Hei's evil men."

"And we must join your gangs of savage

beasts in murdering the men," Klaus added.
    "Away we go," Lin Wu finished off.

***

The sharks, ocean killers and killer reptiles swam past the pelicans' breeding grounds. They sent mind signals to the herbivores, flightless birds, apes and big cats positioned north of the vast flock of pelicans. At that moment, a mass of dark sorcerers appeared out of the mist on the banks of the Mississippi. The Lin Wu Beasts cornered them. Many sorcerers jumped into the river, thinking it was safe, but were horribly savaged by the ocean killers and killer reptiles. Gnashing and chopping with their huge jaws and massive teeth, the enormous sharks bit giant chunks of flesh and bones out of nine men, five of which lost one or both legs. They perished in clouds of crimson blood.

The barracuda and the conger eel severed the arms of two thugs and then savagely mauled two other criminals as the moray eel chewed off the arm of a fifth thug. With repeated slashing blows from their flesh-chopping tentacles, the octopus sliced a sixth crook to death whilst the giant squid and the cuttlefish shredded open another four. Due to excessive loss of blood, all five violent criminals died as horribly as the five men who had been viciously savaged by the barracuda, the conger eel and the moray eel. As the sharks and ocean killers executed this barbaric slaughter, the enormous crocodile spun off a man's leg. The crocodile and the alligator dragged two other men down to the riverbed, drowned and dismembered them. The Komodo dragon attacked two other men in the water with horrific savagery, his bone-crushing teeth mutilating one man as his hideous black claws tore the second man to ribbons.

With all the men in the water ruthlessly slaughtered by the sharks, ocean killers and killer reptiles, the Li Hei sorcerers on the riverbank sprayed lightning at the Lin Wu Beasts on land. The beasts fired lightning back with vicious brutality. The criminals were flat on the grass, and then the beasts pressed home their savage attack against the violent crooks. Stabbing, goring and trampling with enormous tusks, fearsome horns and ground-churning hooves, the elephant destroyed ten men. Within the same two minutes, the rhinos massacred six men and the buffalo murdered two brutes. The zebras, giraffes and ostriches kicked to death fourteen killers within the same three minutes that the cassowaries and kangaroos dropkicked nine murderers and tore them open.

Whilst this carnage was happening around them, the apes took terrible toll of the sorcerers. The giant yetis used their fists and teeth to crush and bite to death nine Nepalese men. Within the same minute that the bigfoot creatures destroyed eight Japanese men, the chimpanzees and orang-utans outnumbered and viciously mauled eight Chinese criminals, two or three chimpanzees or orang-utans to each man. With the same extreme ferocity as the yetis, the gorillas crunched their huge jaws and teeth into the legs of three brutes, breaking their legs like planks of wood, before blows from their enormous fists pulverised the men, smashing their skulls or shattering their ribs.

The bears were also fighting savagely. The black bears broke the neck of one man before mauling five other men, the sloth bears clawed and bit four more, and the sun bears tore the bodies and bit the faces and throats of another five until they died.

The big cats charged and lunged for the last few men with explosive brute power and lightning speed, but the men raised their arms and kicked violently at the massive predators. Two tigers used their claws and fangs to rip off the arms of two men whilst the leopard, the black panther and the jaguar tore off the arms of three other criminals. All five brutes died in agony and shock, pints of blood spurting and gushing from their shoulders where arteries and blood vessels were ruptured. The other three tigers clawed and bit through the stomachs and legs of three other criminals, breaking their legs, rending the men's stomach and thigh muscles and puncturing arteries and blood vessels. The men screamed with horrific agony and shock as blood sprayed onto the grass. All three were dead in a matter of minutes from excessive loss of blood. The five cheetahs outnumbered the last two men and mauled them with devilish ferocity, their claws ripping and tearing flesh to the bone on the men's arms, upper bodies and legs, before their fangs throttled the brutes.

The brown and blue waters of the river churned with clouds and plumes of blood, just as the riverbank and the grass teemed with human corpses. The sight of dark red blood, mutilated flesh and dangling bones was a terrifying, horrific and brutal reminder of that savage battle that had ended in the massacre of Li Hei's dark sorcerers.

The big cats, bears, yetis, bigfoot creatures and chimpanzees began devouring the men ravenously whilst the giant herbivores and gorillas gorged themselves on the leaves and fruits from the trees.

Marion, Klaus and Lin Wu emerged out of thin air.

"It looks like the Lin Wu Beasts did our dirty work for us," Marion said.

"You're damn right they did," Klaus agreed.

"The dangerous beasts in Louisiana are safe," Lin Wu said. "But I sense trouble in Poland and British Colombia, from poachers and their pet rats. They have already shot dead a few large herbivores local to Bialowieza Forest and a forest on Canada's border with Alaska. The remaining herbivores and predators are at risk from two batches of magic gold, which will corrupt them if they kill the poachers and rats."

"Where will we head first?" Klaus asked. "Poland or Canada?"

"We must first head for Poland," Lin Wu decided.

They disappeared into the mist.

***

At Poland's Bialowieza Forest, the two gangs of poachers were on either side of the river, four men on the north side and three on the south, and intended to join up at the bridge crossing the river. But the men on the south side were charged by the European bison and the elk. Blasting with their powerful hunting rifles, the men pumped several shots into the beasts' heads, and the bison and the elk died in a few seconds. The men examined the massive bodies of both magnificent beasts as they lay lifeless, blood running from their bullet-shredded heads and chests.

The pack of pet rats following the men sensed more danger. In nearby trees and thickets, stalking the three men and the rats, were the wild boar, the red deer and the roe deer, backed up by the common otters, rabbits and hares local to Bialowieza Forest. In the next few seconds, the herbivores sprayed lightning at the men's rifles, which burst into flames. The men threw the firearms to the grass.

Charging with tremendous speed, the wild boar disembowelled and killed the first man using his fearsome tusks, whilst the red deer and the roe deer gored and kicked the other two men until they died from fractured skulls. The two male otters clawed and chewed most of the rats to death, and within the same minute, the rabbits and hares jumped onto the backs of eight rats, kicking and slashing with hind and front claws, and broke the rats' necks with their chisel-like teeth.

The four poachers on the river's north side aimed their rifles towards the wild boar and the two deer, but the guns caught fire and burned their hands. Screaming and crying with fiery pain, the men dropped the rifles.

The five large predators, the feral cat and the seven mustelids savagely attacked the criminals and the second pack of rats. The bear and the lynx were backed up by the wolf, the very big mountain fox as large as a Labrador, and the bull mastiff. With terrible blows from his paws and claws, the bear split one man's head open and fractured his spine as the lynx mauled and strangled a second man. The wolf savaged a third's arms and hands before his jagged teeth strangled him, and the last man had his right hand and left arm mangled by the savage teeth of the fox and the dog. The dog switched his attack to the man's neck and throttled him. Tearing and biting at the horde of rats, the feral cat clawed and chewed the necks and heads of five pet rats whilst the common badger, the weasel and the stoat mutilated seven of these evil rodents, biting their necks, and the polecat, the ferret, the pine marten and the beech marten repeated this murderous attack against the last four vermin.

But with both poaching gangs and both packs of rats on the river's south and north sides mercilessly massacred, noble spirits, breeding violent aggression, passed into the three large herbivores, the otters, rabbits and hares. At the same time, evil spirits transferred from the second gang of men and rats into the large predators, the cat and the seven mustelids. Once allies, the herbivores were programmed to slaughter all predators and the predators disciplined to massacre all herbivores on sight. Only the river divided both gangs of deadly beasts.

At that moment, Lin Wu, Klaus and Marion appeared between the forest trees.

"They're about to do battle," Lin Wu stated. "We must warp them to a farmstead outside Bialowieza Forest—that farm over there. And we must reduce the heat of fire we spray from our hands into their heads so we can destroy the noble or evil spirits without killing the beasts."

"The fire will burn their brains, won't it?" Marion asked.

"That's why we must reduce the heat," Lin Wu said. "To the lowest temperature a fire can burn. The fire will be hot enough to kill the spirits without killing the animals or causing brain damage. Do you know how to spray fire from your hands?"

"I've never done it before," Marion said.

"Nor have I," Klaus remarked.

"Think of how cold a refrigerator is, combine this with thinking of spraying fire, and then release the fire," Lin Wu said. "These opposite thoughts of heat and cold as you fire will reduce the heat of the flames. Now go."

Lin Wu warped the herbivores, otters and predators towards the farmstead, and then he, Klaus and Marion made their way there with another spell.

The three sorcerers arrived at the farmstead in a matter of seconds, finding the two otters, the rabbits and hares defending themselves violently against the cat, the badger, the weasel and the stoat, together with the polecat, the ferret, the pine marten and the beech marten. The badger and the latter four mustelids as large as cats outnumbered the otters, attacking them as the weasel and the stoat bit at the rabbits, and the cat spat and slashed at the hares. Outside a cattle barn, which was now empty of cattle, the wild boar fought a running battle with the bear and the lynx at the same time as the red deer kicked at the wolf and the dog, and the roe deer gored and kicked at the mountain fox.

Lin Wu ejected fire into the brains of the cat and the mustelids, which killed their evil spirits and knocked all eight smaller predators out cold. Then he released fire into the heads of the otters, rabbits and hares, killing their noble spirits and rendering the beasts unconscious. Klaus and Marion sprayed bolts of fire at the red deer and the roe deer.

All three humans warped themselves over to the cattle barn's entrance. They were seen by the two deer and three wild dogs and ran inside. They sprinted down the barn past empty cattle enclosures. They reached the furthest enclosure, the deer chasing them with the wild dogs in lethal pursuit.

The bear and the lynx chased the wild boar into the enclosure nearest the entrance. The wild boar's tusks slashed at the bear's flank and then the wild boar was outside the enclosure, hunching his muscular shoulders and lowering his pig-like head and scimitar-like tusks.

In the furthest enclosure, the wolf, the dog and the fox snapped with lethal teeth at the legs and shoulders of the red deer and the roe deer, who gored and kicked at them fiercely. But Lin Wu sprayed flames into the wild dogs' heads, which destroyed their evil spirits. The wolf, the fox and the dog lost consciousness and fell to the ground. Marion and Klaus released flames into the heads of the red deer and the roe deer so their noble spirits were burned up, and both beasts hurtled to the ground, unconscious.

"The wild boar will murder the bear and the lynx," Klaus shouted.

"We must save all three," Lin Wu cried.

Charging outside the cattle enclosure and past the other enclosures, they sprinted towards the entrance. They saw the wild boar facing the bear and the lynx, the deadly wild pig screaming, squealing and grunting with vicious savagery and fury, his bristled fur raised and his eyes fiery and evil.

The bear and the lynx had their backs to the sorcerers as their front paws and slashing claws swiped with speed at the wild boar. Marion and Klaus fired flames towards the predators' heads, incinerating their evil spirits and knocking out both beasts. Lin Wu sprayed fire towards the wild boar's head, burned up the noble spirit in his brain, and the wild boar was on his side, asleep, in a matter of seconds.

"Will all these beasts recover?" Marion asked.

"Yes, they will," Klaus informed her.

"In ten minutes' time," Lin Wu told them.

After ten minutes of sleep, the herbivores, otters and predators recovered and renewed their alliance against future poachers and rats. The predators would never again prey on these particular large herbivores, rabbits and hares, only hunting herbivores not loyal to Lin Wu. The bear and the lynx, along with the wolf, the fox and the dog, nuzzled the wild boar, the red deer and the roe deer with friendship. The cat and the badger rubbed paws with the otters just as the weasel and the stoat, together with the polecat, the ferret, the pine marten and the beech marten, shook paws with the rabbits and hares. The rabbits and hares then squealed and squeaked their gratitude to the cat, the weasel and the stoat for not killing them.

The big predators and mustelids disappeared into the forest, and the large herbivores, otters, rabbits and hares stayed on the farmstead.

"Is this all over?" Marion wanted to know.

"No," Lin Wu replied.

"Let me guess," Klaus said. "The herbivores and predators in British Colombia are at war."

"You guess right," Lin Wu remarked. "But not the herbivores and predators loyal to me. The Kodiak bear of Alaska and the two grizzlies and two black bears from Yellowstone in Wyoming have remembered to avoid killing men and have run away from poachers. The puma, the lynx and the bobcat, together with the wolf, the coyote and the fox from Yellowstone, have also refrained from killing men. So too have the bison and the moose from Wyoming. And the American badger, the mink and the fisher, together with the dogs, cats, rabbits and hares from France and Switzerland, have avoided murdering the pet rats. Two other gangs of herbivores and predators will fight another large gang of poachers and rats on the forest highway further north of Vancouver, the road leading from Canada into Alaska. They will either be shot dead by the poachers or will kill the men and rats and be corrupted by the magic gold buried in the copse of pine trees. We must prevent these animals from killing each other. We've got no time to lose."

***

Lin Wu, Klaus and Marion were in the forest north of Vancouver. They were on the north side of the highway, facing south, watching the poaching gang and their pack of pet rats wander from west to east. These men were from Alaska, and had entered Canada illegally to shoot bison, moose and deer. Two female bison and a cow moose released from Vancouver Zoo were eating grass where the highway separated the south forest from the north forest, and the poachers took aim with their high-calibre rifles. They opened fire, and all three beasts collapsed in spasms of death, blood shooting from their heads, shoulders and chests. The men sprinted towards the carcases, the rats speeding and darting behind them. Making sure the two bison and the moose were dead, the armed men lowered their rifles and sat on the embankment, one man raising his mobile phone to his mouth to call Li Hei. He was going to ask Li Hei to drive over in a truck from Alaska and pick up the three carcases and the gang of poachers and rats. But with their backs turned, the men were unprepared for a savage attack carried out by large herbivores and predators, backed up by a feral cat, three Canadian otters and some rabbits and hares. A male bison and a bull moose plunged their horns and antlers into the backs and kidneys of two riflemen, fracturing their spines, and then trampled and kicked them on the ground, breaking their bones and smashing their heads open. Within the same minute, a giant Kodiak bear, a grizzly bear and a black bear viciously mauled three gunmen. Horrific blows from their paws and claws fractured the men's skulls. A puma, a lynx and a bobcat strangled three armed men and ripped them to shreds as a wolf and a coyote tore the arms and right hand of another man. A large mountain fox and a dog repeated this attack against the last man. The wolf and the Great Dane lunged for the poachers' necks and throttled them in two or three seconds.

The feral cat, the American badger, the weasel and the stoat, together with four mink and five fishers, clawed and bit the necks and heads of thirteen rats. Within the same ten seconds, the three otters, six rabbits and six hares tore fifteen rats to ribbons with their fearsome claws and bit the rats' heads with deadly fangs and chisel-like teeth.

With the poachers and rats massacred, noble spirits passed from the men and rats into the herbivores, otters, rabbits and hares, whilst evil spirits travelled into the bears and large predators, the cat and the mustelids.

Running scared from the cat and the mustelids into the road, the rabbits, hares and otters turned with courage to face the savage cat and the vicious mustelids just as seven more otters darted across the road to confront the seven large predators, and the bison and the moose faced the three bears.

"They'll murder each other," Klaus remarked.

"Where do we warp them to?" Marion asked.

"To a deserted ranch west of here," Lin Wu decided. "On the border with Alaska, but not quite inside Alaska."

"We'll cast our warping spells," Marion said.

The three humans arrived on the ranch four or five seconds after the gangs of herbivores and predators. The bison and the moose fought a running battle with the enormous bears, with the bison confronting the Kodiak bear and the moose facing the grizzly bear and the black bear. The puma, the lynx and the bobcat, along with the wolf, the coyote, the mountain fox and the dog, chased seven otters into the south warehouse as the cat, the American badger, the weasel and the stoat, together with the four mink and five fishers, pursued the other three otters, six rabbits and six hares into the north warehouse. The bison, the moose and the bears were fighting just outside the farmhouse lying east of the two warehouses.

Marion, Klaus and Lin Wu warped themselves inside the north warehouse. As the American badger, the mink and fishers outnumbered the three otters and dealt them deadly bites, the cat, the weasel and the stoat fought a running battle with the rabbits and hares. The three killers spat, slashed and bit; the rabbits and hares inflicted gnashing bites. Lin Wu sprayed flames into the heads of the cat, the badger, the weasel and the stoat, together with the mink and fishers, killing their evil spirits and knocking the predators out cold. Klaus fired into the brains of the otters whilst Marion repeated this attack against the rabbits and hares, destroying their noble spirits and knocking them unconscious.

"The otters, rabbits and hares fought well against the cat and the mustelids," Marion observed.

"But the seven otters in the south warehouse will stand no chance against the much larger wild cats and wild dogs," Lin Wu said.

"We must act," Klaus cried.

In the south warehouse, the otters' speed and ferocity was no match against the larger predators' greater size, speed and savagery, their serrated teeth, killer fangs and razor-sharp claws. The puma, the lynx and the bobcat viciously clawed and bit through the necks of three otters. The wolf and the dog used their jagged teeth to bite two others to death. The coyote and the fox came off worse against the last two otters, but the puma and the wolf leapt onto the otters' backs, the puma tearing with his claws, and then the two massive predators crunched their teeth through the otters' heads, killing them in a matter of seconds.

Klaus, Marion and Lin Wu appeared too late to save the otters, all seven beasts lying mangled on the wooden floor, but the humans fired flames with minimal heat into the heads of the puma, the lynx and the bobcat, burning up the evil spirits and knocking the wild cats unconscious.

With ferocity, the wolf, the coyote, the fox and the dog charged the sorcerers, but Lin Wu sprayed bolts of fire towards the wolf and the dog as Klaus and Marion repeated this fiery attack against the coyote and the fox, destroying the evil spirits and putting the four predators to sleep.

"We couldn't save the otters!" Marion exclaimed.

"Three otters and the rabbits and hares are still alive in the north warehouse," Klaus said.

"The battle between the bears, the bison and the moose could end either way," Lin Wu told them. "But even the beasts who win will suffer crippling injuries. We must act now."

The humans were behind the Kodiak bear, the grizzly bear and the black bear, who reared up onto their hind legs, dealing crushing blows and gnashing bites to the bison and the moose with their enormous paws, deadly claws and huge fangs. As the bears dropped onto all fours, shaking their massive shoulders, necks and heads, the bison and the moose plunged their horns and antlers into the bears' shoulders and flanks. The moose bashed the heads and faces of the grizzly bear and the black bear with his flailing, sledgehammer hooves.

Lin Wu sprayed three bolts of fire into the bears' heads from behind, burning the evil spirits and knocking out the bears. The bison and the moose charged Lin Wu, Klaus and Marion with crushing power and speed, their heads lowered aggressively, but Klaus and Marion fired flames towards the herbivores' heads, destroying their noble spirits. Both awesome beasts were unconscious in two or three seconds.

"That was worse than the battle in Poland," Klaus commented.

"They'll recover in ten minutes' time," Lin Wu remarked.

"Thank God for one thing," Marion began.

"You tell us," Klaus said.

"Those herbivores and predators were not the same beasts as the Wyoming beasts or the dogs, cats, rabbits and hares from France and Switzerland," Marion informed them.

"These particular beasts we knocked out just now are from Alaska," Lin Wu told them. "My psychic mind can now detect where the copse of pines is where the magic gold is buried. And the other batch of magic gold is under a copse of beeches and oaks at Bialowieza Forest in Poland. I must warp myself and the African elephant to Bialowieza, dig up the magic gold, and then the elephant will destroy the gold. Then the elephant and I will return to the copse of pines here in British Colombia, dig up the second batch of gold, and—again—destroy it. That leaves the more dangerous batch of magic gold lying at the Mule Deer Ranch on the state border between Washington State and Oregon, which is well-protected by Li Hei and an army of dark sorcerers.

"But first, I must warp the big herbivores, otters, rabbits and hares, together with the large predators, the cat and the mustelids, over from this ranch to the forest east of Vancouver. All the other large herbivores, predators and mustelids from the tropical regions and from Wyoming, Holland and Belgium will be there. The dogs, cats, rabbits and hares from France and Switzerland will also be there. Let us wait."

As soon as all the beasts recovered without being possessed by noble or evil spirits, the herbivores and predators were on friendly terms. The bison and the moose rubbed heads with the bears, then with the puma, the lynx and the bobcat, together with the wolf, the coyote, the fox and the dog. These large predators would never again prey on the three otters, the rabbits and hares, only hunting herbivores that Lin Wu did not regard as allies.

The American badger, the cat, the weasel and the stoat, backed up by the four mink and five fishers, also formed a bond of friendship with the otters, rabbits and hares. Lin Wu warped all these beasts over to the forest east of Vancouver to join up with the dangerous animals from the Congo, Nepal, Brazil, Europe and Wyoming. Then he, Klaus and Marion followed suit.

***

At the forest outside Vancouver, Marion fell asleep from fatigue. She was unconscious for ten hours, and the last three hours were occupied by two dreams. Both dreams were of two journeys made by the bison, bears and large predators in British Colombia—the first going west towards a park outside Vancouver, the second heading east towards another park and a remote restaurant. The dangerous beasts were sent by Lin Wu to locate his two gangs of noble sorcerers, who were also wildlife policemen from China, Japan, Alaska, Canada and the United States.

In the first dream, at Bialowieza Forest in Poland, Lin Wu followed the African elephant towards the patch of beeches and oaks, the elephant's powerful sense of smell detecting the magic gold. The elephant dug through the soil, unearthed the gold and smashed the hard metal with his heavy left hoof.

Lin Wu warped himself and the elephant back to British Colombia, to the copse of pines, and the elephant's strong sense of smell traced the second batch of magic gold to a patch of loose soil near a flowerbed. After digging up the solid, yellowish-brown metal, the elephant bashed it to smithereens with his powerful right hoof. Both batches of magic gold in Poland and western Canada had been safely destroyed.

In the next scene, the two male American bison and two bull moose, all of them having been warped over from Wyoming or the forest north of Vancouver, were in the forest east of Vancouver. They followed the two Alaskan Kodiak bears, three grizzlies from Alaska or Wyoming and three black bears from Alaska or Wyoming to make sure the eight bears did not mistake any Lin Wu sorcerers for poachers and kill them. The male bison and bull moose were a mile behind the male bears as they made their way towards the park outside Vancouver.

The following scene showed the bison and moose encountering the two American badgers from Alaska and Wyoming, and five mink from both states, protecting five of Lin Wu's sorcerers. The bison and moose were about to attack these wildlife police, who threw down their rifles and showed the large herbivores their police badges. The two bison and two moose thanked the badgers and mink for preventing a tragedy.

The Kodiak bears, grizzlies and black bears faced twelve Lin Wu sorcerers and bellowed and roared at the wildlife police with evil savagery. The American badgers and mink reappeared. They sent mind signals to the bears, telling them the men were friendly. The bison and moose appeared and roared at four men as the bears screamed at eight others, but the men dropped their rifles and showed the herbivores and bears their police badges. The beasts immediately knew the men were not hostile.

The bison, moose and bears continued journeying west, and were greeted by noble sorcerers from India, Nepal and China. The Chinese men were close friends of the top Chinese noble sorcerer, Lin Wu.

Later on, the beasts were waved at by

sorcerers from China, Japan and Australia. Ten minutes after that point, the bison, moose and bears received a warm welcome from sorcerers who had flocked into British Colombia from Alaska and the rest of Canada. The bison and moose had encountered five gangs of sorcerers, who were also animal police backing up Lin Wu in his war against Li Hei's dark sorcerers.

The American badgers and mink walked alongside the bears and herbivores all this time, and then the beasts came to a river. They had to cross. The American badgers and mink swam across the stretch of water first, and then the herbivores and bears followed the mustelids. Because the bison and moose were clumsy swimmers, the bears flanked the large herbivores on both sides to protect them from being carried downstream. Then the bison and moose jumped up onto the riverbank, followed by the Kodiak bears, grizzlies and black bears. The American badgers and mink led the bison, moose and bears towards the last gang of Lin Wu sorcerers, who were wildlife police from the United States.

The six gangs of sorcerers from the Far East, Australia, Alaska, Canada and the United States were reunited, and then Lin Wu and Klaus joined them.

The badgers and mink told the bison, moose and bears that only one more obstacle stood in their way before reaching the park outside Vancouver. This was a mountain that was deadly due to landslides and mudslides. The mustelids would have to make their way back towards the forest east of Vancouver, then join the large predators of Alaska and Wyoming, backed up by the mustelids from Holland and Belgium. The bison, moose and bears would rendezvous with Lin Wu and his wildlife police outside Vancouver, together with the wild boar, the red deer and the roe deer, who had been warped over to British Colombia from the forest in north-eastern France.

The Kodiak bears, grizzlies and black bears led the bison and moose along the treacherous pathway with leopard-like stealth, for the slightest noise could cause vibrations that would trigger a landslide or a mudslide. A black bear trod on a rock, which rolled into the nearby stream. The vibrations caused by the noise of this boulder jumping, bumping and then splashing into the stream aggravated the mountain summit. In seconds, a landslide followed by a mudslide thundered and gushed down the huge mountain with vicious savagery, rage and fury.

The Kodiak bears, grizzlies and black bears sprinted with tiger-like speed towards the end of the pathway. The bison and moose were even faster, gaining distance past the bears. They made it to safety in time.

The landslide and the mudslide crashed with force and fury to the bottom of the mountain and into the stream. The herbivores and bears were relieved that they had escaped death by a narrow margin.

The herbivores and bears met up with the wild boar, the red deer and the roe deer from France. The two bison and two moose greeted the three herbivores, and then the bears welcomed them into their army of Lin Wu Beasts from Alaska and Wyoming. They made their way towards the park outside Vancouver and met up again with the six gangs of Lin Wu sorcerers. Emerging from the vast force of wildlife police came Lin Wu and Klaus.

Lin Wu wanted Klaus to warp himself to the forest east of Vancouver to join Marion. When she was awake, they would travel by magic to a car park and a restaurant lying east of the forest to rendezvous with the wild dogs and wild cats from Alaska and Wyoming, backed up by the mustelids from Holland and Belgium and the dogs, cats, rabbits and hares from France and Switzerland. Inside the car park and the restaurant, Klaus and Marion would set a second trap for another gang of poachers, brutal animal dealers and their army of pet rats.

But before setting both traps, Lin Wu, Klaus and Marion and the wildlife police needed to confront Li Hei and his evil sorcerers at the Mule Deer Ranch in Washington State and destroy the magic gold that had claimed dozens of animal lives in California, British Colombia and Switzerland.

After the conversation, Klaus immediately

disappeared into the mist and reappeared at the forest outside Vancouver.

***

The second dream covered the journey east towards the restaurant, which was carried out by the six wild dogs and six wild cats from Alaska and Wyoming, each state having produced a wolf, a coyote and a mountain fox, together with a puma, a lynx and a bobcat. Two wolves, two coyotes and two foxes flanked two pumas, two lynxes and two bobcats as they crossed a stream and journeyed into pastures of lush green grass in a valley between two rows of mountains.

The wild dogs and wild cats met up with the common badgers, weasels and stoats, backed up by the polecats and pine martens, these mustelids having been warped over to western Canada from Alaska, Holland and Belgium. These smaller killers led the large predators towards a massive pond, where all these carnivores could drink as much water as possible. The pumas, wolves, coyotes and foxes consumed as much water as their stomachs could take before the lynxes and bobcats quenched their thirsts. The badgers, as well as the weasels, stoats, polecats and pine martens, then began drinking. The pumas, lynxes and bobcats were exhausted and had to rest. The wolves, coyotes and foxes told them they would continue the journey towards the remote restaurant. The wild cats would catch up with the wild dogs later.

After sleeping for thirty-seven minutes, the pumas, lynxes and bobcats followed the wild dogs' trail through the valley and encountered six men with rifles. Not knowing whether or not the men were hostile, the wild cats screamed and hissed savagely at the men, but the three weasels and two stoats from Alaska, Holland and Belgium appeared out of the grass and appeased the wild cats. The men stood their ground but did not raise their rifles. They were Lin Wu sorcerers from northern India, China and Japan, and the weasels and stoats reassured the wild cats that the men were not a threat to them. The pumas, lynxes and bobcats journeyed on.

They reached a ranch and saw chickens roaming the farmstead, but they were not hungry. The badgers, polecats and pine martens emerged from the grass overlooking the farmyard and warned the wild cats not to attack the chickens for fear of human reprisal.

More armed wildlife police, from China, Alaska and Canada, came from around the farmhouse with the ranch's owners. The badgers, polecats and pine martens told the wild cats they would meet them at a copse of spruces and firs.

The pumas, lynxes and bobcats encountered the badgers, polecats and pine martens at this copse. The mustelids showed the wild cats the carcass of a wapiti killed and partly eaten by the wolves, coyotes and foxes.

More armed men appeared, and the pumas,

bobcats and lynxes prepared to attack the men in self-defence. But again, the men were wildlife police from Washington State and Oregon in the United States. These uniformed cops would assist Lin Wu, Klaus and Marion and a gang of dangerous animals in attacking the Mule Deer Ranch and killing Li Hei and his mob. The mustelids intervened, and both the wildlife police and wild cats stood down. The wild cats and mustelids consumed flesh from the carcase.

Continuing their trip through another mountain range, the pumas, lynxes and bobcats met up with the mountain foxes. The two foxes had rested whilst the two wolves and two coyotes went on ahead. The foxes would catch up with their fellow wild dogs later.

The pumas predicted a snowstorm, and the foxes led the pumas, lynxes and bobcats towards another ranch where they could all raid a chicken coop, slaughter and eat all the chickens, and then take shelter in the chicken coop through the storm.

On reaching the ranch and entering the chicken coop, the large predators massacred all the chickens. By the time the wild cats and foxes had murdered these poultry, the snowstorm was raging with ferocious fury and intensity outside the chicken coop. To pass the time, the pumas dined on five chickens whilst the lynxes and bobcats consumed two chickens each and the foxes ate three chickens each. Then they rested and fell asleep.

By the time they awoke, the storm had died

down. They knew the farmers would emerge from the farmhouse to feed the poultry in the chicken coop. Knowing the farmers would shoot the wild cats and foxes for killing all the chickens, the large predators pushed open the chicken coop door and made a run for it into the mountains again.

The pumas, lynxes, bobcats and mountain foxes soon caught up with the wolves and coyotes, together with the weasels and stoats. These wild dogs and mustelids were about to attack six Lin Wu sorcerers they had mistaken for poachers, one man from Brazil, two from Colombia and three from Venezuela. But the weasels and stoats diffused the situation and persuaded the wolves and coyotes to put off their attack. The foxes rejoined the wolves and coyotes, and then the wild cats joined the wild dogs and mustelids. The sorcerers from Brazil, Colombia and Venezuela offered the predators friendly nods.

The pumas, lynxes and bobcats discussed with the wolves, coyotes and foxes the need for the Lin Wu herbivores and predators to be permanently united in friendship. This would mean the predators would never prey on the Lin Wu herbivores, only on herbivores not loyal to Lin Wu. Then Klaus and Lin Wu emerged out of thin air and praised the predators for this new alliance.

Taken by surprise by eight sorcerers, three from Chile and five from Peru, the pumas and foxes were about to attack the men from Peru, whilst the badgers, polecats and pine martens would assault the men from Chile. But the badgers, polecats and pine martens persuaded the pumas and foxes not to kill or injure these men. The Chileans and Peruvians sat down and reassured the pumas and foxes that they were working for Lin Wu. As well as sorcerers from Alaska, Canada and the United States, Lin Wu also had allies from Colombia, Venezuela and Brazil, not to mention Chile and Peru. His army was vast.

The lynxes, bobcats, wolves and coyotes, along with the weasels and stoats, faced ten sorcerers from Mexico and were about to attack these men, mistaking them for Li Hei's men. But the weasels and stoats pacified the situation, and the men promised the wild cats and wild dogs they were Lin Wu's men.

Like the weasels and stoats, the lynxes, bobcats, wolves and coyotes withdrew from their deadly attack. The men from Mexico sat down alongside the men from Chile and Peru, together with the men from Brazil, Colombia and Venezuela.

The men from South America and Mexico were joined by the wildlife police and sorcerers from the United States, Canada and Alaska, not to mention India, Nepal, China, Japan and Australia. This whole vast army would take on Li Hei's enormous army at the Mule Deer Ranch on the state border between Washington State and Oregon.

The wild dogs, wild cats and mustelids continued their journey east until they reached the car park and the restaurant, which were remote. The badgers, polecats and pine martens, together with the weasels and stoats, had no knowledge of why these two landmarks were suitable places for Lin Wu to lure one of Li Hei's gangs into a trap.

The pumas, lynxes and bobcats slept under the thickets whilst the wolves, coyotes and foxes rested beside the trees. The mustelids kept watch for friends or foes. At that moment, Marion's dream ended.

***

Marion awoke in the forest east of Vancouver, and standing over her were Klaus, Lin Wu and their vast army from the Far East, Australia and the Americas. Behind them were the large herbivores, flightless birds, apes and Asian bears—the apes including the yetis from Nepal and the bigfoot creatures from British Colombia. Marion knew immediately Lin Wu had formed another dreamworld joining British Colombia with Nepal in order to bring the yetis into Canada.

Marion rose to her feet and greeted Lin Wu and his army. "Good morning."

"Good morning, Marion," Klaus replied.

"And the same from me and my men," Lin Wu remarked. "You dreamt of these sorcerers and wildlife police in your two dreams, no doubt?"

"Your psychic powers do you credit, old man," Marion said. "You know everything that happened in my two dreams."

"My Grand Master in Shanghai passed these powers on to me," Lin Wu told her.

"Li Hei will soon recover from the injuries I inflicted on him," Marion stated.

"Your point being?" Klaus remarked.

"I know what her point is," Lin Wu observed. "We must warp ourselves and our army of men and beasts to the Mule Deer Ranch, kill Li Hei and his men and destroy the magic gold that is fatal to dangerous animals, but not to us sorcerers if we kill the men. Or we will detain most of them after Li Hei is dead."

"But, one question?" Marion asked. "I know the North American bears, bison and moose, together with the wild boar, the red deer and the roe deer, will stay in this forest outside Vancouver as they're needed to trap Li Hei's second gang. The weasel and the stoat of Alaska, together with the American badgers, mink and fishers of Alaska and Wyoming, have been warped over to join Europe's mustelids and the wild dogs and wild cats at the remote restaurant and the car park many miles east of this forest. The common otters from Poland, and the Canadian otters from Alaska who fought the mustelids at the Polish farmstead and the ranch, are here with us and will be needed to massacre the pet rats at the Mule Deer Ranch. The yetis and bigfoot creatures will have to warp themselves to the restaurant, alongside those herbivores and apes who survive the Mule Deer Ranch battle by not killing any men."

"But you have a question," Lin Wu cut her

short. "What is this question?"

"I'm sorry, old man." Marion sighed. "The herbivores, flightless birds and apes are here with the Asian bears and otters. But where are the big cats from the Congo, Nepal and Brazil?"

"You may well ask," Lin Wu began. "They are with the wild cats and wild dogs outside the remote restaurant. The dogs, cats, rabbits and hares from France and Switzerland are with the wild dogs, wild cats and mustelids, and have been joined by the dog, the cat, the six rabbits and six hares from Alaska, who fought each other, the otters and the mustelids at that remote ranch before we destroyed their evil spirits. The cats, rabbits and hares now at this restaurant must assist the mustelids in murdering the pack of rats owned by the third gang of armed poachers. The bears and herbivores from Alaska, Wyoming and France are at the Grizzly Ranch a few miles from Vancouver."

"But I must make another point," Klaus said.

"Go on," Lin Wu invited.

"The bears and herbivores at the Grizzly Ranch don't have to take the lives of the second gang of poachers after we massacre Li Hei's gang at the Mule Deer Ranch," Klaus told Lin Wu. "Although the smaller predators, rabbits and hares at the remote restaurant must kill the third gang's pet rats, the yetis and bigfoot creatures, along with the dogs, wild dogs and wild cats, must refrain from murdering the third gang of armed men. Violence and evil need not be met with more evil or blood for blood. The best justice we can impose on these three gangs is to put them away in a maximum-security prison for many years. Because Li Hei is too dangerous with his powers of sorcery to let live, he and many poachers will inevitably lose their lives as the herbivores, flightless birds and apes massacre them, but to prevent these beasts dying in the process, the elephant must dig up and destroy the magic gold."

"And we must also capture some of these men alive, so they can inform us about other poaching gangs and the names of top wildlife dealers," Marion explained. "Like the two gangs here in British Colombia, and many gangs in Alaska, Canada, the United States and all over the world."

"Okay, you both win," Lin Wu agreed. "They can tell us the names and mobile phone numbers of the fellow dealers leading those two poaching gangs that we'll trap at the Grizzly Ranch and the remote restaurant. And by the way, this remote restaurant is a Chinese restaurant called the Green Lotus."

"The Green Lotus," Marion remarked. "I'll remember that name. Even if Klaus, with his small brain, forgets it."

"With my small brain!" Klaus objected. "I've remembered more restaurants than you! The Green Lotus is not difficult to remember!"

"Okay, we won't argue about it, dear," Marion chuckled. "Li Hei will have recovered from his injuries, so we must make our move now."

"How will you find the buried magic gold?" Lin Wu asked.

"By finding a patch of loose, disturbed soil surrounded by hard soil that hasn't been dug up," Marion said.

"The elephant, the two rhinos and the buffalo will protect you while you search for this loose soil," Lin Wu told her.

"Are you ready?" Klaus said. "Let's go."

***

On Washington State's side of the border with Oregon, the dozens of American and foreign wildlife police and sorcerers closed in upon the Mule Deer Ranch from all directions. Klaus and Lin Wu were already near the farmstead's perimeter, whilst Marion was on the farm's north side, where the elephant's powerful sense of smell had detected the smell of magic gold.

Li Hei's sorcerers were everywhere within the perimeter, and his guards patrolled the area surrounding the ranch. Eighteen armed men guarded the area covered by Marion and the giant herbivores, but she spotted the loose, disturbed soil just inside the ranch. It was between the perimeter fence and the farmstead's thickets, overlooking a green where cattle had once roamed, a green leading to an enormous farmhouse.

Left, right and centre, Marion sprayed

lightning at the eighteen guards' rifles, ricocheting between the weaponry. The guards' arms and hands were fried like chips, and they dropped the formidable weapons.

Charging with awesome power, speed and vicious savagery, but taking care not to kill the men, the elephant kicked and swiped nine guards with his front hooves, tusks and trunk, only injuring them. The elephant cornered them against the fence, and then smashed it in. The men froze with terror and horror, their bones broken.

The rhinos each bashed three men with horns and hooves, winding them and knocking them unconscious without killing them.

The buffalo gently knocked down the last three men with his horns, and then the elephant, the rhinos and the buffalo terrified these men with their furious bellowing, roaring and screaming. The armed men surrendered.

Marion used all her might and speed to dig up the soil and expose the two batches of magic gold. Jumping out of the way of the elephant's huge right leg, Marion displayed the gold. With two ferocious and bone-crushing kicks from his massive hoof, the elephant reduced the strong, hard batch of gold to splintered metal and powder.

The dark sorcerers were on the green in seconds, but Marion ejected lightning with extreme force and fury, throwing them backwards. The elephant, the white rhino, the black rhino and the buffalo also fired lightning. Seeing the great size of the elephant, the rhinos and the buffalo, the sorcerers fled from the elephant's gang. The giant herbivores guarded the eighteen injured men, whilst a horde of Indian, Nepalese, Chinese and Japanese Lin Wu sorcerers joined Marion and chased the Li Hei sorcerers across the green, Marion running behind two Chinese and three Japanese men.

At the ranch's front entrance, five Nepalese men, six Chinese men and four Australians, plus Canadian, American and Latin American men, overcame twenty guards. Led by Klaus and Lin Wu, the sorcerers and wildlife police hurried through the enormous wooden gate into the vast area.

They fired lightning bolts and rifleshots at the Li Hei sorcerers within the ranch, a deadly crossfire of lightning and gunshots lasting for ten minutes.

The criminals' pet rats stormed outside the farmhouse to attack the Canadian otters and common otters, inflicting several bites, but the otters slashed, tore and gnashed with their hind and front claws and razor-sharp teeth, massacring twenty-seven rats. The other thirteen vermin fled through the ranch's gate into the forest.

The herbivores, flightless birds, apes and Asian bears bombarded the Li Hei sorcerers and poachers with lightning, and eventually the gunmen faltered before the ferocious attack. Charging with brute power and speed, the beasts knew the elephant had destroyed the magic gold on the farmstead's north side and its dangerous magical powers would no longer kill the beasts if they murdered the armed men. Kicking fiercely with rock-hard hooves, terrible claws or flying hind feet, the zebras, giraffes and ostriches bashed fourteen thugs and ripped them to death as the cassowaries and kangaroos tore open and pounded nine brutes. The chimpanzees and orang-utans outnumbered ten other crooks, savaging and strangling them and biting through their heads, whilst the gorillas pinned down three criminals and bellowed, roared and intimidated the gunmen without killing them.

As this carnage and chaos was happening around them, the black bears, sloth bears and sun bears savagely ripped, tore and bit the faces of fourteen crooks, their sets of claws and bone-breaking fangs dealing fatal injuries that the men would never recover from. Of all the poachers, only the three men being restrained and roared at by the gorillas were left alive. Three cops thrust handcuffs onto the men.

From Marion's side of the perimeter fence, the Indians, Chinese and Japanese men outran and restrained the Li Hei sorcerers, but Marion was determined to corner Li Hei herself.

As the remaining Li Hei sorcerers were overpowered and hand-cuffed by Lin Wu's men, Lin Wu and Klaus stormed inside the farmhouse as Marion hurried from the farmyard into the kitchen. They found Li Hei alone in the dining room. A ruthless and brutal crossfire of lightning followed between this terrifying wizard and the three noble sorcerers, firing from all directions. Li Hei was the most dangerous sorcerer Lin Wu had ever had to fight, and his lightning bolts were white-hot. All attempts by Marion, Klaus and Lin Wu to fry Li Hei were beaten off with vicious savagery, but then twenty Lin Wu sorcerers, who were Nepalese, Chinese, Australian and Mexican, charged into the room and sprayed lightning bolts.

Li Hei beat off every bolt. He threw back Klaus and the twenty sorcerers, knocking Klaus and eight other men unconscious.

Marion was also thrown to the kitchen floor by five bolts. She crawled across the floor towards a kitchen drawer full of knives. Really sharp knives. She grabbed two of the largest knives and decided to take Li Hei by surprise by stabbing him in the kidneys. Only the element of surprise and a swift, short-range attack where she was up close to Li Hei would kill him. She crawled across the floor, allowing him to think he had knocked her out like Klaus. He had his back to her. And the only vulnerable areas of his back to deal the killing blows to were his kidneys. If Marion's attack failed, she would never have another chance to finish Li Hei. Lin Wu and Li Hei bashed and pounded each other with lightning for what seemed an eternity, and then more of Lin Wu's men from Brazil, Colombia, Venezuela and Mexico stormed into the dining room and released fiery bolts. The police officers from the United States, Canada and Alaska would never bring down this dangerous brute with their rifles and handguns. Li Hei's magical powers were so invincible, he could take on an army of thirty or more noble sorcerers. The men from the Far East and Australia as well as Mexico and South America were weakening from Li Hei's counter-attack, but Lin Wu was persistent.

Klaus came round from his sleep, aimed his hands from the floor and fired at Li Hei's groin. The evil brute doubled up in appalling agony as Klaus and Lin Wu pressed home their savage attack.

By now, Marion was at the kitchen doorway. She tightened her slender hands around both sharp knives and leapt off the floor. It only took a second for her to lunge towards Li Hei's back like a lion, and she slammed into him with brutal force like a locomotive. She rained horrific blows with the knives, chopping, gouging and slashing into his kidneys. Li Hei screamed like a Native American warrior, but his screams were of terrifying agony, not aggression and fury. With one last stabbing blow from the bigger knife, Marion thrust the shining steel through his kidneys, in front of his ribcage and solar plexus, until it penetrated his heart and tore an artery and two blood vessels.

His mouth agape and his eyes dilated with agony and shock, Li Hei crumpled to the floor. He rolled onto his back and aimed his hands up towards Marion. But Klaus and Lin

Wu fired five more bolts, and Li Hei hesitated. His mouth closed and his eyes shut. He was splayed across the dining room floor.

Marion's hands and jumper were soaked with blood, but she ran up to Klaus. Her mouth met his face.

"Are you okay, dear?" Marion cried.

"I'm okay, darling," Klaus told her.

"Were you badly burned by the lightning?" Marion asked.

"No, Marion," Klaus said. "Were you?"

"I'll live." She chuckled. A grin stretched across her mature face as she swept back her long dark hair.

"Two of Li Hei's gangs of poachers are still at large in British Colombia," Lin Wu explained. "And the herbivores, flightless birds and apes, together with the bears and otters, are badly shaken by lightning or rat bites. They need many days to recover from their wounds. Only the elephant, the rhinos and the buffalo, together with the three gorillas, are uninjured. I'll warp the giant herbivores and gorillas to the Green Lotus Restaurant. But, at the moment, the giant herbivores and gorillas are restraining the eighteen guards and three poachers still alive. We must find out from these men the names and mobile phone numbers of the two wildlife dealers leading the two poaching gangs. Are you ready to watch as I interrogate the three men being restrained by the gorillas?"

"We're ready, old man," Klaus remarked.

As the wildlife police and noble sorcerers

ruthlessly interrogated the eighteen guards, Lin Wu used his lightning to brutally torture the three poachers left alive. They all gave the same two names and mobile phone numbers of the wildlife dealers.

"Sato and Ming," the poachers cried. "They're Chinese men."

"What are their mobile numbers?" Lin Wu asked.

"Sato's mobile phone number is six-two-one five-three-four," one man said. "And Ming's number is five-six-three three-one-two. They live in Vancouver, but we don't know what their addresses are."

"That's okay," Lin Wu remarked. He addressed Klaus and Marion and the police officers. "Have you written down the names and numbers?"

"We have," Klaus and Marion both answered.

"And we have," the police sergeant replied. "What's your next plan to trap the two poaching gangs?"

"To warp ourselves and Canada and Alaska's wildlife police back to British Colombia," Marion explained. "You wildlife police and the remaining noble sorcerers must care for the dangerous beasts and otters who have been badly shaken by lightning bolts and rat bites."

At that moment, the elephant, the rhinos, the buffalo and the gorillas wandered towards the three sorcerers at a slow pace.

"These beasts are in perfect shape for the

operation at the Green Lotus Restaurant," Klaus addressed Lin Wu. "To assist the yetis and bigfoot creatures, along with the big cats, smaller wild cats and wild dogs. But there must be no massacre."

"Your morality does you credit," Lin Wu replied. "The giant herbivores and gorillas will travel by witchcraft to the Green Lotus now."

With a warping spell, the giant herbivores and gorillas evaporated into the cool, dry atmosphere. Then Lin Wu, Klaus and Marion, and the wildlife police and sorcerers from Alaska and Canada followed suit.

***

Lin Wu was at a phone booth in Vancouver, his finger pressing the digits 621534.

The mobile at the other end of the line bleeped three times before a middle-aged Chinese man responded.

"Hello there, Sato here. Who's calling?" he wanted to know.

"A dealer in endangered wildlife named Ben Topolino," Lin Wu replied. "Is that Sato?"

"It is Sato," the brute said. "So, Mr Topolino, you deal in endangered wildlife?"

"I do," Lin Wu agreed.

"How did you find out about me?" Sato asked.

"Sometimes a man's life can depend on a little information," Lin Wu said. "Experienced poachers and wildlife dealers told me about you. But let's cut to the chase. You lead a gang of poachers and have claimed several animal trophies."

"There are many trophies to my name," Sato responded.

"Which trophies exactly?" Lin Wu invited.

"Elephant tusks and rhino horns from India and Nepal, powdered tiger bones from China, and the hides of bears, wild boars, red deer, roe deer and serow goats shot in Japan," Sato said.

"I'll tell you what I want," Lin Wu said. "I want two elephant tusks, three rhino horns, and the hides, heads and antlers of a red deer, a roe deer and a fallow deer shot in Japan. How much will that cost me?"

"I'll figure it out," Sato told him. "Half a million Canadian dollars. We'll arrange a meeting place."

"I know the perfect meeting place," Lin Wu explained. "The Grizzly Ranch, three miles north of Vancouver. You got that?"

"I've got it," Sato agreed. "The Grizzly Ranch. What time will we meet at this ranch?"

"Tomorrow morning at ten," Lin Wu decided. "I'll see you there with your men."

At that point, Sato broke off contact.

***

At a roadhouse outside Vancouver, Marion was at the bar's public phone. She dialled the number 563312. A Chinese man of thirty-seven answered.

"Ming here," he said. "Can I help you?"

"It's Barbara Leech from Vancouver," Marion said. "I've heard from wildlife trophy hunters that you have quite a notorious reputation for acquiring trophies. And you have a whole gang with you. You must introduce me to your gang."

"How would this benefit you, Barbara?" Ming asked. "Are you offering to sell me trophies?"

"To buy trophies," Marion remarked. "What have you got on offer?"

"Elephant tusks, rhino horns, animal furs and paintings from South Africa, Zimbabwe, Tanzania, Kenya and Uganda," Ming growled.

"Okay, I'll tell you what I want," Marion began again.

"Go on," Ming said.

"A leopard fur, a zebra-skin rug and a painting of an ostrich," Marion continued. "Can you manage the painting?"

"Yes, I can, Mrs Leech," Ming blurted. "All three will come to two hundred and thirty Canadian dollars. Where and when shall me and my men deliver these items?"

"At the Green Lotus Restaurant, the other side of the forest east of Vancouver," Marion finished. "It will be at eleven tomorrow morning. I'll have the money ready."

"The Green Lotus," Ming growled. "I'll be there tomorrow. Good day."

The line went dead, and Marion lowered the phone onto the hook. She made her way into the roadhouse's bar area and met up with Klaus.

"Let me guess—today is our lucky day," Klaus said.

"You guessed right," Marion said. "He fell for the con. And my cover name, Barbara Leech. Just like Sato fell for Lin Wu's cover name, Ben Topolino. We must join the dangerous beasts and wildlife police at the Green Lotus."

"Hang on a moment," Klaus growled. "What about dinner here at the roadhouse?"

"We'll have dinner at the Green Lotus," Marion explained. "Are you ready? Let's warp ourselves there now."

Within the space of three seconds, they disappeared.

***

Outside the Grizzly Ranch, to avoid arousing suspicion from Sato and his gang, the squad cars drove away from the ranch towards two side roads in the forest. Wildlife and anti-poaching police from Alaska and Canada were hidden in bedrooms throughout the farmhouse and kept a low profile. Hidden inside the barn, west of the house, were the two male bison, two bull moose, the wild boar, the red deer and the roe deer. Obscured behind haystacks in the barn positioned east of the property were the eight male bears—namely two Kodiak bears, three grizzlies and three black bears.

Lin Wu waited on the farmstead. He saw a truck rolling towards the farm. He retreated inside the farmhouse again and retrieved the suitcase containing the money. The half a million Canadian dollars to pay for the two elephant tusks and three rhino horns from India and Nepal, and the hides, heads and antlers of the red deer, the roe deer and the fallow deer shot in Japan. The truck stopped in the farmyard's driveway, and eighteen Chinese men with rifles emerged from the vehicle.

"Get the goods we owe Ben Topolino," the eldest Chinese men ordered. Lin Wu immediately knew this man was Sato.

The Chinese men carried the five crates of elephant tusks, rhino horns and deer hides from the truck towards the house's front door. The door opened, and Lin Wu emerged with the case of money.

Sato and his poachers immediately knew this man was Lin Wu who, aided by his noble sorcerers and formidable beasts, had fought Li Hei's gangs.

"You are Lin Wu!" Sato yelled.

"It is I, your arch enemy!" Lin Wu cried.

"Kill him, men!" Sato shouted.

The poachers focused their rifles, but Lin Wu sprayed lightning, which burned the rifles and scalded the men's hands. Sato and his men threw the weapons to the ground. Ten men, including Sato, ran around the farmhouse towards the barn lying to the west.

Upon hearing the men's running footsteps, the large herbivores charged with tremendous speed out of the barn and galloped towards Sato's men. As the two bison savagely knocked down three men and the two moose viciously gored and kicked three others, the wild boar, the red deer and the roe deer plunged their tusks and antlers into the stomachs and legs of the last three.

In terror at the herbivores' bone-chilling ferocity and fierce aggression, Sato fled around the farmhouse's north side past the barn, but anti-poaching police came out from all the doors, chased and wrestled him to the ground. More cops sprinted towards the nine men being cornered by the bison, moose and smaller herbivores, thrust arm-locks upon the men and handcuffed them.

The eight remaining poachers being chased by Lin Wu and the wildlife police towards the east barn were suddenly confronted by the enormous and vicious bears, bellowing, roaring and screaming as violently as the bison and moose. Swiping with their massive paws and huge, fearsome claws, the Kodiak bears knocked down two men whilst the grizzlies felled three more and the black bears dropped the last three. Lying in heaps on the ground, the men surrendered, and the cops thrust their handcuffs onto the crooks' wrists.

With all these criminals, including Sato, apprehended, the police offered their gratitude to the herbivores and bears.

"It's not only dogs who are man's best friend," the police sergeant added.

"How right you are," Lin Wu agreed.

"A bear, a bison and a moose can prove powerful allies," the sergeant pointed out.

"Not to mention a wild boar, a red deer and a roe deer from France."

"The tusks, horns and hides in those five crates will be concrete evidence to convict Sato," Lin Wu said. "And the fact Sato's men tried to kill me when they found out I wasn't Ben Topolino. There's more evidence of wildlife trophies at Sato's warehouse."

"You'll testify against Sato and Ming when the case goes to trial?" the sergeant asked.

"Yes, I will," Lin Wu promised him. "But first, I must stay behind at the Grizzly Ranch with a few wildlife police to gather food for the bison, moose and bears. And I will warp the wild boar, the red deer and the roe deer back to that forest in Burgundy."

Lin Wu raised his hands, ready to cast the warping spell.

***

In the mountains and forests surrounding the Green Lotus building, Lin Wu had created a dreamworld joining Nepal with British Colombia, for Nepal's Himalayas were the only suitable environment to support the mythical yetis if they were to help Canada's bigfoot creatures, together with the gorillas, the elephant, the rhinos, the buffalo and the big cats. In the restaurant itself, Marion turned towards the chief of Alaska's anti-poaching police, who had cooperated with Lin Wu to hunt down the Lis, Li Hei's family.

"I've thought of something," Marion

addressed the chief. "We must inform the Lis in China that their father, Li Hei, is dead."

"The Lis are no longer alive," the chief explained. "They committed suicide in the dreamworld joining Alaska with China and the Congo. This was before Lin Wu's war against the poachers and criminal developers began, and Li Hei wanted revenge against Lin Wu and the noble beasts for causing the Lis' mass suicide."

"Can you explain what happened?" Marion asked.

"My photographic visions will tell you everything," the chief said.

Visions came up from his psychic mind.

In the first scene, the African elephant and the African buffalo were using mind signals to communicate with the yeti of Nepal and the bigfoot creature of Alaska. The yeti took both giant herbivores to the white rhino and the black rhino, who placed the elephant and the buffalo in charge of leading the noble beasts against the Lis. The rhinos sent the silverback male gorilla to join the yeti and the bigfoot creature, and they would spy out the mountains and forests for any sign of the Li family.

The elephant and the buffalo spotted the Lis hunting with rifles in the Congo's rainforests. They included Li Hei's wife, sister and daughter, his two brothers and two sons. Backing them up were four poachers and three criminal developers. The giant herbivores followed the large gang through the rainforest.

The men and women fired their rifles at the elephant and the buffalo, who used their sorcery to burn up the bullets in mid-air. Then, with thundering hooves, they turned tail and fled from the evil humans. It was lucky the Lis did not share Li Hei's powers of sorcery.

The elephant and the buffalo rejoined the two rhinos in consuming grass and leaves, and then the gorilla was reunited with them. He ate bananas from the forest's trees nearby. The rhinos then guzzled down water from a nearby waterhole.

The elephant and the buffalo were joined by two of Alaska's large herbivores, the bison and the moose. Alaska's herbivores told the Congo's herbivores they must unite against the Lis, but the elephant told the bison this was an act of aggression against humans. The bison and the moose left the giant herbivores to fight the war on their own. Alaska's herbivores approached the top male chimpanzee and the leading male orang-utan, and both apes decided to persuade the Congo's herbivores at a later stage to attack the Lis.

The bison watched the elephant and the buffalo walking down a forest road in Alaska, and then the Lis aiming their rifles from behind thickets the other side of the road. The bison met up with the giant herbivores, warned them they were falling into a trap, and all three herbivores doubled back down the road to avoid the Lis.

The hippo warned the elephant and the buffalo they were in grave danger in the

Congo and told them they must flee across the border into Uganda. The hippo then told the rhinos what he had ordered the elephant and the buffalo to do, and the rhinos took over the leadership of the noble beasts.

The elephant and the buffalo were approached by the yeti of Nepal, who guided them through the mountains of Tibet in China, before the yeti returned to Nepal. The giant herbivores cut south from the border between China and Nepal into Uganda. They could see the Congo's forests to the west and the Himalayas to the north. But when advancing through Uganda, they encountered the bigfoot creature of Alaska. The bigfoot creature guided them into Alaska to meet up with the bison and the moose again, together with the chimpanzee leader and the orang-utan leader. All five beasts persisted in persuading the elephant and the buffalo to attack the Lis, and the elephant told the herbivores and apes he would consider it.

The bigfoot released the giant herbivores, who bade the bigfoot creature, the chimpanzee and the orang-utan farewell, and then crossed the dreamworld border from Alaska into Uganda. Then they faced another dreamworld joining Uganda with Australia.

The giant herbivores encountered the five top male leaders of the herbivores and flightless birds local to these two countries. The zebra, the giraffe and the ostrich were leading the cassowary and the kangaroo. The zebra asked the elephant and the buffalo why they had journeyed from the Congo into Uganda. The elephant explained how the Lis, their poachers and criminals posed a dangerous threat to the giant herbivores, and they were ruthlessly hunting down the giant herbivores in the Congo and Nepal. As the poachers were hunting the beasts, the criminal developers were cutting down the rainforests and mountain forests. The elephant and the buffalo decided it was necessary to massacre the Lis and their gang, and they asked the herbivores and flightless birds if they wished to join their war against the Lis. The zebra, the giraffe and the ostrich, along with the cassowary and the kangaroo, agreed to join the giant herbivores and apes later, on the border between Nepal and Alaska.

The African elephant and the African buffalo were confronted by one of the three gangs working for the Lis, a brutal mob of eighteen criminal developers destroying Uganda's bush country. But attacking from Nepal came the Indian elephant, the Indian rhino, the Sumatran rhino and the Javan rhino. The Indian elephant slaughtered five developers as the three rhinos gored and trampled eight criminals to deaths. The African elephant stabbed and crushed three crooks, and the last two brutes were viciously gored in the chest or tossed into the air by the African buffalo.

The bush country was saved.

The Congo's giant herbivores thanked the Indian elephant, and he returned to Nepal with the Indian rhino, the Sumatran rhino and the Javan rhino. The Congo's herbivores continued their journey towards Alaska to find the bison, the moose and the bigfoot creature, together with the chimpanzee and the orang-utan.

When journeying to Alaska, the elephant and the buffalo passed the foothills of Nepal's Himalayan Mountains. The Himalayas stood tall and impressive, like an enormous fortress. They crossed over mountain paths until they met up with the yeti. The yeti took the giant herbivores along the remainder of the journey to Nepal's border with Alaska and British Colombia in Canada.

The elephant and the buffalo greeted the white rhino and the black rhino again. The rhinos were backed up by the zebra, the giraffe, the ostrich and the cassowary, together with the male gorilla and the bigfoot creature. The gorilla and the bigfoot creature told the yeti accompanying the elephant and the buffalo that the kangaroo was with the chimpanzee, the orang-utan, the bison and the moose, who were about to face the Lis' second gang of five poachers. The elephant and the buffalo told the rhinos and the gorilla that they must give assistance to the bison's five beasts.

The elephant and the buffalo met up with the bison, the moose and the kangaroo, but their arrival was long overdue. Lying in front of the beasts was the second gang of five poachers, who were horribly mutilated. The bison told the giant herbivores how he and the moose had brutally gored two thugs whilst the chimpanzee and the orang-utan horribly mauled and strangled two other criminals. The last brute's stomach had been ruptured and torn open by the flailing hind feet of the kangaroo.

With the eighteen criminal developers in Uganda dead and the five poachers in Alaska also having died, the elephant and the buffalo praised the herbivores and apes for their bravery and ferocity in fighting and massacring the poachers.

But the Lis and their third gang of four poachers and three criminal developers were about to confront the rhinos' gang of herbivores, flightless birds and apes. The elephant and the buffalo had to assist these beasts in their final battle to murder the armed men and women.

The elephant and the rhino joined up again with the rhinos, the gorilla, the yeti and the bigfoot creature, backed up by the zebra, the giraffe, the ostrich and the cassowary. The beasts used their sorcery to melt bullets being fired from rifles in the hands of the Lis and their crooks. The criminals continued blazing fiercely, but the elephant and the buffalo also threw spells, and the brutes each only had one bullet left in his or her rifle.

Charging the Lis with power, speed and ferocity, the elephant targeted Li Hei's wife, sister and daughter whilst the white rhino and the black rhino went for his two brothers, and the buffalo hurtled forwards to attack his two sons. The zebra, the giraffe, the ostrich and the cassowary sprinted towards the four poachers, intent on kicking them until they perished, and the gorilla, the yeti and the bigfoot creature charged the three criminal developers. The apes would tear the men apart in a matter of minutes.

But the men and women of the Lis each raised their own rifle to their head, squeezed the trigger and blew their heads off. The Lis all lay upon their backs or fronts, their heads horribly mutilated by the last bullets from their rifles. The poachers blasted themselves in the chests whilst the criminal developers shot themselves in the solar plexus regions below their chests. All seven men were splayed awkwardly across the snow, their blood and guts smeared all over their bodies.

The herbivores, flightless birds and apes had been saved the trouble of massacring the Lis and their gang, but the elephant and the buffalo warned the rhinos that Li Hei would be bent on revenge for his family's mass suicide. The giant herbivores had to return to the Congo.

At that moment, the visions withdrew back into the police chief's head.

"Do you see now, Marion?" the chief asked.

"I see why Li Hei blamed Lin Wu and the dangerous beasts for the mass suicide of his family," Marion said.

"But now, Li Hei is out of the way," Klaus

said. "And I see trucks approaching the car park."

The giant herbivores, apes and big cats were waiting inside the nearby forest with the smaller predators, rabbits and hares. Wildlife police were positioned inside the Green Lotus restaurant's many rooms, ready to capture Ming and his poachers. But their police vehicles containing more cops were hidden in the forest so that Ming's men would have no knowledge that the anti-poaching and wildlife police were lying in wait with the dangerous beasts.

Several eight-seater cars and trucks drove into the car park and halted. Armed men emerged from the vehicles.

"I'll go into the Green Lotus with nine men and dozens of pet rats to kill Barbara Leech and everybody inside, and to spread disease around all the food in the kitchen," Ming addressed his men. "The rest of you, stay in the vehicles, ready to drive off when we've completed the massacre and make our getaway."

"Why must we kill Barbara Leech and everybody inside?" one of the nine men asked Ming.

"When Barbara made that phone call to me," Ming began, "I recognised a woman talking with a German accent. It was Marion Weisberg. Marion and Klaus have been working with Lin Wu and his men to smash our poaching rings. They're waiting for us in the Green Lotus. If my nine men and I are not enough to massacre any cops protecting the Weisbergs, I'll run out of the building and call all of you to back us up. Now, release the rats."

The men reached inside the trucks and opened the doors of large cages. Swarms of black and brown rats hurried outside the cages into the restaurant's garden area and towards the building's open door. The ten men, including Ming, walked behind the evil rodents, came to the front door and entered the bar area. The rats were eating discarded food in the bar area and the kitchen, but there was no sign of Marion, Klaus or the police.

In the car park outside the restaurant, the men inside the cars and trucks waited apprehensively. Suddenly, they heard thundering hooves and giant fists pounding the ground outside the vehicles. In a matter of seconds, the giant herbivores crashed their heads into four big cars, overturning them. The elephant cornered eight men in the first eight-seater car, just as the white rhino and the black rhino trapped ten men in the second and third cars. Three men in the fourth vehicle were terrorised by the enormous, ferocious buffalo.

Attacking fiercely like bears or tigers, the three gorillas, five yetis and four bigfoot creatures tore off the doors of three trucks and intimidated all the men in the trucks with their bellowing, roaring and screaming. The men screamed with petrified terror. Two brutes jumping out through the front doors were cornered and restrained by the five cheetahs, hissing with fury.

In the fourth truck, three armed men were in the front seats whilst five men were in the vehicle's main compartment. All eight gunmen hurried out of the large vehicle. The tigers lunged towards the five riflemen as the leopard, the black panther and the jaguar sprang against the three gunmen who had jumped from the front seats. All eight big cats fastened their claws into the men's legs, chests and shoulders, threatening the men by bellowing, roaring and screaming, their dagger-like fangs about to penetrate the men's heads or throats. The petrified men surrendered to the big cats, just as the other terrified criminals gave in to the vicious giant herbivores and the fierce apes.

Upon hearing the giant herbivores, apes and big cats attacking and restraining the poachers in the car park, Ming's gunmen inside the Green Lotus knew the odds against them were too great. Ming led the men and rats through the kitchen and out of the back door.

Klaus and Marion faced them and sprayed lightning at their arms and hands. With burning agony, the men dropped the rifles. As the American badgers, mink and fishers used their speed and ferocity to slaughter twenty pet rats, the common badgers, weasels and stoats used their violence and aggression to murder eighteen vermin.

The polecats brought down three, and the pine martens and beech martens viciously massacred another five. Within the same minute that the dogs and cats aggressively gnashed and clawed at twenty-eight evil rats, the rabbits and hares kicked, slashed and bit the last nine rodents to death.

With all his rodents immobilised, Ming and his nine gunmen fled to the left or right of the kitchen door. The wild cats and wild dogs emerged from around the restaurant's corners and obstructed the men's escape routes. The pumas, lynxes and bobcats lunged towards Ming and five other men, restrained the burly men with all their sets of claws and intimidated the horrified brutes by viciously screaming and hissing whilst baring their brutal fangs at their faces and necks. The wolves dug their jagged teeth into the left arms of two other poachers, pulled them to the ground and pinned down the gunmen. Within the same four or five seconds, the aggressive coyotes and vicious foxes outnumbered the last two men, fastening their jaws and teeth into their hands. The four large beasts broke the brutes' hands and caused them to fall onto their backs.

A swarm of wildlife police stormed outside the restaurant and out of the forest. They aimed their rifles at Ming's ten poachers. Producing their handcuffs, they fastened the poachers' arms behind their backs as the leading police officer cuffed Ming.

"Thanks, guys," Marion said.

"It's you, Klaus and Lin Wu who smashed the poaching rings," the leading officer said. "And your armies of vicious beasts."

"You think so, officer?" Marion asked.

"We all played our part," Klaus explained.

"The beasts were not only dangerous, they had plenty of guts to take on armed men." The leading officer praised the giant herbivores, apes and big cats, together with the bears, wild cats and wild dogs.

At that moment, Lin Wu appeared out of the forest.

"This was a job achieved by both beasts and men," Lin Wu said. "And by a brave woman like you, Marion. I owe both of you a debt of gratitude."

"Then can you do us one favour?" Marion asked. "My husband and I don't feel safe with magical powers to injure or kill people. Can you take away our powers of sorcery so we're like normal people again?"

"I have magic bananas with me to take away your powers," Lin Wu promised them. "You each ate three bananas to gain magical powers. You only need two bananas each to remove these powers. Take them."

Unpeeling the bananas, Marion and Klaus ate the fruits with gusto. They felt their magical powers leaving their bodies.

"There's more positive news," Marion finished off. "The sharks, ocean killers and killer reptiles in Louisiana's Mississippi River and the Gulf of Mexico have stopped attacking humans. Despite their reputation for ferocity and bloodlust, I knew they would come round to our side and end their violent attacks on men. The other vicious beasts are only aggressive towards evil men who try to harm them the way Li Hei, Sato and Ming attempted to. They are not dangerous.

"I want the otters returned to British Colombia and Poland and the mustelids returned to Wyoming, Holland and Belgium. Apart from one dog, one cat, six rabbits and six hares local to British Colombia, I want all the other dogs, cats, rabbits and hares sent back home to France and Switzerland. The gorillas, yetis and bigfoot creatures must return to the Congo, Nepal or stay here in British Colombia, the chimpanzees and orang-utans returning with the gorillas.

"You must also warp us back to the Mule Deer Ranch to check if the herbivores, flightless birds and Asian bears have recovered from their battle injuries. The giant herbivores and big cats must be sent home to the Congo, India and Brazil, the beasts from Alaska and Canada must remain here, and the herbivores and predators from Yellowstone should be sent back to Wyoming."

Then Marion was interrupted. The bison and moose emerged from the forest, alongside the Kodiak bears, grizzlies and black bears.

"Greetings, fellow beasts." Marion laughed.

The pumas, lynxes and bobcats, together with the wolves, coyotes and foxes joined the herbivores and bears. The dogs, cats, rabbits and hares, as well as the mustelids, were ready for the return to Wyoming, France and western Europe.

Lin Wu cast a warping spell, and all these beasts found themselves back in Wyoming and Europe, the dogs, cats, rabbits and hares joining the wild boar, the red deer and the roe deer. By sorcery, the yetis were warped back to Nepal, and the bigfoot creatures returned to Alaska, but the three gorillas had to check on the chimpanzees, orang-utans and bears recovering at the Mule Deer Ranch.

Lin Wu and his noble sorcerers gathered around the Weisbergs, the giant herbivores, big cats and gorillas, and they all disappeared into the mist. Lin Wu, Marion and Klaus knew they would have to attend a criminal court case in Vancouver to testify against the gangs of poachers they captured.

***

At the Mule Deer Ranch, the elephant, the rhinos and the buffalo poured out their love to the otters, knowing the otters had recovered. Then they offered their affections to the zebras, giraffes and ostriches, together with the cassowaries and kangaroos, who were now fit enough to return to Uganda and Australia.

The gorillas gave their sympathies to the chimpanzees and orang-utans, and these apes consumed fruits from a nearby village market. The tigers, the leopard, the black panther and the jaguar exchanged growls of respect with the cheetahs and then praised the tigers.

They nurtured the black bears, sloth bears and sun bears, who were also healthy, and then the bears and big cats roared or hissed with respect towards the giant herbivores led by the elephant.

Lin Wu, Klaus and Marion were relieved that all these beasts had recovered from the last battle against Li Hei.

"Are you both ready to attend the trial in Vancouver?" Lin Wu asked.

"Yes, we are," Marion agreed.

Author Profile

Michael Elia was born in Southampton in 1968. He was educated at Eynsham's Bartholomew School near Oxford. He has autism and Tourette's syndrome and lives in accommodation for people with autism in Maidenhead. He has written *A Trio of Cartels*, *Web of Crime*, *Nature's Revenge* and *Fear of the Unknown*.

Publisher Information

Rowanvale Books provides publishing services to independent authors, writers and poets all over the globe. We deliver a personal, honest and efficient service that allows authors to see their work published, while remaining in control of the process and retaining their creativity. By making publishing services available to authors in a cost-effective and ethical way, we at Rowanvale Books hope to ensure that the local, national and international community benefits from a steady stream of good quality literature.

For more information about us, our authors or our publications, please get in touch.

www.rowanvalebooks.com
info@rowanvalebooks.com